BEYOND THE RIO GRANDE

WILLIAM MacLEOD RAINE

SAGEBRUSH
Large Print Westerns

First published in Great Britain by Hodder and Stoughton
First published in the United States by Houghton Mifflin

Published in Large Print 2011 by ISIS Publishing Ltd.,
7 Centremead, Osney Mead, Oxford OX2 0ES
by arrangement with
Golden West Literary Agency

British Library Cataloguing in Publication Data
Raine, William MacLeod, 1871–1954.
   Beyond the Rio Grande.
   1. Western stories.
   2. Large type books.
   I. Title
   813.5'2–dc22

ISBN 978–0–7531–8755–5 (pb)

Printed and bound in Great Britain by
T. J. International Ltd., Padstow, Cornwall

CHAPTER
ONE

Against the adobe wall at the corner of Papago and Fourth Streets leaned a brown-faced man in chaps. So long had he stood there that the descending sun sent a shaft of light creeping into the shadow almost to his worn and dusty high-heeled boots. Motionless as a peon taking a siesta, there was, even in his stillness, a promise of dormant power not to be ignored. It could be read in the flow of packed muscles sloping from the throat, in the confidence of the careless ease, in the cool steadiness of the steel-blue eyes noting impassively the tide of humanity which swept up and down the thoroughfare. Tourists and Mexicans, Indian women with pottery and papooses, giggling school-girls, shoppers and loungers, all the details that went to make up the atmosphere of Spring River, were absorbed by his keen, indifferent gaze.

That he was a cynical observer rather than an actor in the drama might be guessed. His detachment held a touch of the sardonic, a suggestion of wary wisdom bought by experience, in odd conjunction with such obvious youth. Back of the recklessness lay a grimness, tight-lipped and hard, astonishing in one of his years.

He watched two horses coming down Papago Street, a bay and a claybank, in the saddles a man and a woman, knee to knee. The woman was in riding-breeches, a gay silk shirt, and a fancy beaded vest of deerskin. Beneath the expensive sombrero a small blonde head showed lovely as an exquisite cameo. Tendrils of tawny gold shot with copper escaped in impudent, upturned curls. She was smiling at her companion, and the smile was an enchanting gift. It made the baby-blue eyes sparkle with vivacity.

The man in chaps decided that she was a "Dude" at one of the neighboring guest ranches, from New York, Philadelphia, or some point not far from the Atlantic Coast. But the man beside her was no tenderfoot. He was obviously indigenous, the bronzed leathery product of many summer suns. Large, Roman-nosed, broad shouldered, in the arrogant strength of the late thirties, he was one to claim and hold attention. Not a corral dog, the watcher felt sure. He was far too assertive for the cowboy rôle. More likely a cattleman who had taken to wrangling dudes as a means of self-preservation against the dry lean years.

An automobile snorted down Fourth. The claybank did a nervous little dance, decided to get frightened, and went sun-fishing. Its rider gave a small cry of dismay.

The statue against the adobe wall woke to action. Like a coiled spring released, the body shot forward. Strong brown hands caught the bridle rein as the forefeet of the horse came down. Frustrated in an attempt to rise again, the claybank backed to the sidewalk. An arm of the rescuer swept up, encircled the waist of the young woman, and lifted her to the ground. To a Mexican standing near he released the horse.

She lay for a moment against his shoulder, supported by it, clinging to him while she gathered assurance of safety. Her laugh was a little tremulous, her voice not quite sure of itself, though the words she spoke held a note of friendly derision.

"Thank you, kind sir, the rescued maiden said."

A sardonic smile offered a glimpse of strong white teeth. "Dragons slain to order for lovely ladies," he assured her.

Ranse Brennan pushed forward. He was annoyed, unreasonably so. He objected to strange waddies introducing themselves to Doris Silver in such dramatic fashion. There had been no need of it. Given another second, he would have had the bridle rein himself without all this grandstanding. But that was the way of this young lady, to dramatize herself and her little adventures, to brush aside preliminaries and let a picturesque scamp forget the social distance between them.

"Does one just look up Saint George in the telephone book?" Mrs. Silver asked demurely in a low, melodious voice. Her soft eyes were shining. They were quick with invitation, filled with excited laughter.

"Poppycock! No danger at all. I was looking after you," Brennan blurted out.

He handed the cowpuncher a dollar. The gesture was born of an irritated impulse to put this meddler in his place.

The man in leathers looked at the coin lying in his brown palm, turned a slow, cool gaze on Brennan, then tossed the dollar to the Mexican.

"For holding the bronc, I presume," he drawled.

It was done with an easy insolence as disdainful as the arrogance of the older man.

The two measured each other, eye to eye, both recognizing an instinctive hostility. Brennan saw a young man of medium height, slender but well-built, with an appearance of sunburnt competence. So much this stranger had in common with many Arizona youths, but there was in the steady regard a quality of frosted granite that served as a warning.

Brennan was of uncertain temper, accustomed to bullying his way through opposition. He knew himself more forceful than most men. "I reckon you're too good to hold a lady's horse," he said, a rasp to his voice.

"I reckon you're wrong — both times," the answer came quietly.

Brennan did not need to ask information as to the other time. He had yielded to the self-indulgence of a gratuitous insult. To offer such a man money for a service done a woman was to violate unpardonably the code of the outdoors West. But it was written in the horoscope of Ranse Brennan that he must blunder through errors with a high hand rather than try to rectify them.

Then, with the irritation of the big man, there mingled a more disturbing sensation. Some vague fugitive memory, as yet too indefinite for recognition, something threatening out of the sinister and buried past, looked out of the steel-barred eyes at Brennan. For a moment fear, stark and naked, tightened the stomach muscles of the bully. Swiftly he brushed this aside. It was an emotion with which he was not familiar and did not intend to be.

"What's your name, fellow?" he demanded.

The cowpuncher ignored him and the question by turning coolly to the lady. A little crowd had gathered. The incident was due to close.

"If you're quite all right," he suggested.

"Quite. Thanks a lot." She offered her hand.

His palm met hers. They looked into each other's eyes. Once more his smile derisive showed a flash of pearly white against a background of brown. He dropped the small hand and turned away.

The gaze of Doris Silver followed him down the street. He was a man women looked at twice — and then again.

"This town is getting too full of tramps to suit me," Brennan said offensively, for all to hear. "Let's go, Mrs. Silver. The express office is round the corner. Juan will hold the horses."

Doris moved beside him, smiling to herself. Who was this stranger, dusty and travel-worn, with all the casual insolence of a young French aristocrat in the pre-revolutionary period? How had he acquired that manner which imposed on one a sense of the conflict between his youth and worldly wisdom, between the almost ragged clothes he wore and the consideration one was forced to grant his personality?

"If I had my way I'd put fellows like that on the rockpile," Brennan fumed, striding along the sidewalk with salient chin thrust forward.

The whole episode still irritated him — the service done her by another man, her treatment of it, the cowpuncher's manner, a sense of having come out second best, anger at having for a moment been disturbed by a chill wind of warning that had swept his heart. He was one whose vanity resented the acceptance of any but first place with the women he fancied.

Doris brought herself back from vagrant musing. She did not object to his jealousy. That was the natural tribute paid her charm, the symbol of success with men.

"Do you think you were quite — nice to him?" she asked, by way of probing his annoyance.

"Why should I be nice to every Tom, Dick, and Harry?"

She dropped a step or two behind him. "Please, you're going too fast for me."

Brennan slackened his pace ungraciously. "Didn't notice."

"Because he's a special Tom, Dick, or Harry. He helped me."

"Grandstanding. Any one could see that but a woman. I was reaching for the bridle when he butted in . . . You oughtn't to pick up a scalawag like that and treat him like your equal."

"But after he had done me a service — at some risk to himself," she demurred gently.

"No risk at all. Damned impudence . . . And you encouraged it."

The smallest of smiles twitched at her mouth. She slanted a quick look at him. "Was he impudent? I didn't notice it."

"You wouldn't," he said sourly. "If a man throws a big chest, a woman always falls for him."

"Oh, that's the way of it," she said innocently. "I've wondered about that. Do you explain Mr. Ranse Brennan that way?"

"I'm not talking about Ranse Brennan."

"Well, I think you're a little hard on my picturesque tramp. I thought he was quite nice."

"If you'd had as much experience of his kind as I have, you wouldn't think so. He's a bad lot. Take it from me."

A murmur of indulgent laughter welled from her soft round throat. "No doubt you're right. Anyhow, he doesn't matter, does he?"

Her words carried almost the effect of a caress. They dismissed the stranger as unimportant and reproved Brennan for not appreciating the special niche of favor he held with her. She was a master of the art of letting men believe that they came first among her friends.

Brennan felt a glow of anticipatory triumph. But he felt it necessary to stress his intuitive perception of the stranger's quality.

"A sure enough bad lot. What's he doing here? Who is he? He doesn't belong in this country. Probably one of Manuel Megares's ruffians."

Megares was the bogy man of the border, his name one with which to frighten naughty children to good behavior. Sometimes outlaw, not seldom rebel, always the villain of the plot, his name connoted theft, robbery, and murder.

"Do you really think so?" Doris cried. "I'm thrilled to death! I've heard Megares has Americans in with him. Let's go back and ask this man if he is an outlaw. If only I could believe it — well, I wouldn't have come West in vain."

He looked at her, annoyed. He preferred her not to think of other men when she was with him. "You don't know what you're talking about," he said. "Megares isn't any comic-opera bandit. He's a bad *hombre*."

"But it would be quite nice to meet him, wouldn't it — with you along to protect me." She beamed, eyes dancing. "They say he's quite a ladies' man."

"If you want to call it that," he said grimly.

"He speaks English fluently. So I hear. Went to school in this country. Quotes the poets. And is graceful and handsome."

He grunted. "Matter of opinion." Then, bluntly, he added: "You'd flirt with the Devil himself if you had the chance."

"Mr. Brennan," she reproved with mock coyness.

Along one of the nomadic roads of the border-land a horse ambled at a road gait. The rider sat the saddle with the careless ease of long habit. He was in no hurry. While he jogged along, his mind milled over a recent incident not clear to him.

8

A shimmer of heat danced above the sun-scorched plain. Now and again a dust eddy, an inverted cone, whirled across the desert sand. The vegetation had stamped upon it the stark gray look of life that has fought to endure. The clumps of cholla and prickly pear bristled with thorny defiance. The hole-pecked sahuaros were like grim old sentinels ready to succumb to years. Even the Apache plumes were dry and desiccated. There was something fantastic about the jigsaw line of hills standing against the horizon, as though they had no depth and substance, but were a stage property without reality.

Why had an instant dislike flared up in him at sight of Ranse Brennan, the rider asked himself? Before the man had said a word, before the insult of the offered silver, he had known they were to be enemies. The feeling still existed, and it was unreasonable. Was there not room in this wide world for each to go his own way and never meet the other?

The road ribbon wound up a hill shoulder and dropped abruptly to cross an arroyo. Beside a sandy wash a small car stood. One wheel was jacked up and a spare tire leaned against the running-board. From the interior of the car a pair of shapely legs projected. The owner of them seemed to be searching for a tool. Judging by the fervent "Damn!" he heard, the horseman guessed she was not finding it.

"Have you lost something?" he asked politely.

A slim body and a brown boyish head emerged from within. The look that swept over him was keen and swift.

"My temper," she said shortly.

"May I help you find it?"

She smiled, and the amber eyes beneath the dark lashes became warm as molten gold. "You have," she told him.

He swung from the saddle, dropped the bridle reins to the ground, and came forward. Both of them took it for granted that it was his job to change the tire. Inside of ten minutes he had the last bolt tightened. He removed the jack and replaced it with the other tools underneath the seat.

The girl had been watching him, curious in spite of herself. His worn clothes proclaimed him a cowpuncher, but he did not look like an ordinary waddy. What was it about him that gave the impression almost of distinction? Was it the careless good looks? The poised grace with which he carried himself? The expression so recklessly sardonic and yet so engaging?

"Are you with some outfit near here?" she asked. "I don't think I've seen you before."

"I'm riding the chuck line." He said it lightly, as though his bread and butter were a matter of the least consequence in the world.

She frowned, studying him. The man was competent. That was stamped all over him. What was wrong with him, then? Why did he have to go to a country where he was not known to look for a job? How explain the discrepancy between the apparent facts and that manner he had of riding the top wave?

"Where do you come from?" she asked curtly.

10

He waved a hand that might include all the points of the compass in its circuit.

"Where did you work last?" she insisted.

"I fixed a lady's tire on the Palo Duro road," he said blandly.

"Which reminds me. I haven't thanked you — and I do."

"Pleasure was mine," he drawled.

"I'm not just being inquisitive," she went on. "If you're looking for work, I know of a place."

"I'm looking for the kind of work I'm looking for," he answered, smiling at her.

"Do you drink?" she wanted bluntly to know.

"I thought this was a prohibition country."

"You're going at it a queer way to get a job," she said coldly. "I need a man myself to help on a guest ranch I run near here, but if I employ you, I'll have to know more about you."

"Yes, ma'am," he admitted.

A change had come over him. His manner had taken on the simulation of the humility of labor looking for employment after many rebuffs. It was apparent even in his voice. But the eyes were still full of gay impudence.

"Why did you leave your last place?"

"Had a few words with the boss, ma'am. He canned me — gave me my time."

"You oughtn't to be looking for work, a man like you. You can ride and rope, I suppose."

"Yes, ma'am."

She made a characteristic swift decision. "I own the Lazy R. It's three miles up the road. I'll give you sixty dollars a month and board to ride for me."

The question he asked seemed irrelevant. "Do you know a man called Ranse Brennan?"

"He's my foreman. Why?"

"Oh, nothing."

"Do you know him?"

"Met him this mo'ning, ma'am. You've hired a hand."

"All right. Report to Mr. Brennan."

She nodded a little farewell and got into the car.

"Who shall I say hired me?" he asked.

"Lee Reynolds. What is your name?"

"Call me Slim, ma'am."

"I prefer to call you by your name, if you're not ashamed of it." She gave him a look severe with reproof. What right had he to mock her with this pretense of humbleness, with this relapse into the voice and manner of an unlettered cowpuncher? She did not propose to put up with any nonsense from him. If he worked for her, he would find that out. He could reserve his humor for the other boys in the bunk-house.

"Yes, ma'am." There was a momentary hesitation before he suggested Smith. "John K. Smith," he added an instant later.

That was not his name, of course. She knew that. The way he had almost chuckled over it told her so. But she was a product of the Old West which carefully refrained from curiosity about a stranger's past.

"Very well. Since that name suits you, it does me."

Her foot touched the starter. The car moved down the road.

The man who had adopted the cognomen of Smith crossed the dusty track to his horse. "I shouldn't wonder, Blaze," he drawled to the animal, "if there wasn't fireworks around the li'l' boss once in a while."

The silky nose of the horse nuzzled his shoulder.

"An' her foreman is Mr. Ranse Brennan. Well, well, I reckon he's going to be real pleased to meet the new Lazy R rider."

Dipping down into the valley where the windmills of the Lazy R flashed sun signals at her, Lee Reynolds took herself to task.

"Now, why did you do that?" she asked herself. "Why did you hire that impudent, good-looking young scamp? There's something wrong about him. There must be. You deliberately insulted him, to make him fly up and get angry — and he didn't. He stood for it. Why? You've probably bought trouble, Miss Reynolds. Why-for did you do it?"

She did not know why. Her offer had been born of one of her fool impulses, as she called them. Ranse would not like it. She knew that. He would feel she was infringing on his rights as foreman. Lee shrugged her shoulders. If Ranse did not like it, he could do the other thing. She had a crow to pick with him, anyhow, on another matter.

Lee drove into the courtyard of the Lazy R and left the car under the shade of a huge live-oak. In the corral three men were busy with some wild young colts.

"Ranse back yet, Dunc?" she called to one of them.

An old man came to the fence and answered. "No, Miss Lee, he ain't."

"Will you tell him when he comes I want to see him?"

"Sure will."

He watched her walking to the house, a light, trim figure that moved without effort, springily, as a young deer does. She was a recent product of an Eastern finishing school, but that free gait had found its genesis in the untamed heart of the girl. It was an expression of her spirit. No schoolmarm had taught it to her.

Old Dunc Daggett's eyes followed her with a pride in them he did not attempt to conceal. Ever since she had been a baby he had served first her father and then her. He had taught her to ride and to rope and to shoot. She was the ewe lamb he cherished above all living things.

"Something seldom about that girl," he boasted to the perspiring youth who joined him at the fence.

Kansas mopped his face with the sleeve of the shirt he wore. "It don't hurt a fellow's eyes any to look at her," he agreed. "Funny about her. She's pretty as a new painted wagon, but she ain't what you'd call feminine in her ways. Me, I like a girl that waits for a fellow to take the lead, a girl —"

"Hmp!" snorted Daggett. "Who cares what you like? Why you cain't even rope a bronc. You don't know sic' 'em. Nothing but a brakeman. Call yoreself a cowboy, an' just now missed yore throw three times. In my time you would have been in a livery stable. If there were any good top hands left, I'd certainly send all you corral

14

dogs high-tailin' to town. But the country ain't what it usta be."

"I don't claim to be a champeen roper," Kansas demurred. "That ain't what we was talkin' about, anyhow. I claimed Miss Lee was a right nice good-lookin' girl, but in no ways feminine. You can't tell me different either. Why, if she sent Ranse down the road tomorrow, she could darn near run the ranch as well as he does."

"Better!" the old man cried, in the high falsetto that always seemed on the edge of excitement. "A doggone sight better! Lemme tell you about that girl, young fellow, me lad. Her pappy Lee Reynolds wanted a boy, an' he was plumb disapp'inted when the stork dropped in with the third girl runnin'. Then Mrs. Reynolds died an' the two oldest little girls. Got diphthery, they did. Lee was left alone with one little tyke six months old. Well, sir, he called her Lee an' started in to treat her like she was boy. It was duck soup for her. I never did see her heat. Pretty soon she was racin' all over Arizona, wild as a colt. She got so she could ride anything on four legs. She hated to think any boy could do something she couldn't. So she'd fork a pitchin' bronc an' stay with him to a fare-you-well. I've seen her throwed a dozen times. Usta be always black an' blue. But she never cried an' she never quit. Old Lee just lived in that kid. Hated to let her out of his sight for long. She was sure a handful."

"I've heard she could swear a blue streak," Kansas suggested.

15

"Gosh all hemlock! It was plumb funny to hear all that language comin' out of the mouth of such a li'l' trick. When she got mad, she'd stand with her feet straddled out an' cuss. Gentlemen, hush! One day a sky pilot come along an' listened in. He went straight to the Old Man an' had it out with him. Did he want his daughter to grow up a wild heathen like these fool cowboys? The Old Man packed her East to school. She let out an awful holler about goin'. That's one time she cried aplenty. Cain't blame her, can you? Every colt on the place was a personal friend of hers. She hated like sin to go back an' learn to act like a lady. But o' course what the Old Man said went . . . Too bad, one way lookin' at it. He died just before she graduated. An' both of 'em just lookin' forward to the time when they could be together again."

"Then she come home," Kansas prompted.

"An' found Arizona dry as a lime kiln. No rain for years. Fillaree burnt out. Cows' bones all over the range. Rustlers right busy helpin' themselves to what's left. A nice cheerful welcome home for a girl who would be nineteen comin' grass."

"Kinda tough," the younger man agreed.

"She was drug into it, but I wantta tell you she'll go through from hell to breakfast. Got sand in her craw, Miss Lee has. An' brains. Set you brakemen to wranglin' dudes instead of calves. Got her rich school friends an' their friends out here at sixty a week per and made 'em crazy about it. She ain't outa the timber yet, but you can bet that lone four bits in yore pocket that

16

she will be one of these days. Outside of her dad, Miss Lee is the best man I ever worked for."

"She's full of dynamite. My point is —"

"Nothin' to it. Trouble is you don't know a lady when you see one. Because Miss Lee don't doll up with all these dofunnies like the dudes —"

"I ain't a-claimin' Miss Lee is no lady. Don't you go puttin' words in my mouth, Dunc. All I said was she ain't no clingin' vine type."

"If you mean the p'ison ivy kind you're used to —"

"Listen, old hell-a-miler. When Miss Lee marries, who'll run the Lazy R? You darn well know who. The happy groom will be Miss Lee's husband, an' that's all he'll be. Now, me, when I pick me a wife from the Christmas tree, she'll understand I'm the head of the family."

"I'll tell the li'l' boss there's no use her pinin' for you any longer," the old man cackled, deep sarcasm in his toothless grin.

"You don't need to trouble yoreself," Kansas told him calmly. "I got reasonable good horse-sense. She wouldn't look at me in a thousand years. And that's that. I'm for Miss Lee all the way down the road. But I don't have to wear blinders, do I? Most usually her mind acts like a man's does. You heard her blister Stumpy with her tongue so he most shriveled up."

"What for?" old Dunc shrilled. "Left five calves in a corral without water, didn't he? For two days. Forgot 'em, he said. An' if you hadn't happened to be ridin' out Three Pines way, they would have died, wouldn't they? Sure I heard her. If you ask me, that boy was a leggin's case. What he needed was a pair of leathers laid on where they would do the most good. Forgot, huh!"

The third man in the corral drifted toward them, rope in hand. He had heard his name mentioned. He was a short, squat youth, bow-legged and fair-haired, with a face modeled so carelessly that the features lacked outline. Stumpy went through life with the helpless conviction that he was of no importance. He had heard it so often that he did not doubt it.

"Ranse," he said, with a jerk of the thumb toward a cloud of dust moving down the road.

Two riders were cantering toward the ranch house. One of them was Brennan, the other Doris Silver.

"I wonder where that lady's husband is at," Kansas murmured to the world at large.

Dunc Daggett's faded eyes jumped at him. "Some one elect you chaperoon of the Lazy R, Kansas?" he demanded with acerbity.

"Me? No." The cowboy looked at the boss of the remuda with an assumption of mild surprise. "I was jest thinking that if I was a judge at a beauty contest she'd win first place. She's real feminine too."

Old Dunc's snort was eloquent.

CHAPTER
TWO

Brennan lifted Doris Silver from the saddle. She flashed on him the enchanting smile that had worked mischief ever since she had been old enough to know its value, a date so remotely in the past as to be beyond her memory. It had been effective with nurses, parents, and teachers. Among her boy friends and the slim young college men she knew later there had been devastation in its wake. That smile, and the beauty back of it, had won for her everything she wanted in the world, or at least what she had thought was her heart's desire until she had it.

"A lovely ride," she murmured, and raised the blue eyes to let them rest for a moment in the bold, possessive ones of the foreman.

He felt himself lifted on a wave of triumph. "We'll go to Point of Rocks tomorrow," he promised.

"If you have time," she said, with the mental reservation that it might be better to have other plans. He was the kind of man who could get out of hand unless she was careful.

"I have twenty-four hours a day," he told her, largely.

She turned and ran lightly up the porch steps, waved an "*Adios!*" to him, and vanished into the house.

Daggert had called to him that Miss Lee wanted to see him, but he was in no hurry. He wanted to let his mind dwell for a while on the little affair he was promoting with Doris Silver and its promise of excitement for the future. He strolled over to the mail-box, glanced through the contents, and pretended to be busy reading a circular. That the little boss, as the men called her, was waiting for him in the office did not disturb his equanimity. She could wait. It would do her no harm. Recently she had shown irritation toward him once or twice. It was about time he gave her a lesson.

A long shadow crossed the line of his vision. He glanced up from the paper, to see Dunc Daggett approaching. He frowned. That Dunc did not like him he knew, though the old range rider was always scrupulously polite.

"Miss Lee, she said for me to tell you —"

"I heard you the first time, Dunc," the foreman interrupted rudely. "I'll see her when I'm ready. Don't get on the prod."

"— to tell you the claybank was her own private riding-horse not to be used for any of the ranch guests."

Daggett finished his sentence in an even monotone that carefully expressed no personal satisfaction in delivering the message.

A purple flush spread beneath the tan of Brennan's face. It was a rebuke, one she had chosen to make emphatic by delivering it through a third party. He knew why. In taking Nugget for the use of Doris Silver, he had deliberately ignored the fact that the gelding was for the sole service of his mistress as much as her toothbrush.

Brennan shifted from defense to attack. "Where's the rest of that bunch of broomtails I told you to run up?"

"In the big pasture."

"I see. We'll have to waste time running them up again. Nobody on this place knows how to take a straight order."

"I thought you said —"

"I'm paid to do the thinking, Dunc."

"In regards to that, Mr. Brennan, as the old sayin' is —"

"Are you foreman of this outfit or am I, Daggett?" Ranse demanded bleakly.

"You're foreman, an' I'm no eyeballer buttin' into yore business. Likewise an' also, Mr. Brennan, I'm boss of the remuda at present. When I don't cut the rust to suit her, Miss Lee will gimme my time, I expect."

The old man turned on his heel and walked away jauntily. To make it quite clear that he did not consider he had been called upon the carpet, he lifted his voice in a high falsetto chant, an old dance-hall refrain.

> Ducks in the river going to ford,
> Coffee in a little rag, sugar in the gourd;
> Chicken in the bread tray kicking up dough.
> "Granny, will yore dog bite?" "No, by Joe."

Brennan looked after him angrily. "Too many favorites in this outfit to suit me," he said, with bitterness.

21

The foreman strode across the open to the little adobe building used as an office. Lee Reynolds was at her desk looking over some bills. She glanced up.

"Dunc tell you I wanted to see you?" she asked.

"Yes."

"Good of you to come when you found time." The sarcasm was obvious.

"I stopped to look my mail over. Were you in a hurry?"

His voice was sullen. He was not used to being disciplined and he did not intend to get used to it.

"It doesn't matter." She put on the desk the bill that was in her hand. "I wanted to tell you that I've picked up a man to help Dunc."

"Hired him, you mean?"

"Yes. He'll be along in a little while."

"Thought I was majordomo of this ranch," he said, stiffening.

"You're the foreman — and, by the way, I'm the owner." The eyes that looked directly into his showed a touch of frost.

"Does the owner do the hiring?"

"When she wants to."

"Who is this fellow you hired?"

"He says his name is John Smith."

"Where did you run into him?"

Lee did not like his manner. Since he was an employee and not a partner, he had no right to put her on the witness stand. But she did not care just now to raise that issue and obscure a more important one.

"I met him down the road. He fixed my tire."

"What do you know about him?"

"Nothing. If he can't do the work satisfactorily, we'll let him go. By the way, he says he met you today."

"Where?"

"He didn't say."

As he looked down at her, there leaped into his mind a suspicion. "What kind of fellow? A brown impudent guy in shiny old leathers and gray shirt?"

"That does for a rough description," she admitted.

"I won't have it! That tramp can't work for me!"

Lee felt a touch of angry color in her cheeks. "He's not going to work for you, but for me, Ranse."

"He's a bad *hombre*. I knew it soon as I saw him. A troublemaker. I don't want him here."

This time she ignored that first person singular pronoun of his. "If he makes trouble, he can go down the road. What do you know against him?"

"He annoyed Mrs. Silver — dragged her from the saddle when Nugget pitched a little — then got sassy."

"He won't need to drag her from Nugget's back again," she said pointedly.

"One of these fellows that don't know their place." He yielded to a sudden irritation. "What's eatin' you, Lee? You've got mighty cranky lately. Ain't I runnin' the ranch right? Have you got any kick coming?"

"Yes, I have a kick," she told him flatly, her gaze steadily meeting his. "We'll come to that presently. You asked another question. I'm not running cows for my health, Ranse. My ledger tells me that ever since I came home, the Lazy R has been in the red. I've been carrying the cattle deficit out of the profits of the guest business."

"I'm not God Almighty," he flung back at her. "I don't make the drought. It's not my fault we've had three short-feed years on end and the range is baked like an oven."

"No," she assented. "You're not to blame for the activities of rustlers either, but you're responsible for seeing they don't get my stock. Over a hundred head have been driven across the line this year. I don't find it profitable to raise cows for Megares."

"Can I help it? What can I do more than I've done? They raid our range in the dark of the moon. I can't close-herd all the Lazy R cattle."

"If you can't help it, you are unlucky," she said deliberately.

"What do you mean by that?" Brennan demanded roughly.

"Perhaps if you gave more of your time to the cattle and less to the guests, it might be better. You forget I'm not employing you to run the guest ranch. That's my particular job. You have nothing to do with it."

Again a deep flush suffused the foreman's face. His mouth set to an ugly line.

"You've got uppity since you went off to school and got in with your rich friends," he told her. "I can remember when you weren't too good for me."

It was the girl's turn to flush. There had been a month, during the first summer vacation home from school, when her eager eyes had seen him through a glamour. He had seemed to typify that West to which her nostalgic mind had turned all year. Shrewdly he had capitalized her sentiment to his own advantage. Secretly and doubtfully she had let herself become half engaged to him. There had been a hurried kiss or two, virginal and reluctant on her part. Then she had come to her senses.

"I was fifteen and you were thirty-five," she said. "Nice of you to remind me what a fool I made of myself. You don't need to be afraid I'll do it again, Ranse."

"You act like I'm poison," he growled. "It's you that's changed, not me."

She turned her back on that subject. "You asked me if I have a kick. I have. One sure way to wreck a guest ranch is to play favorites among those who come to it. I won't have flirtations between the help and the guests. You may tell me some of the women who come to the Lazy R want the excitement of foolish little affairs. They are bored and like to get interested in outdoor men. I'm not concerned about that except so far as it gives the Lazy R a bad name among the nice people who come here. I want my boys to be friendly and courteous to all the guests, not to single out individuals for their attentions. Do you understand?"

Brennan was furious. "Are you trying to tell me what I can and can't do?"

"As long as you're my employee — yes."

"Meaning Mrs. Silver?"

"It's not necessary to name anybody in particular."

"She can look out for herself. I won't do her any harm."

Lee smiled, not without malice. She understood Doris Silver a good deal better than Brennan did. They had been roommates at school, and Lee had been the confidante of a never-ending series of episodes with various youths. If one point stood out of them, it was that Doris would not be the one hurt in case there was a casualty.

"I know all about that. It's my business I don't want harmed."

The foreman slammed a big fist down on the desk. "Don't talk that way to me, girl. I won't have it. No woman alive — and no man either — can lay down the law to Ranse Brennan. It's not being done, never has been and never will be. You've got another guess coming if you think you can tell me who my friends are to be. Might as well get that straight now. I'm free, white, and twenty-one — and I'm a he-man. Understand?"

With a scornful little lift of the hand she brushed aside what he had said. "I care nothing about your friends. What I'm getting at —"

"You did once," he reminded her with a sneer. "I'm not so sure you don't now. Listen, Lee. When the time comes I'll have something to say to you. It's going to be with us the same as it was once. You can't turn me down the way you do these knot-heads that fall for you. I'm not that kind of a bird. What I want I get."

Her eyes blazed with cold anger, but she did not raise her voice. "Are you telling me that you will look with favor on me again — after you're through with the other women you find more interesting?"

"Don't get jealous. What I say is —"

"You've said too much already. I never saw such insolence. Will it be convenient for you to leave the ranch today?"

"What do you mean, leave the ranch?"

"You've talked yourself out of a job. You're fired."

"Fired?" He glared at her. "Don't be a fool, Lee. You can't run this ranch without me. You know that."

"Can't I? We'll see. You overestimate your importance. I'll send a check to the bunk-house. One of the boys will drive you to town."

"What are you trying to do?" he roared. "You can't kick me out like an old shoe. I won't have it."

She rose, a straight, slender young creature, brown and hard as most of the wild life of the desert. "I'll add two weeks' pay to the check," she said quietly.

A savage anger mounted in him. This was a totally unexpected finale and one that did not suit his plans. "Forget it. You can't get funny with me. I'll not stand for it. I'm dangerous. Understand? Do me dirt, and I'll ruin you."

"Yes? How will you do that?"

She tossed the question at him with careless contempt. Why not? She was youth in the saddle. The only defeat she had ever known was that disastrous one when Death had snatched her father. Then her strong arrogant will had been powerless. Brennan was only a bully making futile threats.

Enraged, he was not a sight pleasant to look upon. His empurpled face was a picture of ugly passion. As he moved around the table toward Lee, she did not back away. Steadily she faced him, with eyes unafraid.

"I'll show you how. Before I'm through, you'll beg for mercy."

"Interesting if true!"

"When I snap my fingers, you'll come like a whipped cur."

"Shall I?"

Her cool scorn fell on him like the lash of a whip. That she was so indifferently sure of being beyond the reach of his revenge fanned the flame of his fury. He caught her by the shoulders and shook her.

"Damn it, yes! With your head and your heels dragging, scared to death."

"Take your hands away! Don't you dare touch me!" she warned.

He was beside himself, beyond caution. "I'll show you!"

An arm encircled her waist and dragged the slim body to his. Roughly he tilted up her chin so that his eyes could meet and challenge hers.

"I tell you to let me go, you fool!" she cried.

His snarl disregarded her protest. "Too good for me, are you? We'll see about that, missie. From right damn now."

The man's kisses stung her cheeks and lips and throat. She did not spend her strength in resistance, though the anger in her was like a fire. The groping fingers of the girl found and opened a desk drawer, closed on the handle of a small revolver, and pressed the end of the barrel against his ribs.

Brennan struck down swiftly at Lee's wrist. There was an explosion and the foreman staggered back. He caught at his thigh.

"You damned wildcat!"

He stood glaring at her, ready to plunge like a wild bull if she wavered. The hand back of the weapon was steady, though she felt the pounding heart in her bosom.

"Stay back there! Don't move!" she ordered; voice shrill with excitement.

"You've shot me, you hellion."

Lee became aware that some one was standing in the doorway, though her back was turned to it. A voice made itself heard, one politely interested and just a little amused.

"If I'm intruding, just let me know," it said.

The young woman backed from the desk in order to be able to see the newcomer without lifting her gaze from Brennan.

"He says I've shot him," she panted, lips bloodless. "It's his own fault."

A brown-faced man in worn shiny leathers moved forward.

CHAPTER
THREE

If the new Lazy R rider was surprised to see the foreman with a bullet in his thigh and the boss with a revolver in her hand, he gave no evidence of it. Nobody could have guessed from his manner that such acute differences of opinion were not a part of his daily life.

"You told me to report to Mr. Brennan, ma'am, and one of the boys said he was in here," he explained.

"You don't have to report to him. He isn't foreman now," Miss Reynolds snapped. She was frightened at what she had done and the fear sharpened her voice. "Better see how much he's hurt. One of the boys will get a doctor."

"Or an undertaker, ma'am," the man in chaps suggested pleasantly. He was already convinced that the wound was not a very serious one.

"He isn't badly hurt. Is he?" The question followed the statement, forced from the girl by terror. Surely she had not killed the man.

"I reckon not, ma'am. Looks to me like a nice clean flesh wound. When I spoke, I didn't know whether you were through with him."

"He made me do it. He struck my arm." Lee shuddered.

"That's a lie!" Brennan flung back, showing his teeth.

"Sho! That's no way to talk to a lady," the cowpuncher admonished genially. "Never contradict 'em. Give 'em the last word. If you'd listened patient to the li'l' boss, she wouldn't have had to puncture one of your tires."

"Get out of my way — both of you!" the ex-foreman roared. He walked, limping slightly, to the door. There he turned, to shake a fist savagely at the owner of the Lazy R. "Just wait. See how far you get with this. You've bought trouble today will last you long as you live."

The cowpuncher smiled. "Ideas don't seem to get across to you very well, Mr. Brennan. If I were in your place I'd gather, in a sort of a general way, that the lady was annoyed with me. I expect that's why she sent you the little pill, as a reminder that you were getting on her nerves. Time for you to say *Adios*."

"Don't get funny with me, fellow. It ain't supposed to be safe. For half a cent I'd work you over right now."

The other man drew a hand indolently from the pocket of a pair of Levis and tossed a dollar on the table. "Don't let any good notions like that go to waste," he drawled.

For the second time Brennan felt the chill of ice traveling down his spine, of something menacing reaching toward him from the past which he had buried. It spoke out of the cold steely eyes of the stranger. He was puzzled and disturbed by the strange warning. What was there about this youth that set a bell tolling in him?

With a sound from his throat that was both an oath and a snarl, Brennan turned and left the office.

Lee dropped the revolver on the table and looked at her new rider. "He can't be badly hurt," she said, asking reassurance.

"Don't worry about that *hombre*. If he's not a bad egg, the break was sure against him when he got that plug-ugly face. How come you to start the fireworks? Or is that none of my business?"

A tide of pink washed into her cheeks. "He . . . forgot himself," she said.

"Well, he won't forget you, ma'am — not right away. I didn't like that look he gave you before he left. I'd say he was a vindictive devil."

"What harm can he do me?"

"I don't know," he smiled. "But maybe you do."

She shook her head. "I don't see what he could do."

"Plenty, if he sets out to get even."

She drew a deep breath. "Anyhow, I'm glad I didn't . . . hurt him worse, even though it was his own fault."

"I reckon he had it coming."

"Maybe, but — Wouldn't it be awful to kill some one . . . not meaning to, and yet in anger?" The horror of the thing she had escaped stared at him out of her brown-flecked eyes. All the arrogance had for the moment been shocked out of her. She was a child who had been playing with edged tools and had grazed the skirt of tragedy.

"Not so good," he agreed, looking into her blanched face. "But you needn't waste time over what might have been."

32

"No."

From her forehead she brushed back a truant lock of wavy hair, a tawny gold shot through with copper. The gesture had its touch of boyishness, the frank unconsciousness of sex.

They heard the clump of boots. Dunc Daggett came into the office, his eyes big question marks.

"Everything all right?" he panted.

"I shot Ranse," the girl answered.

The old fellow needed no explantion in justification. "Good for you!" he cried in his high shrill falsetto. "I'll bet he asked for it. Me, I never did take a smile to that moke. He's a bad outfit."

"I discharged him. He's not foreman any more."

"I knew it had to come, Miss Lee. None too soon, I say. He's out there in the corral, with hell in his neck, spillin' a mess of cuss-words while Kansas runs him up his bronc. He can't rattle his hocks away from here any too fast to suit me. Got fresh with you, did he? Wisht I'd of been here with a six-gun in my hand. You're damn whistlin'! Excuse me ma'am. I meant to say doggone."

"Does he seem much hurt?"

"No, ma'am, but sore as a toad on a skillet. He'll hive-him off to a ginmill in the nearest honkatonk town an' fill himself up with coffin varnish. If you ask me, I'm sure pleased you handed him that pill from yore little tried an' true. He needed it, that bird. I never did see such a bully puss fellow. Been actin' like he owned the whole place, you an' the dudes to boot. Always runnin' over someone for no reason a-tall except that he's sull an' overbearin'."

"Let Buck take him to town in a car. He ought not to ride. And see his leg is fixed up before he goes."

"Hmp! You know him, Miss Lee. He'll do as he doggone pleases, bull his way through to suit his own self."

"Yes, but give him a chance to refuse. Even if we're through with him, I don't want him to fall off his horse on the way to town. This is our new rider, Dunc. His name is John Smith. He'll help you with the remuda at present. Kansas will go back to fencing. Will you please see that John is looked after at the bunk-house?"

"Yes'm. Pleased to meet you, Mr. Smith. Hope yore corporosity will sagasuate nice at the Lazy R. It's a right nice ranch." Daggett's chin fell. He stared at the man whose hand he was shaking. Then a yelp of recognition leaped from his wrinkled throat. "Dog my cats, if it ain't —"

"John T. Smith, known as Slim," the young man cut in.

"The middle initial is T now, is it?" Lee asked. "It was K a little while ago. At least you told me so."

"Did I? I'm mighty careless sometimes. My brother is Jule K. We're twins. Folks are always mixin' us up."

"And sometimes you mix yourselves up. Are you quite sure now you are John T and not Jule K?"

"Positive, ma'am. Reckon I must have been thinking of something else when you asked me down the road. I'm kinda absentminded sometimes, as you might say."

34

"Yes? Which brother did you think he was, Dunc?" the girl inquired derisively.

Daggett was not ready for this direct thrust. "Well, Miss Lee, I wasn't right sure. I thought maybe —"

"Don't forget that our one is John T. T for Truthful, I dare say."

"T for Theocritus, ma'am," the new employee corrected. "My father was kinda fond of those old Greek poets."

"And his son is fond of the fables, I think."

That was her parting shot. She drew a chair up to the desk and reached for a pen.

The man who had fastened upon himself the name of John Theocritus Smith followed Daggett from the room. As soon as they were out of hearing, Daggett sputtered an indignant protest at his companion.

"What's the matter with you, boy? Ain't yore dad's name good enough for you?"

"I didn't expect you'd know me. It's been fifteen years since we last met. I was a little chap then."

"Know you? Why, you're the spittin' image o' Jack Hadley, the way he looked when he was a young colt before he raised a beard . . . I'm plumb glad to see you. Where you been all this time?"

"A lot of places, Mr. Daggett."

"Dunc," the old-timer interposed.

"Dunc, then. I'm here on a little matter of very private business."

"Hmp! Got anything to do with a sheriff trying to locate you?"

"No."

"Glad to hear it. What's all the mystery about, Jack Hadley? If you're tryin' to fool the li'l boss, you can try something easier. She's got you pegged right now. John T. Smith! Hmp!"

"I'm not trying to fool her. But I've got reasons for not telling every one I'm Jack Hadley."

"You in trouble, son?"

"No. A man died in a Los Angeles hospital the other day. Just before he passed out his mind got to wandering. He told me about my father's death."

The old man drew a plug of tobacco from his hip pocket and cut off a chew. His eyes gleamed savagely. He had personal reasons for interest in this subject. "What did this fellow say? Was he one of the bunch of lousy coyotes that did it?"

"Yes. It was on his conscience. He was a renegade serving with Francisco. It got him to see an American lined up and shot, but he daren't let out a peep. Francisco wouldn't have stood it a moment. The point of his story is that the man who led the outlaws to the mine used to work for my father and is now living on a ranch near Spring River."

Daggett spat at a flat stone and made a center shot. "Dog my cats! Who is this bird? An' where does he live? At which ranch?"

"Don't know. When this sick man began to talk, the nurse thought his mind was wandering. She didn't pay any attention until he mentioned my father's name. She's a friend of our family. The man died without repeating the name of the betrayer. She says it was an American name, not Mexican."

"Would she know it again if she heard it?"

"She thought so."

"Hmp! Worked for yore dad, he said. Quite of lot of scalawags did that, off an' on. So that's why you're here — to find this lousy lobo?"

"That's why I'm here."

The old-timer looked at him curiously. In this young fellow's quiet manner was a threat more deadly than bluster. It occurred to Daggett that a tiger on the trail would be less dangerous.

"An' of course you don't want this skunk to know yore name?"

"Not till I'm ready to balance accounts."

"At which time he'll turn up his toes to the daisies. Is that to be the way of it?"

Hadley looked at the horse wrangler and said nothing.

"Count me in, son, long as there's a button on Jabe's coat," Daggett continued.

"No, I'm playing a lone hand. All you can do is give me information. You've been here a long time — know everybody in the Spring River country?"

"All the old-timers. I don't claim to know all these one-gallus plowhands that call themselves cowboys nowadays. Yep, I drifted here to the Lazy R right soon after what happened at the mine. Been here ever since, first with her pappy Lee Reynolds an' then with the li'l' boss."

"I'll want to check up the whole list." Abruptly the young man tossed a question at his companion. "What do you know about this fellow Ranse Brennan?"

"I know he's mean an' ugly as galvanized sin." The startled eyes of Daggett sought those of the man in chaps. "You ain't suspectin' Brennan, are you?"

"I suspect every possibility, till he ceases to be one. What about his past?"

"He came here soon after I did. I ain't got any medicine on his past. Ranse don't talk about it. But he ain't yore man. He can't be. It ain't reasonable that I'd spend fifteen years with a fellow who helped kill my best friend an' left me for dead without me gettin' hep to him."

"Why? It took place after dark. You couldn't identify the murderers, could you?"

"No — except one, maybe. He was a Mexican. Had a scar above the left eye. He was the one put me out when the attack first started. There was a full moon."

"I know that. I was there."

"Sure enough. You an' yore dad an' Big Bill an' me. I always figured it was some of the Mexicans workin' at the mine betrayed us to that devil Francisco. An' it was a white man, by this fellow in the hospital's story?"

"Yes. This outlaw Megares was a lieutenant of Francisco at that time, wasn't he? Did you ever hear whether he was in that raid?"

"No. Maybeso he was, maybe not. Those fellows were always scatterin' an comin' together again. Son, I'll never forget that night, an' I don't reckon you will."

"Never."

The young man looked grimly across the saffron-hued desert to the porphyry mountains. He did not see the shriveled greasewood, the parched mesquite, the gray-green cholla, nor did he see the shilvery sheen of the sun rays streaming over them. He was not aware of the opalescent mirage that lay like a lake in the hollow between two hills.

What he saw was the stark setting of that red tragedy which many years ago had leaped out of the night and changed his life.

The mine lay far up in the Sierras. Jack Hadley was resident manager, and at this time he was working only a small force, all natives except Daggett and Big Bill. Hadley's motherless little boy was with him.

That little boy, now a full-sized man, still remembered fragments of the talk in the cabin before he fell asleep.

Daggett had rambled on in his garrulous fashion, discussing a projected railroad through the hills. Big Bill, who had just returned with the monthly payroll for the men, had heard there was a party of surveyors in the mountains.

"Don't get excited, Bill, about that railroad," Daggett advised. "I got all het up about one comin' into Ajo twenty years ago an' most rode a mustang to death to beat it into town an' buy me some lots. It ain't there yet, nor liable to be. A railroad ain't ever built till you see the choo-choo trains runnin'."

Hadley rose, walked over to the bunk where his small son lay, and tucked him in. "Sleep tight, Jack," he said, with the warm smile which promised love and protection, the smile that within a few minutes was to be blotted out forever.

The eyes of the boy dropped. He fell asleep.

And awoke to the sound of crashing guns. Daggett was sinking down upon the bunk, smothering him where he lay. He caught a glimpse of brown men charging at his father, who stood in the center of the room with a smoking revolver in his hand.

It seemed forever to the small boy before he could burrow out from under the body of the man pinning him down. He heard voices outside the house as he worked to free himself. One was harsh and dominant, the brutal voice (so he learned later) of Francisco, the outlaw chief. The other was that of his father, quiet and steady.

"So. You keel my men, two of them. You tell me lies — lies, Meester Hadley. You say this is all the money your man bring. I do not believe, but if so you are sairtainly onlucky." The man interrupted himself with a savage laugh. "You have thirty seconds, Meester Gringo. Where iss that money?"

"You have it all. Figure it out, you fool. We are working thirty-five men. If you multiply —"

"Poof! You beeg man there! Can you talk?"

Big Bill let out a cry of rage cut short by the roar of guns.

When little Jack Hadley crept out of the cabin, the raiders had gone. He found the bodies of Big Bill and his father.

Ranse Brennan straddled the horse Kansas had run up and saddled for him. The animal was a square-built, short-backed bay with a deep barrel body.

"He ain't hurt much," Dunc volunteered, watching him.

"No," agreed young Hadley, and added, "If he's not a crook, he's got all the earmarks of one."

"I never liked him, not from the first. Always knew there was something shady about him. I'll bet he's swung many a wide loop in his day."

"Queer. Soon as I saw him this morning, I felt hostile. Hated him *pronto*. Why?"

Daggett did not answer. He was watching the ex-foreman.

"See how he forks that bronc, boy, draggin' savage at the bit an' driving in his spurs. He's mean, I tell you. Never did treat a horse right . . . By Jinks, Tequila is sure enough pitching. Hooray! He's done piled the slit-eyed son of a gun."

Hadley grinned. "Hats off to Tequila. He certainly let Mr. Brennan have a bird's-eye view of the scenery before hitting the dust."

The old-timer's voice grew squeaky with excitement. "Ranse is some covered with Arizona. He's gonna try it again. Listen to him cuss a blue streak. Didn't I tell you he was mean? See him kick Tequila in the belly. I wisht that barrel-bodied bay would kick his lights out. He's on again. Here he comes! Look out!"

The last words were a shout of warning. In the saddle once more, his face a map of purple rage, Brennan caught sight of Hadley's scoffing grin as the horse plunged forward. With a jerk of the rein he guided the animal straight at the cowpuncher.

Jack ducked, just in time. In a cloud of dust horse and rider swept past at a gallop and dashed down the road.

"He tried to run you down!" Dunc screamed.

"I noticed it," returned Hadley evenly, his hard eyes on the diminishing figure of Brennan. "I think I've found the man I'm looking for, Dunc."

Dunc tilted back his chair and stroked a lean gray jaw rough as a field of wheat stubbles. "Looks like it's neck meat or nothin', Miss Lee. Country's dry as a cork leg. No fillaree. No six-week grama. The desert ain't been as baked as this since the Rincons were a hole in the ground. No use tellin' you that, though, after you've seen the bones of yore cows bleachin' in the sun. So you done got the Costillo Ranch?"

"On a year's lease."

"Good. When do we drive?"

"Soon as we can round-up. I'd like to start by Thursday." Lee turned to the other man in the room, a tall thin young fellow with delicate shadows under his fine dark eyes. "I'm going to leave you in charge of the guest ranch, Hamilton. The season is nearly over. After next week, nobody will be left but Mr. and Mrs. Ensworth. Kansas and Buck will take care of the remuda. You won't have much to do. Just keep things going and answer the correspondence. I'll go over everything with you."

Hamilton was a "lunger," exiled from the East for his health. Already he knew that the fine dry air of the arid Southwest was going to make a new man of him.

"I'll try to keep things up as you want them," he said.

"You'll go with me, Dunc, unless you'd rather stay here," the girl continued. "It may be a tiring trip. If you think it would wear you out —"

"Wear me out!" the old-timer snorted. "Are you just puttin' on, Miss Lee? To hear you talk, a fellow would think I'd been around since the first mornin' star riz. Ridin' don't faze me none. Since I'm drug into makin' my brags, I'll say that I'll be sittin' high an' handsome when the tails of yore dude wranglers are draggin' in the dust. An' you need someone of experience with you. These kids don't know any more about cows than a hog does about a side-saddle. Me, I was a brush-popper in Texas, ma'am, in the good old long-horn days."

"You qualify, Dunc," his mistress said, smiling at him. "We'll have with us Smith, Rusty, Stumpy, Jim Yell, and Stan Ritter. That will make seven of us. Had I better pick up a couple more men in town?"

"How big a herd do you figure on drivin'?"

"About twenty-five hundred."

"Hmp! Stumpy don't amount to a barrel of shucks. He can't even throw a rope. Smith is a top hand. Jim Yell and Stan Ritter are all right as riders go nowadays. Rusty ain't so bad if he'd get a move on him an' not act as sleepy as a snail climbin' a slick log. I'd say we better have a couple more, or even three. We can use 'em on the round-up too."

"All right. I'll get three. We start rounding-up tomorrow. You'll be wagon boss, Dunc. I'll send Charley out to cook for you. Better ride circle from Cottonwood Buttes first."

Busy days at the Lazy R followed. Riders combed the shale ridges and the water-gutted arroyos, dust caked on their unshaven faces. They plunged through the prickly pear and the ocotillo, both now abloom with lovely scarlet flowers that not even the long drought had been able to prevent. They followed flying two-year-olds among the cholla and the bisnaga.

At the round-up grounds, fires were lit, irons heated, and calves branded. Cows bawled their anxiety, the young blatted fear. Men roped, threw, tallied, and applied the redhot ~.

The crew was aroused before daybreak. In the gray light of pre-dawn they swallowed hot coffee and ate biscuits and strips of steak that had been cooked in pots of boiling lard. They rode from camp into a desert touched to magic by the dim, mysterious morning light. The sun came up, and the plain was no longer a sea of swirling mist.

All through the sultry hours the dust and noise of cattle milling as they were worked filled the air. In the untempered light the desert showed its teeth, every gaunt detail visible. The cruel sting of both animal and vegetable life made clear that here nothing existed except by struggle. So it was till sunset, when the dusk blurred harsh realities and softened the landscape to a violet haze. Then the hard dry mountains wore vivid scarfs and the hollows of the far hills became reservoirs of color beautiful and rare.

It was long after nightfall before the weary punchers, like tired schoolboys, rolled into their blankets and fell instantly asleep. Almost before their eyes were closed, so it seemed to them, by turns they were aroused to circle the sleeping herd.

Hard work, long hours, little rest, but always much laughter and joking and rough horse-play. And day by day the herd grew, as each drive brought in from prong and arroyo more Lazy R cattle.

By Wednesday night the country had been combed and a chuck-wagon loaded with supplies. Saddles had been checked up and the remuda run into a pasture.

To Lee, making a list of first-aid medical supplies, came Doris Silver with word that she wanted to go along.

"Thought you were going home," the mistress of the Lazy R said.

"I did think I would, but I've had a letter from Harold and I've decided I don't want to go back just yet."

Lee looked at her in surprise. "Doesn't he want you?"

"Yes. That's just it."

Which cryptic remark Lee understood without explanation. "Of course. If he didn't want you, a plane couldn't take you home too fast. You ought to be paddled, Doris."

"I'm sure I ought. I'd probably love Harold if he'd do that. But he won't. He's too much the little gentleman."

"He's far too good for you. I wish you had a brute for about four months to abuse you. It might make a reasonable human being of you . . . Why don't you stay here, then? We're not going on a picnic, you know."

"I'm bored here, dear. I think it would be fun to go to this hacienda. You told me yourself it was a delightful place."

Lee covered her annoyance under a manner of explanatory patience. "Did I tell you that we are all going to be very busy, fifteen or sixteen hours a day in the saddle, swallowing dust and baking in the heat? Did I mention that we'll live on rough food and bed on the ground with ants and bugs and mosquitoes to make the nights pleasant?"

"I wouldn't like that," Doris admitted. "But I could stay at the hacienda and drive out sometimes to see you in the car."

"We'd be too busy to spend time amusing you. Then you'd be bored again."

"No, I won't. I promise not to be any trouble."

"Oh, promise! If you'd only understand that we're not going on a yachting cruise with a lot of servants to wait on you."

"Of course I know that. I'm not a child." Doris reflected that with seven or eight men in the party, no matter how busy they were, she would have plenty of attention. Also, the Costillos were leaving a cook and a maid at the ranch.

With the forthright directness of one used to this lady's vagaries and not intrigued by them, Lee flung out a question. "Who is the man, Doris? Ranse has gone and isn't within reach to be made a fool of. It can't be old Dunc or Stumpy. Or Jim Yell. Rusty doesn't seem to have a romantic manner. Is it this new man Smith?"

Doris pouted. Even the pout was charming. The lovely lips had a little twist of humor that denied the petulance. "Must there be a man? Sometimes I'd like to see them all transported. Men aren't the only thing in the world. I want to catch up with my reading."

"Yes, you do!" derided Lee. "All right. I've warned you. Come if you like. I'm driving through the first day in the car. You may go with me if you like, though I can tell you I'll not be much of the time at the ranch for the first month."

Doris conjured visions of moonlight rides in the soft languorous air of Mexico, knee to knee with a brown-faced man whose flashing smile suggested mockery rather than deference. Here was a foeman, she felt, worthy of her steel. His indifference, amounting almost to insolence, piqued her vanity and stimulated her interest. When they met, as they had done three or four times in the course of the week, imps of deviltry danced in his cool eyes and made clear that he understood perfectly that she would like to chain him to her chariot wheels, and made it equally clear that he had no intention of being her slave. Doris longed for a chance to show him.

"You ought not to be down there with all those men, all alone except for a servant or two," Doris said smugly. "It will be better if I'm there."

"Flapjacks!" Lee scoffed. "Madam Grundy has nothing to do with the etiquette of the cattle business. But come down if you like and be the chaperone, or, if you prefer, the Lovely Lady of the Hacienda. You'll do that last to perfection, though I don't think there will be any Spanish dons to stand under your window and sing passionate love-songs."

"Nor any bandits in sombreros and sashes to hold us for ransom?"

"Afraid not." Lee shook her head, smiling at her. "You're going to be so terribly disappointed, my dear."

Doris denied this, nodding brightly. "We'll see. I've been to too many movies. I know."

And as the sequel developed, her guess was a good deal closer to the truth than that of Lee.

CHAPTER
FOUR

For weeks the long line of gaunt cattle had moved south across the baked desert. Weakened though the herd was, Dunc had to make forced marches to distant water-holes. More than one night he had been obliged to loose-bed at a dry camp. Along the trail behind them were the skeletons, already picked bare by lobo and buzzard, of a score of Lazy R cows that had collapsed.

The trail herd was in a bad way. Hip bones stood up like revolver butts of a two-gun man. Ribs were furrowed like washboards. The black tongues of the plodding beasts hung out from drooping heads. Hunger gnawed at every stomach. The continuous bawling from swollen, thirst-tormented throats was piteous.

Lee rode along the straggling line, observing with anxious eyes. She put Nugget to a lope and joined Dunc at the drag. Rusty was with him. The men were gray with alkali dust. Their red-rimmed eyes turned toward her, those of Rusty drowsily half-shut.

Daggett's high cackle was jubilant. "We're gonna make it, Miss Lee. Ten miles now till we strike the Santa Cabrillo. Looky!" His wrinkled hand pointed to the hillside rising from a distant valley. "The country's greenin' up. Come night the leaders will be rattlin' their hocks down to the river. It won't hurt my feelin's none to quit spittin' cotton an' swallowin' dust. They say a fellow has got to eat a pint of dirt, but I done chewed more'n a bushel of Sonora already. I could drink right now prob'ly a keg of beer."

"I was worried yesterday," Lee admitted. "I didn't think they had another day's travel in them. But you've prodded them along fine, Dunc. The leaders are smelling water already. They are stretching their necks and moving faster. Think I'll throw off and give the herd a day or two to rest and feed when we reach the river."

"Good. How far is the rancho from here?"

"Not more than forty miles. Plenty of water and good grass all the way down the river."

"I've got to wonderin' if there's any such things in the world." Daggett looked around in disgust. He saw a hard turquoise sky, a copper sun, a cracked plain where even the dust-covered greasewood looked shriveled and parched. "Seems like I been travelin' in a frypan 'most all my life. Did you say honest-to-God grass, Miss Lee?"

"Fillaree, Dunc, and grama." The young woman turned to Rusty. "What did those Mexicans want, the ones you were talking with this morning?"

"Nothing, I reckon, ma'am. Claimed they were hunting horses. I asked one of 'em about that rumor of a revolution brewing we saw in the 'Star.' He grinned and shook his head."

"Probably he would know nothing about it even if it were true," Lee said.

"An' if he did, he wouldn't tell you," Daggett added. "A greaser can be awful dumb when he's a mind to. But, by Jacks! I ain't worryin' about no revolution. They're always hatchin' one here, but it don't most usually break till *mañana*."

The eagerness of the herd to reach water became apparent. The long line of travel lengthened as the leaders began to move away from the main body. Even the drag made an attempt to hurry, though some of the weakest could hardly scrape one foot in front of another.

A fiery sunset set the western sky ablaze. The valley of the Santa Cabrillo could be seen through a lilac envelope of air. The desert lost its harshness. The thorny ocotillo blossomed with banners of purple and scarlet, the cholla with red and crimson, the greasewood, the prickly pear, and the palo verde with yellow blooms or scarlet. The floor of the plain was patterned blue and pink with alfilaria. Winter and spring rains had made an oasis of a sandy waste.

Night had blanketed the desert long before the herd had been watered and bedded. Moonlight was drenching it with soft silver by the time the riders sat down cross-legged to a welcome supper.

"If anyone was to ask you," Jim Yell said, fighting mosquitoes away with the tattered hat he wore, "you can tell 'em I sure earned my two bucks today, an' some."

Yell was a tall lank man, loosely built, a Texan. Daggett had once described him as "long like a snake an' draggin' the ground when he walks."

"Me," said Rusty, easing his stiff limbs into a comfortable position, "after this drive is over, if it ever is, I'd like to lay like a lizard on a rock for about a week."

From a pup tent set a little way from the camp a contralto voice could be heard singing softly a trail song. Jack Hadley listened. It had not been cultivated, and it held no unusual range or quality, but there was a note in its throaty sweetness he liked.

"Listen, boys, the li'l' boss is singin'," Stan Ritter interrupted. "I reckon she's right glad to have got over the desert."

"She's done forgot we're here," Daggett explained. "Don't all quit gassin' at once or she'll stop. Kinda ease up some."

> Last night as I lay on the prairie,
> And looked at the stars in the sky,
> I wondered if ever a cowboy
> Would drift to that sweet by and by.
>
> Roll on, roll on,
> Roll on, little dogies, roll on, roll on,
> Roll on, roll on,
> Roll on, little dogies, roll on.

There was a soothing anodyne in the chorus as it fell from Lee Reynolds's lips into the soft Mexican night. The words and tune had been used by each man present a score of times to quiet a restless herd at night. It had been sung for sixty years by trail-drivers from

52

Lockhart, Texas, to Billings, Montana. But there were two men present who would always associate it henceforth with Lee Reynolds.

One of them was the snub-nosed, bowlegged little puncher dubbed Stumpy. It was his dearest secret that he loved the li'l' boss — loved her dumbly and hopelessly. For one wild absurd instant he let himself believe that she was singing for him, then laughed at himself for a fool. But often in that short stretch of life left him he dreamed of the song, the voice, and the singer. He was to hear her sing it again once more, on that day when he was to go to swift and tragic death, and he was to know that this time she lifted her unsteady voice for him alone.

An hour later, Daggett touched Jack Hadley on the shoulder.

"Miss Lee she wants to see you," he said.

Hadley walked across to the small camp-fire where she was sitting alone. "Sit down," she told him.

At such a command Stumpy would have reddened to the ears and sat down awkwardly tailor fashion. Hadley dropped gracefully to an easy lounging position. He smiled at the girl.

"Tough a drive as I've ever seen," he said. "There were a few hours when the odds were against us, I thought. Good we had a boss who knew her own mind and kept going."

"Good for her she had men who knew their business," she answered quietly. "If you and Dunc hadn't nursed the herd along the way you did, knowing when to drive and how hard, we would never have got through."

"Oh, I was just one of your waddies. Give Dunc the credit."

"I'll give you both credit — and thank you. You may be just one of the waddies, but — don't you think I know who brought this herd over the desert? I was brought up with cows. I ought to know."

"If you're pleased, I'm satisfied," he said.

She passed, rather hurriedly, to another subject. "Do you know much about Mexico? What do you think of this revolution they are talking about? Will it amount to anything?"

"I don't know. You never can tell about this country. The revolutionary pot is always simmering. Usually it doesn't boil over. I notice the authorities went to the trouble to deny there was any danger of an uprising. That looks as though there might be something doing, doesn't it?"

"You saw that copy of the 'Star,' then. I didn't like the way the governor put it in the statement he made. It sounded as though he were covering up."

"Yes. If there's trouble in this state, Megares will be in it, of course. He's been a nuisance ever since he killed Francisco and took his place."

"It may be very awkward for me if fireworks are started," Lee said, looking into the fire. "Megares doesn't care for Americans. He might levy toll on me — make me contribute some cattle to the support of his command."

"Yes." He added a word of comfort. "The authorities have been warned. They'll probably scotch the rebellion before it gets started."

"I expect so." She passed to another matter. "I want you to ride to the rancho and see that things are ready for us. Better look the range over and decide where we'll throw the cattle. There are two large fenced pastures. And you'll probably have to drive in to Palo Duro for supplies. We're out of a lot of things. I'll give you a list. The car is at the ranch. Probably Mrs. Silver would like to drive in with you. Tell her I'll be there within a day or two after you."

"When do you want me to start?"

"In the morning. While you're at Palo Duro, keep your eyes and ears open, please. I mean about this revolution talk. If it amounts to anything, we'll have to drive out again. We'll be between the devil and the deep sea. We're not getting the breaks exactly, are we?" The smile she flashed at him was a little weary. She had been fighting ever since her return from college, and it seemed to her that a change of luck was about due. She wanted to be a good sport, but enough punishment was enough.

"Sometimes a fellow has to make his own breaks."

His smile was a little cynical, a little grim, but she got a thrill from it. Back of the sardonic harshness of the man she felt a sense of comradeship. He understood her. He was there to lean on at need. It came to her almost with a shock. Amazing what comfort it brought her. She had resented the pictorial picturesqueness of this nut-brown rider, the dare-devil impudence that challenged response, but she recognized an arresting force in his personality not to be denied. Unless she missed her guess he was strong, with a strength that could be patient as a cat at a mouse-hole, lithely tigerish as a crouched panther.

"I'm glad you're with me" she said.

"I'm with you," he answered quietly.

Doris was bored. Time had taken the edge from her rhapsodies about the Rancho Costillo. It might be a Garden of Allah, as she had exclaimed in her first glad excitement at its loveliness, but it was not in her nature to enjoy for long any garden with nobody to walk there beside her. Except for old Juan, whose face was like a wrinkled parchment map, males were conspicuous only for their absence. She held within herself no capacity for enjoyment. The fillip of social contact was necessary to her. Men preferred.

To talk about reading was all very well, but books were for diversion, to be skimmed over, taken in homœopathic doses. She was beginning to wish she had gone back to Harold — to good old Harold who was devoted to her just as he was to his business. Soon she would be getting lonesome for him, as she always did after she had been away for a time. That was one of the nice things about him. She could always go back and find him just as fond of her. He might not be exciting, but he was necessary to her life.

She picked up an old magazine, riffled the pages, glanced at an illustration or two, read an advertisemnt, and let it drop into her lap. She yawned, stretching herself in the long wicker chair with the slow, indolent grace of a cat. In the shade of the long piazza the *patio* was cool. A fountain splashed agreeably in a pool where pond-lilies bloomed. Doris shrugged her shoulders deeper into the pillows and nestled down for sleep.

The clip-clop of a horse's hoofs scarcely roused her. It was, of course, some peon dropping in to see old Juan. They would sit down and exchange the gossip over a glass of *tequila*, then the visitor would remount and vanish into the desert.

A house door opened and a man came out to the *patio* and moved down the tiled floor of the piazza. That it was a man Doris knew by the sound of jingling spurs. Lazily she turned her head.

Into her eyes life leaped. This was not the man of all men she would have chosen to see, but he was better than none.

"What are you doing here?" she asked.

"I might say I'm here because you are."

"Which would be very pretty, but not true. You didn't know I was here."

"I know a lot more than you think I do."

"Enough to take your hat off when you meet a lady, Mr. Brennan?" she tossed at him lightly.

He flushed with anger, but removed the hat. In fact, he flung it to the floor. "We're not indoors," he growled.

She laughed. It pleased her to watch the effects of her darts on this hulk of a man, to see rage stir in him and vanity purr.

He was her dancing bear, she had once told Lee when the girl had remonstrated with her.

"You haven't answered my question," she reminded him. "I didn't know you were welcome on Lee's ranches since — By the way, is your wound quite healed?"

"If you're being funny at my expense —"

"Oh, but I'm not. I think it was very brave of you to try caveman stuff with Lee. But not very good judgment, perhaps." Her eyes bubbled to mirth. "There's a little bit of the wildcat in Lee. But of course you know that — now."

"She's a hellion," Brennan bit out. "And one of these days I'll tame her with a whip."

"Will you? When will you do that? I'd like a seat in the parquet, if you please."

"She'll beg a-plenty before I'm through."

The savagery of the man daunted Doris. "Don't be silly," she said severely. "She didn't mean to hurt you. There's no sense in blaming her for what was your fault. Some women don't happen to care for primeval brute stuff."

"She's going to care less about it," he threatened.

Watching him, it seemed to Doris that there was something oddly like triumph in his manner, as though he already held the whip hand. What did he mean by it? Why was he so sure his vengeance could reach her? She decided to find out.

"Oh, any one can talk big," she said, tilting her chin derisively toward him.

"Stick around."

"For how long? I'm about fed up with Mexico. Never have I seen a place where so few interesting things happen."

"They'll begin happening soon."

"What sort of things? The taming of the shrew, Mr. Petruchio?"

"Listen. Whatever happens I'm going to look after you."

"That's very nice of you, though I suppose I'd appreciate your kindness more if I needed any looking after."

"You will," he said ominously. "Hell's going to pop in this country. It has started already."

"What has?"

"A revolution."

Doris sat up, her indolence banished. "A revolution!" she repeated, eyes shining brightly. "No! Nothing so interesting as that. You're fooling me!"

"That's why Miss Lee Reynolds gets down off her high horse and says 'pretty please' to the man who wasn't good enough to be her foreman."

"But even if there was a revolution, they wouldn't bother Lee. That would be absurd. She hasn't anything to do with it."

"You know so much about it," he jeered.

"It wouldn't be reasonable. There wouldn't be any sense to it. She isn't taking sides."

"She's over here with the permission of Governor Gabilondo, isn't she? That's enough. If he's for her, Megares will be against her."

"Megares! Good gracious! Is *he* in it?"

Brennan had said too much, a good deal too much. He knew it, since the revolution was not yet actually under way.

"No need going into that. What I've been telling you is a secret. I've told you so you won't worry when you hear about it. You'll know I'm going to look after you. Me, personally."

"Why should I worry about their old revolution? I think it'll be lots of fun."

"Get that out of your head," he said harshly. "It's war. A lot of people will be killed, and some of 'em won't be in the fighting line either. What I'm telling you is that I'm for you. I'm gonna look after you. Behave nice to me and you won't be hurt."

"I'm not afraid of being hurt. I'd like to meet Señor Megares. We'd probably get along fine."

"You're not gonna meet him," Brennan said with finality. "Not if I can help it. I think too much of you."

"It's sweet of you to feel that way," she said, with her sudden devastating smile. "Just the same I'd like to meet him."

"You've got him wrong. Megares is a devil. You wouldn't play with a tiger, would you? Keep close and let him forget you're here. That's the best bet."

"Unless I can get you to shoot the tiger for me."

"Sh-h! Don't pull any talk like that. Walls have ears in this country, girl. It's not safe to make fun of Megares."

"Isn't it? Not even with you to protect me?"

"You've got to do as I say."

"It's worse than if you were my husband," she murmured, with a little laugh.

"Whatever you do, don't leave the ranch. Lie low and don't let yourself be seen. I'll take care of you."

"What can you do — a lone American in a foreign land? Will you detour the war if it comes this way?"

"Trust me. That's all you've got to do. And do as I say. I'm the one man in this country who can and will protect you now," he boasted.

"If I'm nice to you," she added, not without irony.

He broke away to ask a question that seemed to her wholly irrelevant. "How many Lazy R cattle on the drive?"

"I don't kn ow. Seems to me Lee said something about twenty-five hundred. Why?"

"How many men with the herd?"

"Eight or nine, I suppose."

"This new rider Smith with them?"

"Yes. What do you want to know for?"

Abruptly, after a moment's silence, he flung another question at her. "Who is this fellow Smith? What's his real name? Where did he come from?"

She shook her head. "It's odd, but he hasn't confided in me, I'll ask him when I see him."

"When will that be?"

"Soon, I hope. He's the best-looking man I've seen since I came West, a real answer to a maiden's prayer."

She said it to tease Brennan, and she knew by the snort he gave her that her enthusiasm for the new rider had annoyed the ex-foreman. Before he could answer,

Juan opened a door leading into the *patio* and stood aside to let a man enter.

The man was Jack Hadley.

At sight of him Doris clapped her hand. "Prompt to your cue again, Mr. Dragon-Slayer," she cried gayly. "We were just talking about you."

"Saying pleasant things about me, I'm sure," he said lightly, bowing over her hand.

"Just as well you didn't hear. You're probably vain enough, anyway," she answered. "As it chances, Mr. Brennan hadn't reached the compliments yet."

The hard, cynical eyes of the young man rested on the ex-foreman. "No? I'll be pleased to listen to any he has to offer," he said, almost in a murmur.

"You'll hear 'em when I'm ready," Brennan retorted.

"You're the mysterious rider, you know," Doris said audaciously. "We were wondering who you really are, and where you came from. Since the war there have been so many exiled princes. One can never tell, can one?"

Brennan snorted. "Most of the fellows traveling under an *alias* in this country got here three jumps ahead of a sheriff."

"Meaning nobody in particular, of course," Hadley said gently.

There was in his eye a gleam more potent than threats at repressing insurgent impulses.

"I didn't hear any names mentioned," Brennan growled. "Don't put words in my mouth, young fellow."

"Mr. Brennan just happened to be passing down the street and dropped in for a cup of tea," Doris explained. "Wasn't that nice of him? We've been gossiping. He thinks we'll have a revolution. But if there's one, he has promised to save me. He's the only man in Mexico that can, he says."

The former foreman of the Lazy R darkened with anger. He understood that she was laughing at him, rejecting any alliance with him. What mild interest she had once had in him had evaporated. There was malice in the look he flung at her.

"All right, if that's how you feel," he told her.

"So there's going to be a revolution," Hadley commented, his gaze on the other man.

"I'm not discussing that with you, fellow — not now."

"Some other time, perhaps?"

"Y'betcha!" Brennan agreed fervently.

"But even if there is, you'll look out for Mrs. Silver?"

"Just you mind your own business, Mr. Smith, and I'll mind mine."

Brennan turned on his heel and swaggered out of the *patio*.

"Exit the villain," Doris said, with a smile, leaning back indolently and knitting the fingers of her well-cared-for hands behind her head of coppery gold. Nobody knew better than she did how great a lure her lovely lines and opulent charm held for the masculine eye.

Unfortunately, Jack Hadley was not looking at her, but at the maguey plant in a corner of the *patio*. He was frowning at it without seeing the long starlike branches. His mind was intent on something else.

"So he said there was going to be a revolution and that he could save you. Now I wonder how he could do that." He spoke aloud, but not to her. It was apparent he was asking himself the question.

"I asked him how. He said just to be nice to him and trust him. If I'm nice to you, will *you* save me, Mr. Smith?"

His eyes came back to her, a soft, delicious creature, feminine, magnetic, instinct with sex, and in them a devil-may-care light danced.

"We might talk about that on the way to Palo Duro," he suggested.

"Are we going to Palo Duro?"

"I'm going to get supplies. Miss Reynolds said you might like to go along."

"You've saved my life, dear man," she told him fervently.

"Already?"

"I've been almost bored to death."

"Maybe I can cure that ailment," he cheerfully replied.

"I'm sure you can."

They looked at each other and laughed. She felt the little waves of excitement pulsing through her that were always heralds of a new flirtation. Maybe Mexico was not going to be so disappointing after all.

CHAPTER
FIVE

Hadley spent a busy afternoon in the saddle. He rode through the two immense pastures and decided how many cattle should be thrown into each. It was a country of mesquite and cactus — of cylinder-shaped bisnaga, rounded neatly as though trimmed by the shears of a gardener, of graceful ocotillo, tall and sweeping like great plumes; of sahuaro, desert sentinels branched like candelabra. All of them flowered gloriously and all bristled with thorns. But in the uplands there was grama, and lower down were the fillaree and bear grass. It rejoiced his heart to see green feed in plenty. The starving herd would take on flesh rapidly here.

Returning to the house, he explained to the little Mexican maid that he wanted a bath. Ysela was her name, and she was a granddaughter of old Juan. Seventeen years old she might have been, all soft curves and shy smiles and dark, long-lashed, liquid eyes. She heated water for Hadley, after which he bathed, shaved, and dressed from the skin out in clean clothes taken from the roll he had brought with him on the back of his horse. Doris had explained that tonight he was to eat with her.

At sight of him Doris opened her eyes. He was no longer a beggar on horseback, a dusty, unshaven cowpuncher in shiny leathers, hickory shirt, and ragged hat. The young man who moved across the floor to meet her so lightly and so confidently was in sport shoes, belted cricket flannels, white shirt, colorful tie, and soft brown coat. He might have been at a hotel in a summer resort.

She was curled on a lounge. He took her hand, bent low, and kissed it.

A lively interest rippled through her, stimulating as wine. "And all this treat for me!" she bantered, a gay smile in the eyes lifted to his. "What have I done to deserve it? Who am I, my lord, to be honored with purple and fine linen, and a scarf like a Rocky Mountain sunset?"

"*Porque ño, corazón?*" he said.

"No fair," she cried. "Are you making fun of me or love to me?"

They made a jolly evening of it, the more so because Doris had been deprived of the attentions of an attractive man for so long.

Since Doris was a late riser, it was well on toward noon before they started in the car for town. The road was rough and often narrow. It wound up into the moutains and along ledges. Hadley drove with the skill and assurance of one used to cars of many makes.

They had brought a picnic lunch with them. They ate it far up in the hills among the pines and afterward smoked companionable cigarettes before they renewed the journey.

66

Palo Duro they reached in the middle of the afternoon.

Before he had been in the little city half an hour, Jack Hadley knew there was something unusual in the air. When he stopped to ask directions of some natives chattering on a street corner, they stared at him with scarcely veiled hostility. He knew that whenever there was political unrest in Mexico, it was accompanied by distrust of the gringos. Half a dozen armed men crossed the parked square in front of the government building and hissed maledictions at the sentry standing there. Even the clerks at the stores where he made his purchases were preoccupied with the volcano simmering just below the surface of the town's life.

Hadley became uneasy. He wished he had not brought Doris Silver with him. Mexico in revolt was altogether too volatile for an American woman, especially an attractive one like Doris, who insisted on making audible comment upon what she saw.

He warned her against this. "You are not at home. Mexicans are suspicious and easily offended. When you look at one and laugh, she thinks you are making fun of her. Please be more careful. We don't want to draw any more attention to ourselves than necessary."

"Does it matter what they think?" she asked carelessly.

"Yes," he told her curtly. "I don't like the atmosphere. We'll get out as soon as I can get my business done."

"You're as bad as Mr. Brennan," she pouted. "He told me to stay at home and not leave the ranch."

"Did he? Why didn't you tell me that? He knows what he is talking about. I can't get out of Palo Duro too quick to suit me."

"And I think you're both scared-cats," she said, shaping her pretty lips to a mocking moue.

"I hope so. In a few minutes now I'll be through. Don't leave the store."

It was a command, and she chose not to like the tone of it. When Jack looked around a few minutes later from adding up the cost price of the supplies he was purchasing, Doris was not in sight.

Sharply he asked a clerk where she had gone. The man shrugged his shoulders and said he did not know. Another clerk pointed to the door. She had stepped out two or three minutes ago.

Hadley strode to the front of the store and looked up and down the street. Doris was nowhere in sight. The road was a narrow one, the buildings on each side flush with the street. Had she turned to right or left? Had she gone into some house or store?

A dog lay in the sun searching himself for fleas. Two men lounged in front of a house. A barefooted beggar crouched at a corner. There was no other sign of life.

Hadley's searching eyes found a sharply indented heel-print in the dust. It told him in which direction Doris had gone. He walked down the street and stopped to make inquiries of the men who were taking the sun. One of them, he thought, was a villainous-looking specimen.

Had they seen an American lady on the street within the past few minutes, he asked in Spanish. They had

68

not. They had, in fact, just come out of the house. Hadley hesitated, not satisfied. Had the explanation been a little too blandly pat?

He made as though to move on, then looked back quickly. The man who had answered him was grinning. That grin was altogether too knowing and on a face altogether too sinister. And it was no certificate of innocence that when caught the grin went out like the light from a blown candle. Corroborative evidence stared up at the young man from the dusty street, in the form of a dainty footprint with the toe pointed toward the house.

Doris was inside the house. She had entered it of her own volition or by force.

If Jack's fears had been less active, he would have hesitated. This was no time and no place to make trouble. In five minutes he could stir up a nest of hornets that might sting him to death. It was quite possible that Doris was in no danger, that she had walked into the house of her own accord and for reasons of her own. But why had the man denied it? Why that smirk of triumph on his face, wiped out instantly as soon as detected? Instinctively the young American realized that neither diplomacy nor bribery would avail him. What he had to do must be done quickly.

Lightning-swift he went into action. Two brown heads crashed together. A limp body sank on the step, another went catapulting into the dust of the street.

The door opened to his pressure. He walked into an empty room. Beyond this was the *patio*, surrounded by a two-story building, a gallery running around the upper story. To this a flight of stairs ran from the court.

Jack stepped into the *patio*. There were doors, four of them, on the ground floor. He opened one and then another. Nobody at home.

Putting two fingers to his lips, he gave a shrill whistle. Some one came out on the gallery above, leaned over the rail, and called sibilantly, "*Quien es?*"

That was a question which seemed as well not answered. Jack kept close to the wall and trod softly toward the stairs. Again he heard the "*Quien es?*" of the inquirer on the gallery, followed by the sound of his footsteps moving back into the house. The man had probably made up his mind that the whistle had come from the street.

Stealth became of no importance. A man burst into the *patio* from the door by which Jack had entered. He held one hand to a bleeding head while he shrieked a warning.

Swiftly Jack took the stairs, three at a time. When he reached the top, men were pouring out of a room like seeds pressed from a squeezed lemon. At sight of him one gave a shout to let the others know.

In his college days a prize-fighter had once given Jack the most important rule of *mêlée*. It was to hit the other fellow first, unexpectedly, and hard. As the natives waited, uncertain what to do, young Hadley charged. In his plunge he caught up a chair and flung it at the huddle. The impact of it hurled the nearest man against the others. They gave ground, and before they

70

had recovered, one hundred and sixty pounds of fighting energy was upon them.

Jack lashed out with his left at a brown face and it went back as though a battering-ram had struck it. His shoulder caught a foe in the midriff and sent him crashing through the flimsy rail to the ground below. A short arm jolt lifted to a chin, and the owner of the chin lost interest in the battle.

The Mexicans recovered from the surprise and closed in on him. He was the active center of a compact group of struggling men, each unit of which was trying to strike or drag him down. They flung maledictions at him as they crowded on one another, seven or eight in all, impeding the efforts of those nearest in their eagerness to get at this human wildcat who had launched himself upon them.

They tore the shirt from his back. They scratched and hammered his face and body. Their arms went like flails as they beat upon his flesh. The deep panting of their lungs and the shuffling of moving feet accompanied the cries they uttered. But as they clawed at him, as the mass swayed to and fro, he struck and struck and struck again.

Hadley realized there could be but one ending to this. His attack had failed. He was growing weaker. Presently he would sink down and the life would be pounded out of him by the wolf pack. The odds were too great.

Yet the fact of the great odds saved him. His enemies had no singleness of mind except the desire to tear him to pieces. They hauled this way and that, one neutralizing the force of another. The weight of the scrimmage crashed against the rail. It gave as though made of paper. Those nearest could find no footing. They clutched at others. Two of them went plunging down into the century plant below.

The American found himself free for the moment. He hurled his weight against the nearest man, who in turn was flung against the next, already tottering on the edge. Both of them lost balance and went over.

Jack turned snarling on another. The fellow wanted no more. He stumbled back, turned, and ran. His friends followed. Panic is contagious. Except for one swarthy little chap lying on the floor, Hadley was alone.

He had been aware of cries from the room out of which the men had come before the battle. Now he staggered through the doorway and looked around. Doris, face colorless to the lips, eyes dilating with horror, was shuddering in a corner of the room back of a bed.

She stared at him, a picture of disheveled and bruised victory. His shoulders and torso were bare and bleeding. A knife wound disfigured one shoulder. Head and face were battered and discolored.

His mouth shaped to a distorted but indomitable grin. Then, with an amazed glad cry, she recognized him.

"You!"

"Still dragon-slaying," he told her with sardonic irony.

She sank down on the bed and wailed.

72

The young man spent no time in comforting her. He went to the window and flung it open. The back of the house faced a garden. Behind it was a path which ran along a little creek.

He caught a spread from the bed and tied one end around her waist.

"W-what are you going to do?" she sobbed.

"Lower you from the window. They'll be back. Here. Put your legs over the sill. Now slip off. I'll lower you."

Hand over hand he let her down as far as he could before releasing his hold. She dropped into a flower bed. In a moment he was beside her.

She swayed. "I'm faint," she told him. "I — I — I — can't —"

He neither comforted nor argued. What he did was to slap her cheek sharply.

"None of that!" he ordered roughly. "This is serious business."

Catching her wrist, he started to run. It was an ocotillo fence, but he found a break in it and bundled her through regardless of the thorns. The shock of the slap he had given her had driven away the faintness. She ran beside him, her hand in his.

They came to a lane and turned up it toward the street. Shouts drifted to them. Looking to the left, Hadley could see men craning out of the window from which they had just dropped. The pursuit was on.

Doris lagged. "I can't keep going," she panted.

"As far as the car," he urged. "Stick it out."

Two women looked out of windows and shouted at them. A man came to a door and shook a fist. A second one, the street beggar Jack had seen before, made as though to stop them and thought better of it.

Without stopping, the young man snatched from him his heavy walking-stick.

They reached the car at the same time as a man in uniform came running down the street. The officer flung a spurt of Spanish at Jack and barred the way into the car. Out of the tail of his eye the cowpuncher could see others closing in on them. It was no time for argument. He swung the walking-stick and brought it down on the head of the policeman. The hands of the officer dropped. He swayed, then staggered across the sidewalk to collapse against the wall.

Jack pushed Doris into the car and clambered over her. Fortunately he had not removed the key. He turned on the ignition switch, put his foot on the starter, and let in the clutch. The car moved forward.

Someone leaped on the running-board and demanded that he stop. The driver shifted to second and then to high, swung around the corner, increased his speed. He was on a narrow side street.

For the first time he found leisure to attend to the incubus clamped to the running-board. The man was leaning past Doris trying to get at the wheel. As Jack's left hand crossed in front of his body swiftly to the man's chin, he realized that the fellow was the same villainous-looking specimen he had met in front of the house at the beginning of the adventure. The man slumped down and slid off the running-board.

Hadley realized he might be blocked in this narrow street by a cart or a wagon, and at the earliest opportunity he swung back into a main street. He turned his head to see if there was any in pursuit. There was, he thought, an eddy in the distance, but he had so far outstripped it that none of the people they were passing had any idea that there had been trouble.

Ten minutes later, Palo Duro lay back of them, with only the cottonwoods to mark its location.

Hadley drove fast. For a time he gave his attention strictly to the road. It was full of chuck-holes, as Mexican roads are likely to be. He did not look at the woman beside him, but he knew she had withdrawn to a far corner of the seat. It was possible that he was being punished for his presumption, but that did not seem important.

"Our luck certainly stood up fine," he presently said cheerfully, slackening the pace a little for a series of bumps. "All the way. Lucky I got gas when I went into town instead of waiting. Lucky I parked where I did. Lucky those fellows didn't have guns and the cop didn't think of drawing his until it was too late. Every break came our way."

No answer from Doris, unless a deep sob was one. He looked at her, the smile sarcastic on his battered face. Big tears rolled down from the baby-blue eyes. She was, he guessed, feeling sorry for herself.

"What's the matter, lady?" he asked. "You were looking for an adventure, and you've surely had one."

It occurred to him that even now, though she had been so frightened, she did not realize how closely both of them had skirted the edge of disaster.

"I'll never forget it!" she wailed. "Never as long as I live. They pawed me. One of them carried me upstairs and held his dirty hand over my mouth to keep me from screaming. He smelt of garlic . . . or something. It was horrible!"

There was a flash of sardonic mirth in his eye, the one that had not been closed. He had barely escaped with his life, and she from agony unthinkable — and what impressed her was that one of the ruffians smelt of garlic.

"Think how you'll enjoy telling the story," he said. "Over the cocktails. An audience enthralled. Lovely heroine abducted by band of villains. Plot foiled. Escape of heroine. Flight in high-powered car from pursuers."

"It's not a high-powered car," she objected.

"It will be when you tell the story," he said dryly.

She pouted. What he said was quite true. It was going to be a lovely adventure to talk about . . . some day. But just now she could not get that slant on it. She had grievances. He had had such a chance to be gallant and romantic. Instead . . .

"You struck me — in the face," she charged, and again her eyes were flooded with tears.

"Treatment recommended by the best doctors," he defended. "I couldn't have you fainting on my hands just then. It would have spoiled the whole story. Don't you see that?"

"You didn't have to hit me. You could have talked to me." The indignity of what she had endured flamed up in her. "I never was so insulted — never in my life. And you don't even apologize. Are you used to striking women, Mr. Smith?" she queried contemptuously.

"Not as a rule. One can usually handle them better without it."

"I think you're hateful."

"And I think you're lovely. So now we've both freed our minds."

He looked at her and laughed. It was as though he found in the situation some source of amusement hidden from her. This made her furious.

"Very well," she said, with cold dignity. "Since you think it's funny to strike me. Since you're so far from being a gentleman."

"Oh, I'm no gentleman," he admitted carelessly. "I'm just one of Miss Lee's waddies. It wasn't a job for a gentleman back there. Too much garlic in the atmosphere."

For as much as ten minutes she said nothing. Then she spoke in a small, contrite voice. "I'll forgive you if you ask me pretty please."

"All right." He grinned. "I'm sorry I had to hit you."

"You're not — mad at me?"

"I? Not at all. I never strike a woman in anger. It hurt me more than it did you."

That he was laughing at her she knew, but she did not any longer mind. She wanted to be friends again.

"I expect I'm selfish," she told him. "I do appreciate what you did. You look awful. I never saw anybody so . . . so bruised and everything. They must have hurt you dreadfully."

"I didn't even feel it." The unholy light of reminiscent battle gleamed in the eye he turned upon her. It reflected sheer savage joy. "But, lady, it was a beautiful scrap. I would have enjoyed it more at the time, though, if I'd known how it was coming out."

"How did you get that cut on the shoulder?"

He looked at the clotted blood below the wound. "Fellow did it with a knife. Only a scratch."

"And you were wounded and beaten up for me," she said.

"Now don't go making me a hero. I just hadn't sense enough to talk those fellows into being decent. I get no medal for that."

"You think they wanted to hold me for ransom?"

He looked straight at her. "What else could they have wanted?" he asked.

"I don't know." She shuddered. "I was afraid. Just sick with fear. Then you came — and fought them all. How did you do it?"

"You know how hard I can hit," he told her.

"Yes. You did sting me, too." She put a hand to her soft cheek. "Did you leave a mark?"

"No. Shall I kiss it to make it well, *muchacha?*" He made of the last drawling word almost a caress.

"Please."

His cut lips touched lightly her cheek. "Must be a good deal like being kissed by a gargoyle," he suggested. "They didn't work over my mug into a thing of beauty."

Her eyes passed over him. Bruised and battered and gory though he was, he was still a prince of vagabonds.

78

The bare arms and shoulders revealed long rippling muscles lithe as those of a panther. She thought she had never seen a head set so gracefully on a finer neck column. He was one of those rare men who strip well. A hot flash passed through her. He had fought for her, against overwhelming odds. Let him make light of it. That was the sporting thing to do. None the less it did not alter the fact. Because of it he was in a way sealed to her. She had a claim on him he could not ignore.

Tenderly she put her hands on that hammered head and drew it to her. She kissed, very softly, the closed eye, the bruised cheek, and the cut lips.

"Account squared," he said gayly. "I'll have to hunt up some more villains to put you in my debt again."

She preferred to keep him a creditor. "I'll be in your debt forever and ever," she said fervently.

"I hope, then, you'll pay installments on the bill occasionally," he said, with a smile.

For the first twenty miles Hadley kept going. He did not know whether there would be any pursuit, but he did not want to take any chances.

Then he drew up on the edge of a brook. "Ten minutes for repairs," he announced.

The cool water was very soothing to the fevered face and body. When he returned to the car, he was a less gruesome individual, though he still looked much the worse for wear.

CHAPTER
SIX

They found Lee at the rancho upon their return. She had just come clean and fresh from her bath after a long desert ride.

At sight of her battered *vaquero* the girl's brown eyes opened wider. She did not ask any immediate questions. None were necessary. Doris flung herself upon her with exclamatory explanations.

"Darling! Darling! The most awful thing happened! You would never guess! Some brutes lured me into a house. They said they had some lovely shawls to sell. They carried me upstairs. I couldn't even scream. I nearly died of fear. Then Jack came . . . and fought them . . . and got me out. And afterward he knocked down some more men . . . and brought me home. Oh, it was terrible, Lee. If he hadn't saved me . . ."

Lee looked at Hadley. She had listened to her friend's exaggerations too long to accept her version of any occurrence at face value.

The young man grinned. "That's about the way it was," he agreed.

"You mean they took her by force?"

"Yes."

"And you had to fight to rescue her?"

"A bit of a scrimmage."

"How many of them?"

"I was too busy to take a census."

"There were eleven," Doris said promptly. She was not sure just how many there had been, but eleven would do as a round number.

"Eleven," echoed Lee. "You fought eleven men. What with?"

"With a chair and a beggar's stick and whatever else came handy. But I don't think there were eleven. I'd guess eight or nine."

"But eight or nine of them. Good Heavens! No wonder they nearly murdered you. I don't understand how you got away. Doesn't seem possible."

"Luck," he told her jauntily. "We were on a *patio* balcony, and while we were waltzing around, the rail broke. Four or five of them went down with it. That discouraged the others some."

"And after he'd whipped them all," Doris went on in a single breath without stopping for periods, "he came and lowered me from the window and pushed me through a cactus fence and got to the car and knocked some more down and if you don't believe it look at the scratches on my arms and how the sleeves of my dress are torn."

"It does sound a bit like Falstaff's story, doesn't it?" Hadley admitted, with a smile apologetic. "Incredible. Maybe we dreamed it all."

"You didn't dream all those cuts and bruises and the slash in your shoulder, did you?" Lee asked.

81

"They seem quite real," he assented. "But they might have been a lot worse. I took the gentlemen by surprise, and they didn't have much room to work. We got all jammed together in a huddle. Then, as I said, the rail broke. After that Mrs. Silver and I beat it through a window . . . By the way, I didn't get all the supplies. Some were in the car, but the last lot I couldn't wait for."

"I should think not. You must be all in. Better let me do some first-aid work, unless Doris is handy about it."

Doris shook her head decisively. "I couldn't take a splinter out of a finger."

"Then let's go inside," Lee suggested. "You'd better lie on the lounge while I get ready."

"What would buck me up most would be a good stiff drink of *tequila*," he said.

"Straight or with orange juice?"

"Straight. I'm taking it as medicine."

He had his *tequila*, and afterward Lee looked his wounds over and did what little could be done for them. Most of them were bruises and surface cuts. Even the knife thrust had been a glancing one.

Lee was brisk and business-like, but her fingers were not quite so deft as usual. It was all in the day's work of a ranch woman. At any time a cowboy was likely to have a broken arm or a sprained ankle. No sense in getting flurried, she told herself severely. Yet she was a little tremulous with excitement. There was something about him that quickened the pulses, a charm of personality not quite explainable. The smile, both cynical and gay; the mocking eyes; the fine slope of the splendid shoulders rising to the throat; the impression one got of stark courage born of a dare-devil soul: it might be all or none of these that affected her when her sensitive finger-tips contacted with his flesh. She was aware of a fierce joy, and of a scorn of the idiocy in her that allowed it.

"Now you're all right," she said when she had finished. "All you need is a night's good sleep."

"I wonder if I'll get it," he said dryly. "It wouldn't surprise me if a few *rurales* dropped in and had a few words to say about that."

"You think they'll arrest you?"

"*Quien sabe?* There are probably one or two broken legs or arms in Palo Duro tonight. And one policeman must have a sore head. Someone will make a row about it, and they can find out from the store who I am and where I came from."

"Tell me the whole story from the beginning," Lee ordered.

He told it, very briefly. Once she stopped him, to ask a question. "Why did you let Doris go into the house at all?"

The young man hesitated. He had not want to tell tales out of school.

"I hadn't finished in the store yet," he explained.

"And you let her go wandering around alone, feeling as you did that there was danger?"

The sharp voice of the girl accused him. He did not look at Doris as he answered.

"Not so good of me, was it?"

"No. I should have thought you would have kept her near you." Lee's forehead knit in a little frown. She looked at Doris — and continued to look at her. A small suspicion was born in her. "Didn't he tell you to stay near, Doris — not to leave him?"

"Yes," Doris admitted defensively. "But I didn't see why I couldn't go out. How was I to know that —"

Lee interrupted rudely. "I see."

That was all she said, but it was enough.

After Hadley had concluded the story, he and Lee turned to a consideration of possible consequences.

"It's unfortunate," he said. "With so many witnesses against me, it will be difficult for me to set myself right with the government here. I'm a gringo, despised by most good Mexicans and therefore discredited even before the evidence is in. The question is how it will affect you."

"That's one point, but not the most important. If you're flung into prison here, you may not get out for years. You know how it is with foreigners accused of crime in Mexico. I wonder of you hadn't better take the car and get across the line while there's still time. Doris can go with you, too. I don't know that she'd be disturbed if she stayed here. But you can't tell what lies they'll cook up. Yes, I think that will be best. You'd better pack and go at once. I'll have Ysela put up a basket of food for you."

"You mean — go tonight?" Doris asked.

"I mean go now. Soon as you can get packed. In ten minutes."

84

"But I can't even change my dress in ten minutes, let alone pack all my things," Doris protested.

"One suitcase will be enough. You don't need to change your dress."

"But —"

"If you'd rather stay and run the risk of a Mexican prison," Lee cut in brutally. "It will be very dirty and there will be lots of vermin, and the food will be unspeakably bad, and of course anything may happen to you there."

"Oh, I'll go. I didn't mean that, Lee." The lovely Cupid's-bow lips trembled and the blue eyes misted. "But I don't see why you speak that way to me, after all I've been through today. It's not my fault those horrid men insulted me. I didn't ask them to . . . to . . ."

Lee repented her harshness. After all, she was primarily to blame herself for ever having let Doris come into the country, even though she had had no faintest suspicion that a revolution was in brew. It was not fair to blame Doris because she was what she was.

We take our friends with capitulation, as they are, in spite of their faults. Lee had known for years that Doris would not tell the truth when a lie was easier, that she was not very scrupulous in regard to other women's men, and that she was not a very good sport. None the less she had liked her, had found her amusing and entertaining. To continue to show irritation at her now would be unjust.

"Forgive me, dear. I was too brusque. What I mean is that if you're going with Mr. Smith, you'll have to hurry. Every minute counts. Even now it may be too late."

Lee's voice and manner were gentle. In that they did not reflect the annoyance that seethed within her. For this indulgent self-willed woman had come near to wrecking the enterprise they had undertaken. Perhaps she had done so.

"I'll hurry," Doris promised, and left to pack.

"I'd better go and get some clothes on," Hadley said. "They didn't leave me much."

"No." Lee drummed with the tips of her fingers on the table in front of her. "I ought not to lose my temper with her, but she's so exasperating. You might have lost your life, for no reason except some whim of hers. Even now she doesn't realize what she's done."

"As a botanical specimen I suppose she would be catalogued decorative rather than useful," the young man volunteered. "But she would come at the top of her class. Did you ever see anything more lovely?"

"Never. And she's all right. There's no harm in her. Even her flirtations don't go very far usually. They are to satisfy her vanity . . . Have you gas enough to get through?"

"Probably not. I'll pick some up on the way." He broached what was on his mind. "Fact is, I hate to leave you holding the sack. I wouldn't go, except that I'll make you more trouble if I stay. Of course my name isn't Smith, as I told you. It's Jack Hadley. Dunc knows all about me. Ask him. I have a reason why I don't want my real name known just now."

"Thanks for telling me," she nodded.

86

"That's all right. Dunc can tell you why I have an alias. I haven't time now." He rose stiffly, and moved toward the door.

"You're quite able to travel?"

"Quite."

Doris came running back into the room. "Why don't you go with us, Lee? I wouldn't stay in this horrible country if I were you — not another hour. I thought of it just a minute ago."

"That's nice of you, Doris. But I can't go."

"Why can't you? There's lots of room in the car."

"Because I've got to stay here. Because I've leased this rancho, and my cattle and my riders are here."

"Let Dunc look after your cattle. You don't have to stay yourself. They might make you some trouble about what happened in Palo Duro today."

"Probably not. Anyhow, I'll have to risk that. Hurry up and pack, dear. I'll see about a basket of food and a water bottle."

"Oh, I wish you'd go, Lee, dear. If anything happened —"

"Nothing will happen. I can't go. I've got to stay."

Jack Hadley wished, too, that Lee could go with them, but he did not say so. He knew she wouldn't go, had known it without even broaching the subject. He would have thought less of her if she had deserted Dunc and the enterprise to which she was pledged. But he worried about her future, especially if the revolution developed, and he was sorry that he had to desert her just when she seemed to need him.

His reluctance at leaving was so great he could not quite understand it. He had to go, as much on her account as on his own. If he stayed, the authorities would find some way of bringing the responsibility home to her. If he fled, taking her car with him, she would be by that very fact acquitted of complicity. But his whole desire was to stay. She was so gallant, such a good sport. She was hard, of course. All good fighters have to be. There did not seem to be anything romantic or sentimental about her. The men who worked for her had to do a day's work. They could not slough on her. But Jack knew that in spite of the hard-baked crust she was a woman in ten thousand.

The night fell chill on the hills. A full moon rode the heavens and softened the harshness of the desert. Its silvery light drenched valley and mesa, lending to the landscape the touch of romance possible when grim details are blurred. Palo verde and Spanish bayonet and ironwood took on the indefinite outlines of a Corot. A thicket of wild cherries billowed with vague blossoms.

They drove along the shoulder of a hillside, above them a ghostly grove of sahuaro. Doris shivered closer to the man at the wheel.

"Cold?" Jack asked. "Shall I wrap my slicker around you?"

"No-o," she murmured. "It's this giant cactus. I feel as though I were in a graveyard and the dead might begin to walk."

"They'd have to run to catch us," he promised her. "And fast, too. See, we're leaving your graveyard behind."

"I feel so safe with you," she said sleepily. "As if I were a little girl and you my big brother. You'd take care of me, wouldn't you, and not let danger touch me?"

"Would I?"

"Yes. You can't deny it, because you've fought for me already."

"Said the heroine, sentimentally but drowsily."

"Oh, you needn't laugh at me. I'm not going to waste this gorgeous moonlight thinking about practical things like — oh, baked potatoes and the price of beef in Chicago. I'm going to let dreams happen if they will. Maybe when we drove through the purple sunset we came into a wonderful new world, just you and I, and nobody else within a thousand miles of us."

She did not see his ironic grin. "Just you and your big brother," he reminded her.

"I don't have to think of you as a big brother all the time. There wouldn't be any fun in that . . . You're not like any one I ever met before. You're different."

"There's a reminiscent sound about that," he said, aloud, as though to himself. "Where have I heard it?"

"Oh, but you are! It's not a line. Do you know, I have a queer feeling that Lee has fallen in love with you? You're just the kind of a man she'd fancy. That's why she was so cross with me a while ago."

"She's begun to dream already," he commented dryly. "Just a minute ago she and I were in a wonderful new world alone, and now she has dragged another girl into it. I always thought Lilith and Eve were too much for one poor Adam. In the Garden of Eden three was a crowd."

"Three always is," she nodded. "So we'll leave Lee out of our paradise. She had her chance to come and she didn't take it. Only . . . before we shut the gate on her . . . I do think if she ever woke up, she'd make a wonderful lover. I'm just light-minded and trifling, always wanting the moon and then not caring for it so much after someone has got it for me. But Lee — she always knows what she wants and usually gets it. And she's different, too. When I tell fibs, with her around, I feel mean somehow, though she doesn't say anything."

"She's a thoroughbred."

"Yes. When she's really angry, it scorches. I'll bet if she loved a man — Wow!"

She yawned, drowsily.

"Better sleep," he told her.

With one hand he tucked his slicker around her like a blanket. She snuggled down in it and leaned comfortably against his shoulder.

"Aren't you going to kiss me good-night?" she asked, tilting her golden head at him with a most inviting smile.

He kissed her.

"Hmp! I don't think much of that as a kiss," she criticized.

"Little girls never do think much of their big brothers' kisses, do they?"

"But you're only a kinda big brother. You could forget it sometimes, couldn't you?"

"I've forgotten it already. Is this better?"

She flashed a swift sidelong look at him as she emerged breathless from his embrace. It asked a question, not of him, but of herself. Was she playing with fire when she tempted this hard, reckless man to put a sting in his kisses? She had called him safe, but of all the men she had known, he seemed to her least calculable. Most lovers were alike. You could predict what they would say and do, when it was time to call a halt. It was her habit to start fires and let them die for lack of fuel when the blaze threatened to grow dangerous. But this man — so prodigally endowed with good looks, so almost insolently indifferent to her charm, so much an Admirable Crichton of the frontier — could she be sure enough of herself with him, of the even coolness of her blood, to be certain she would have the will to deny him what he might claim? He was no tame drawing-room cat, but was more related to the jungle breed which takes what it wants with savage force. It was no part of her plan of life to give or even to pay for what she received. She had not found it necessary even to promise in words. Usually it had been sufficient stimulant to lift shy long-lashed eyes and let them meet helplessly the sultry gaze of a wooer. But her instinct told her no tricks would serve her with this polished barbarian.

"I don't think you need any lessons," she said. "Now you may be a big brother again, please."

She settled herself for sleep. Her deep, even breathing presently told him that she had dropped off.

The road was bumpy and he drove carefully. After a time he became aware that he had got off the main road, though he was going in the right general direction. He stopped, uncertain what to do.

A glimmer of light came to him from a hillside. Someone lived in this sea of land waves. He started the engine and moved slowly toward the light. A fence of mesquite poles and barbed wire crossed the road, but there was a gate and it was open. The road terminated at a barn built of sahuaro poles and mud. Hadley turned the car, so that it faced in the direction from which he had come. It might be necessary for him to get out in a hurry. "Where are we?" Doris asked drowsily as he gently removed his supporting shoulder.

"Don't know. We've got off the road. I'm going to find out."

He left her in the car and moved toward the house, making sure that his revolver hung easily in its scabbard.

Someone flung the door open and called a question. "Who's there? Don't come any nearer."

The man was an American. He carried a rifle.

Hadley explained that they had lost their way. There was a lady with him in the car, he said.

"Come into the light and don't make any breaks. That's right. Stop right there. Now tell your story, young fellow."

The story passed muster. As Hadley came forward, the man apologized.

"Have to be careful these days. We won't be so popular now this darn revolution's started."

"Has it started?"

"Went off with a bang yesterday. Met a fellow down from Nogales. The rebels have taken the city and that whole section. They're going strong down at Palo Duro, too. I left there after dark. There had been fighting and they had seized the government building."

The man was middle-aged and bearded, apparently a miner.

"We're headed north," explained Jack. "How about getting across the border?"

"Couldn't possibly be done. It's closed. They're not letting any Americans through. So I hear."

"How about slipping through by some of the smugglers' roads?"

Doris emerged out of the shadowy moonlight to stand beside Hadley. The miner stared at her. In the silvery atmosphere her blonde beauty was startling. It seemed too amazing to be a reality.

"Like I said, the border's closed tight as a drum. Several Americans have been arrested and flung into jail. Barela is mighty particular about what news gets to the U.S. these first days. After he has got away with his coup — if he can pull it off — he'll do his own explaining to Washington, I reckon."

"Who is Barela?" asked Doris.

"He's the high mogul among the rebels in this part of the country, from what I can hear."

"What about this Megares? He's in it, isn't he?" Jack queried.

"Up to his neck. But Megares is an outlaw. You know how it is. He's got a following, and a lot of the peons are for him. But he has no standing. His name at the head of the revolution would queer it with lots of respectable people and maybe with our government. So he'll stay in the background awhile and let Gomez and Barela and the others take the limelight in the press dispatches. After they win, in case they do, the big bugs will scrap it out among themselves as to who'll be chief."

Doris slipped her arm under that of her companion. "And you don't think we can get across into Arizona?"

"No, lady, I don't."

"We're awf'ly anxious to get to our own country," she pleaded.

"Lots of Americans are right now. I guess they'll have to wait till things clear up." The man grinned. "I'd just as lief spend a little vacation in Tucson myself."

"You said the rebels have control at Palo Duro, didn't you?" Hadley questioned.

"They've won the preliminary scrapping. Some of the government troops went over to Megares, I was told. The others have fallen back into the barracks. It's too early yet to say who'll win. There's always a lot of jockeying to and fro in these risings. You hear all kinds of stories and you never know who is winning at first."

"Ever met Megares?"

"He was pointed out to me once. A bad hombre. But sauve and smooth when he wants to be. Quite the gentleman. Not at all like Francisco was."

"As I understand it, Barela is up at Nogales. He isn't down here?"

"Barela is in command there and Megares here. That's what they say."

The arm of the young woman tightened on that of Hadley.

"What'll we do?" she asked.

"Can't tell yet. But don't worry. It'll work out." Hadley turned to the miner. "While you were at Palo Duro, did you hear anything about a row today between an American and a bunch of Mexicans?"

"Did I? I'll say I did. The town was buzzing with it. I don't know who the guy was, but he sent about four greasers to the hospital. He was crazy with *tequila*, I guess."

"He wasn't either," Doris denied indignantly.

The man looked at her in surprise. "Maybe not. I'm telling it the way I heard the story."

"Mr. Smith here was the man. They tried to abduct me and he rescued me. He wasn't to blame at all."

"I see." The miner understood now why they were so anxious to get across the border.

"What I wanted to ask you was whether you know what the authorities are doing about it," Hadley went on.

The bearded man shook his head. "No, I don't. I expect maybe your little row got lost in the discard when the rebellion broke later. I expect both sides will have their hands full for quite some time."

Hadley had been thinking the same thing himself. Events are important in regard to their relativity. A week ago his little fracas might have caused no end of trouble. There was a good chance it would be entirely overlooked now.

"Much obliged for what you've told us," he said. "We'll move along."

"Won't you come in awhile? I'll make you some coffee."

"No, I think not, thank you. We have some in a thermos bottle. We can't miss the main road if we backtrack, can we?"

"No. Keep going till you hit it."

"Where are you going now?" Doris asked, as Jack started the car.

"Back to the Rancho Costillo. Since the revolution has started, we're in an entirely different situation. Nobody will bother much about us. We're too small fry."

"I wish we could have got out," she said.

"Yes."

Absently he agreed with her. But the warm little glow inside was contradicting the assent. He was glad the border had been closed. He was glad circumstances were driving him back to the rancho, to whatever adventure might be waiting there for him and for the girl who had driven her cattle across the thirsty desert with such pluck and competence. He had a strong sense of kinship with Lee Reynolds. She was game — no quitter. There was a quality of steely resolution in her born of her heritage. It made her hard, buried deep in her the feminine softness that might be a part of her nature. But it gave her character. And there had been moments to remember, few but significant, when the amber eyes under the long lashes had warmed to molten gold as they turned to him, and had given her a loveliness far more precious than the largesse of beauty scattered so prodigally by Doris Silver.

CHAPTER
SEVEN

Dunc Daggett met his boss about three miles from the rancho. She had been riding out to meet the herd and he in from it to report progress.

"Miss Lee, there's a bunch of about twenty-five hundred whitefaces in the Lazy R brand headin' thisaway, maybe ten-twelve miles back. The boys are driftin' 'em along kinda easy, but you'll see an' hear 'em before night."

"How do they look?"

"Fine as the wheat, some gaunted yet, but give 'em time an' they'll be slick as split silk . . . We had a visitor last night."

"Who?"

"Mr. Ranse Brennan."

"What did *he* want?"

"I'd like to know. I asked him if he wasn't a long ways from home. He gimme one of those black looks an' told me where I could go. Miss Lee, that bird is so mean that if a skunk bit him, the skunk would die. By Jacks, it kinda give me a turn to see him. What's he roostin' down here for? Howcome he to know where our herd was? He's here to do you dirt, I'd say, an' if he gets a chance he'll turn his wolf loose."

"What can he do? Do you think he's in with this crowd plotting the revolution?"

"I dunno." The old man's unshaven jaw fell. He sat there staring at her. "Dog my cats! D'you reckon that flop-eared hound has been in with Megares all the time, that he was in cahoots with him to rustle Lazy R stock even while he was yore foreman?"

"Don't let's be too suspicious, Dunc. Ranse worked for the Lazy R more than fifteen years. Just because he got to feeling his oats, we don't need to think he is a dirty thief."

"Prob'ly you're right," the old man assented reluctantly. "Only I never have been satisfied the rustlers weren't gettin' information from someone on the ranch. They knew just when to time their raids. My notion was some of the boys talked too much when they went to town. Not on purpose, y'understand. Just innocent blabbers . . . Say, Miss Lee, where's that double back-action, adjustable fraud Jack Smith? Is he settin' around on a porch fannin' himself? If so, I'll sure tell that boy I've had an elegant sufficiency of his loafin'."

"He is heading for Arizona as fast as a car will take him there."

"What?"

She told him of what had taken place at Palo Duro.

Daggett slapped his thigh with a wide-brimmed dusty hat. "Fought eleven Mexicans! Wow! Doggone it, he'll sure do to ride the river with, that boy. Cleaned up on 'em an' then lit a shuck with the young lady. If it was anybody else but Jack Hadley, I'd sure say that story sounds to me." His voice rose to a high cackle of excitement.

"Hadley said he thought there weren't more than seven or eight. It was Doris guessed eleven. He gave explanations of how he managed to escape with her. A rail of a porch broke and some of them fell, he said."

"Smith I meant, Miss Lee, not Hadley."

"Why not Hadley? That's his name. He told me so."

"Did he? Well, I'm right glad he did. It's no name to be ashamed of. He's got reasons why he ain't usin' it just now."

"He said you'd tell me what his reasons are. He hadn't time himself."

Daggett told her the story of his friend's death and what the son had learned from a dying man after many years.

"I knew all the time he wasn't just a cowpuncher," she said. "Anyone could tell that by looking at him . . . What's that dust over there? Isn't that a car coming?"

"Sure is."

Her eyes watched the approaching car. It was in the valley below them, still a mile and more distant. "Did he find out who the man is, the one working on a ranch near Spring River who was implicated in the murder of his father?"

"Not yet, Miss Lee. But he's done made a guess."

The quick brown eyes of the girl came back to meet the faded skim-milk ones of the old man. "Who?"

"We're back again to the gent the skunk would die from biting."

"Ranse?"

"Yes, ma'am."

"Why? Has he any evidence?"

"I dunno as he has. Onct in a while a fellow feels a thing in his bones."

"That's nonsense . . . Suppose he found the man who helped kill his father. What does he mean to do about it?"

The old Texan looked at her bleakly. "Yore guess is as good as mine, Miss Lee."

"Yes, but — you don't think he has any silly idea of personal vengeance, do you?"

"I think I'd hate to be that man. Jack will hang onto his trail like death to a nigger's heel. He cut his teeth on cartridge shells, that boy did."

"I hope he never finds him," she said fervently.

"He'll find him. Don't make any mistake about him, Miss Lee. When his dad ran cows, he never blocked a brand or ran one over, never bought a wet horse. It didn't hurt him any to eat his own beef. But he was the kind of man I liked to have with me in a tight. Jack's thataway, too. Straight. But he'll go through to a fare-you-well."

Looking at the car, Lee gave a little exclamation of surprise. "It's my Packard!"

She was right. The car presently drew up beside them. Jack grinned across at his boss.

"Can you use another puncher, ma'am?" he asked.

"What's wrong?"

"They've turned the key in the door that leads to the U.S. We're locked in here with you."

"The border is closed?"

"That's it. The revolution has started."

"I'm sorry you didn't get through," Lee said.

That was true in a way. In another way it wasn't true at all. He had come back to her. The joy of it warmed her slender body, though the glow did not reach the surface.

"One good thing is that everybody will be too busy to pay any attention to my little party at Palo Duro yesterday."

"I hope so . . . You must be all tired out, Doris."

The young woman in the car nodded. "Just a bit. A bed and a bath will do wonders for me. It was rather a lark, though." Doris showed her perfect teeth in a smile. "Mr. Smith looked after me like a big brother. He was so nice about it that I learned to call him Jack."

Lee guessed there was an inner meaning in her friend's explanation, one meant for Hadley alone. No doubt they had been carrying on the little affair she was promoting. For the first time Lee felt a pang of envy at her former schoolmate's beauty. Doris could turn any man's head if she set out to do it.

But Lee wanted to be a good sport. She smiled cheerfully. "Run on, you and your big brother. Have a bath and breakfast, both of you, and then sleep round the clock. We working folks have got to get busy."

She jogged back to the hacienda beside Daggett at a road gait. They were going out to help bring the herd in later in the day, but they had a lot of bills and accounts to work over together first.

"Like he says, both the rebs an' the government party will be too doggone busy to worry any about him.

I'm sure glad. I'd hate to have him get his tail in a crack on account of puttin' up a good scrap with a bunch of Mexicans. Say he stove up a few of 'em. That's all right with me. You know what us Texans think of Mexicans."

"Yes, I know, Dunc, and your thinking is all wrong. The Mexicans are a pretty good people."

"Now looky here, Miss Lee. I know 'em. Me an' my folks have been fightin' 'em nigh on to a hundred years. Quite a spell before the Alamo —"

"You Texans were just as much to blame as the Mexicans were. I've read my history. You were a wild, hot-headed lot of mavericks who wouldn't wear another country's brand. Now I've known a lot of Mexicans. I've had them for neighbors since I can first remember. All this stuff about their being treacherous and sticking a knife in you when you're not looking is just nonsense. They are quiet, peaceable, and easy-going. You know that as well as I do. They have fewer criminals according to population than we have. They are friendly and full of smiles. I grant you they're indolent. Maybe that's where they show good sense. We're always so busy rushing around. What does it buy us?"

"You're judgin' em by particular individuals," the old Texan protested.

"I'm judging them by the ones I've met, just as I do our own people. Did you ever meet nicer folks than the Ainsas and the Oteros and the Ochoas?"

"They're high class, an' they've lived forty years in the States, but I've met a chance of 'em that ain't thataway. Take these revolutions. They're always betrayin' each other, ain't they? An' linin' up prisoners before a wall with a firin' squad in front of 'em?"

"Officers, mostly. That's politics. It's the way they play the game. For that matter our wars are just as bad, only different. They have their own rules and they don't happen to be the same as ours. One of theirs is that the officers of a defeated army if captured will be shot. They don't complain about it. I'll admit it seems cruel, but it's all perfectly aboveboard."

"You done got the bit in yore teeth," he said with a grin. "My pappy told me never to argue with a woman. She's right when she's wrong. All I got to say is I hope a passle of yore quiet, peaceable, friendly Mexicans won't take a notion to visit our hacienda an' prove to you that an old donker from the Brazos knows what he's talkin' about."

After they had finished checking up bills and accounts, Lee and Daggett rode out to meet the herd. They drew off to one side and let the leaders pass. Stumpy was at the point and he waved a hand to them as he passed.

"They don't look quite so much like horned skeletons," Lee told her foreman, pleased at the appearance of the Herefords. "Surprising what three or four days of good feed will do."

At the ranch they split the herd and threw half into one pasture and half into the other. Jack Hadley was on hand to help. He and Daggett kept tally as the animals poured through the gates. They did not differ by ten in their count. The loss on the trail, not counting a half-dozen newborn calves they had been unable to load on the wagon, amounted to less than thirty.

While Lee sat on Nugget watching the cattle as they were driven into the second pasture, a rider came up at a lope and drew up beside her. She glanced at the man.

"You've got a nice herd of scarecrows," he jeered.

The girl looked at him with level eyes. "That needn't worry you, Mr. Brennan," she said quietly.

"It doesn't. Not a bit. I just thought I'd like to take a look at 'em." There was a scarcely concealed triumph in his heavy mirth.

She wondered what was the source of his amusement. It puzzled her, and somewhat it disturbed her.

"That's twice you've taken a look at the herd and twice you've honored us with a visit at the rancho. I think that will be enough," Lee told him curtly.

"I'll be the judge of that," he cut back arrogantly.

"I thought it was my ranch."

"It's a difference of opinion that makes horse-races. You'll see me again, right soon, looking the herd over here at the ranch."

"I'd advise you not to come," she replied, with studied carelessness, her gaze on a young steer starting to bolt.

A moment later, Nugget was off on the jump, pounding over the ground in a half-circle to head back the three-year-old. The girl swung the loop of her rope in front of the animal and crowded it back to the herd. This done, she joined those holding the circle.

105

Brennan was annoyed at her cavalier departure. He had come to gloat over her, to make covert threats that would fill her with fear. He had expected to taste the anticipatory joy of her defeat. Instead, he had been warned, like some casual tramp to keep off her property, and had been left to digest it without being given a chance for a comeback.

Angrily he jerked at the rein, turned his horse, and rode away. He did not leave the ranch, but went to the house. Not waiting to be announced, he pushed through the outer court and the door opening to the *patio*.

Doris Silver reclined in a hammock back of the cerise-blossomed bougainvillæa. Just out of a hot bath, after a sound sleep, she lay luxuriantly among the pillows, her blonde loveliness set off by delphinium-blue silk pajamas and gold-kid mules above which could be glimpsed bare ankles and insteps.

"Look who's here!" she cried gayly. "The only man in Mexico who can protect me!"

"Go ahead," he said sourly. "Laugh. I'll have my turn later."

"But I'm not going to laugh," she said, with her most engaging smile. "I ought to thank you for your advice. You told me to stay at the ranch. I didn't, and had the most terrible thrilling adventure."

"So it was you. I figured it must be."

"If it hadn't been for Mr. Smith, if he hadn't been so brave, I don't know what would have happened. He saved me, so you see you're not the only man in Mexico who can."

"Smith was the fellow, eh? Well, he hasn't heard the last of that. I wonder if he can save himself."

She realized her error and attempted to remedy it by placating Brennan.

"He wasn't to blame at all. Those horrible men dragged me upstairs, then he came in and fought them and rescued me. Nobody could have done it better — except maybe you, Mr. Brennan, because you are so fearless and powerful. I wouldn't have worried if you'd been there."

"You wouldn't have needed to worry. I'd have fixed it all right. Next time maybe you'll listen to me and do as I say."

"Yes," she promised meekly, her big innocent eyes raised humbly to his.

"You're going to see a lot of me these next weeks, and you're going to be mighty nice to me."

"Am I?"

"You bet you are, Doris. Lucky for you I'm fond of you. I'll say that right now. Maybe you don't know it, but the war is on here against the present government. The revolutionists are winning everything. You'll need a friend, and a powerful one. I'm that friend. I can look out for you, and I will. It'll be known that I take a particular interest in you, and nobody will touch you. See?"

Doris saw, quite clearly, and chose not to discuss that aspect of the subject. She had had one lesson on the ruthlessness of social conditions here. It might be just as well to have a friend to windward as an anchor in case the political winds went wrong. When the time came she would no doubt be able to regulate the tempo of the friendship.

"It's awf'ly good of you," she thanked warmly. "You big outdoor Westerners are so chivalrous. It's men like you, Mr. Brennan, who have made the West and given it the name it has."

"Ranse," he corrected.

"Ranse," she repeated obediently.

"Don't get me wrong. I'm not chivalrous. I know what I want and mean to get. Any man who doesn't play his hand for himself is a fool. I always have, and I always aim to do it."

"Yes . . . You must have a great deal of influence with the revolutionists."

"I'll say I have. Listen, girl. Your friend Lee Reynolds got gay with me a little while ago and practically ordered me off the place. Now I'll leave a message with you for her. See you give it to her straight. Tell her that the third time I come here it will be for business. Can you remember that?"

"Yes. What business, Ranse?"

"You don't have to tell her what business. Just say it will be soon."

The sound of voices from outside came to them. He moved closer and stood over her.

"I'll be going," he said quickly.

"Must you?" she murmured politely.

His sultry gaze drank in the rounded curves outlined against the thin silk of the pajamas, passed down the slender, gracious figure. He stooped and kissed the bare instep above the mules.

"Don't!" she warned hurriedly. "Someone's coming."

The fragrance of amber wafted from her to his nostrils and filled him with a heady intoxication. His arms swept around the hammock and lifted her, pillows and all. Savagely his lips pressed against her soft breasts.

When Lee opened the door to come into the *patio* with her foreman, Brennan was moving across the tiles to leave. The girl glanced at Doris, a lady of flushed fury, and back at the man striding across the court. The fellow seemed to her to exude triumph.

"I told you to go!" Lee cried. "Get out, or I'll have you whipped off the place!"

He stopped, and glared at her. "Me! Ranse Brennan! I'd sure work you over if you was a man."

Lee turned to Daggett. "Go bring three or four of the boys."

"It'll be a pleasure, ma'am," the old man cackled.

Brennan did not wait. He flung himself into his saddle.

Twenty-four hours later, a dozen horses clattered up the road and stopped at the Costillo Hacienda. From them descended ragged peons and one man dressed as a cattleman. He was an American, big and brown and rangy, clearly the leader of the expedition.

"Stay here till I come back," he gave order in Spanish, then rang the bell at the gate.

Juan answered the ring.

"Tell your mistress," the big man said brusquely, "that Colonel Brennan, of the Mexican Army of Revolution, wishes to see her at once."

"*Si, señor,*" Juan replied, and vanished into the house.

Brennan did not wait for an answer. He followed the old servant. In the long living-room he stopped. It was dark and cool. He sat down in a comfortable old chair, put his boots on another, and lit a cigarette.

When Lee came into the room, he removed his feet from the second chair and rose, to bow to her.

"Back again, as I promised," he jeered.

"What do you want?" she asked.

"Always the little business woman. Good enough. I have come to get two things."

"What are they?"

He looked at her, malice smoldering in his eyes. "I'll tell you, soon as I get ready, missie. First off, meet Colonel Brennan, aide-de-camp to General Megares, Commandant of the Revolutionary Army in the District of Southern Sonora."

"I'm not surprised," she said, very quietly.

It was amazing how much of contempt she got into those three words. Not an overt criticism, he yet could read in her remark a volume of disdain. She conveyed her meaning without laying herself open to reprisal. Aide to a murderer, the foe of law and order and decency! A renegade driven to join the scum of civilization!

Some one knocked on the door and at Lee's invitation came into the room. It was her foreman,

Dunc Daggett. She had sent for him as soon as Juan had announced the guest.

"I think you've met each other before," Lee said, with an ironic smile. "But Mr. Brennan has risen in the world since you saw him last, Dunc. He is now Colonel Brennan, aide-de-camp to General Megares, Commandant of the Revolutionary Army in the District of Southern Sonora. Am I quoting you correctly, Colonel?"

"Go ahead. Be funny. You'll pay for it," Brennan growled.

"The Colonel was about to tell me why he is honoring us, Dunc."

"I've come to get the body of a fellow who claims his name is John Smith. He's wanted for raising a riot at Palo Duro and attempting to kill good Mexican citizens."

"What do you mean — get his body?" Lee demanded.

"I mean I want him dead or alive, and I don't care a billy-be-damn which."

"He didn't raise a riot. You know that very well. He defended a woman against dishonor, a woman you say is a friend of yours." The young ranch-owner's voice was still steady, but there was a rising wave of alarm in her heart. This man hated her, hated Jack Hadley. He would direct against them the power of the rebel forces. He would use his influence to pay off private grudges, to destroy the friend who was already so much more to her than a friend.

Brennan's malicious smile was hateful. "Maybe he'll be able to prove that after I've taken him to Palo Duro. Of course he'll have a perfecly fair trail. You understand that."

"He's not going with you to Palo Duro."

"I've got a different notion. Outside I have a few soldiers waiting."

Daggett spoke for the first time. "I seen 'em as I came in, a bunch of ragged ornery scalawags."

"Are you maligning the Army of the Revolution?" Brennan asked, with acid mirth. "Have you forgot that Washington's army at Valley Forge was ragged and had no uniforms?"

"Hell, Brennan, what's the use —"

"Colonel Brennan," the big man interrupted harshly.

"All right. Suits me. Colonel Brennan, then. You know doggone well this Smith boy didn't do a thing any man with guts wouldn't do if it was put up to him. You'd do it yore own self. I'll say that for you, though you an' I ain't friends an' never have been. Let's be reasonable about this here matter, fix up a compromise over a drink of Bourbon. Dawged if I'd want to see that boy in a Mexican jail. Now what I say is —"

"It doesn't matter what you say, Daggett," the other man interrupted brutally. "I'm dealing with principals and not with a cowhand. And I'm telling her that this Smith goes along with me to Palo Duro. If he or you make any trouble, I'd as lief take him dead. He'll pack easier that way."

"I won't give him up!" Lee cried, a little wildly.

112

"No? You set yourself against the revolution, then?" Brennan grinned. She was on the edge of a trap. Would she put her foot in it?

"I do not," she protested. "It's none of my business. I'm a foreigner and a neutral. I won't interfere in any way."

"But when an officer of the revolution comes and demands you give up a criminal, you refuse. What do you call that but interference?"

"He isn't a criminal. I don't believe he is wanted by the authorities, not unless you've stirred them up. You are paying off a personal grudge. Because you don't like me, you're trying to take it out of one of my men who has never done you any harm."

"Don't I like you, missie?" he said, and showed his teeth in a grin. "You'd be surprised if you knew what good intentions I have toward you."

As though to punctuate those good intentions, his quirt rose and fell heavily to wind the lash around his boot.

"We needn't go into that," Lee said, flushed and disdainful. "The question is this man Smith."

"Right. I want him. I'm going to have him. Colonel Brennan talking."

"So you say. I don't know that you're an officer in the revolutionary troops. I have no proof of it."

He drew a document from his pocket. "Here's my commission."

Lee looked it over. "I don't understand Spanish very well. Maybe it is, but it's not on official stationery."

113

"It's signed by Megares. That makes it official enough."

"May be a forgery. How do I know?"

She handed the paper back to him.

"You don't have to know. I know. And I'm going to take this fellow Smith back with me. You can lay a heavy bet on that and win. That's not all I'm going to take. We're going to cut out twenty-five of your fattest steers for the army."

"Rob me of them?" she asked.

"Commandeer them." He grinned, then recited as by rote what were evidently instructions from headquarters. "This revolution is of and for the people, to redress unbearable wrongs inflicted by the tyrants who have usurped the power. Supplies at times must be requisitioned, but officers of the patriot forces will issue warrants in payment to be redeemed at the national treasury in Mexico City one year after order has been established."

"Which means never if the present government wins."

"All good patriots will gladly take their chance of that," he parroted with huge enjoyment.

"And very likely never even if your friends succeed."

"Have you no faith in human nature?" Briskly he came back to business. "While it's still light enough we'll cut out the cattle we want. After we've secured the man."

He turned and walked out of the room. Lee followed him, Dagget at her heels. The old man was grinning as

114

he hobbled after them. He had an idea that part of the program at least would miscarry.

Outside, Brennan turned to Lee and indicated his men with a wave of his quirt. "Members of the patriot army," he said, jeering both at them and at her. "Detailed for special service. A picked squad."

Daggett took a squint at them. They were a nondescript lot, ragged and poorly clad, none of them in uniform, mounted on scrub stock and armed with such weapons as they had been able to find.

"Kinda hand-picked," the old Texan suggested. "You'd ought to left some tail-feathers on 'em, Colonel. Some time you come north of the line, señor officer, if you ain't ever been in the States, an' I'll show you —"

"Don't get funny with me, you old mossback!" roared Brennan. He got and resented the full implication of Daggett's innuendo. The old man was hinting that he must be a Mexican, since he could not be an American without being a renegade. "I'm boss here now, and don't you forget it. Padlock that tongue of yours."

"That's good advice, Dunc," his mistress told the garrulous old foreman.

A shot sounded. They turned, all three of them. A hundred yards distant, in a little grove of live-oaks, a small group of men were apparently practicing with rifles. Brennan knew them all, with the exception of two. There were Rusty, Jim Yell, Stan Ritter, Stumpy, and the one who called himself Jack Smith. The others were men picked up for the drive.

115

Brennan looked blackly at Lee. "Trying to pull something on me, are you?" he demanded.

"The boys got to makin' their brags this mornin' about how good shots they are," Daggett explained. "I reckon maybe they're kinda demonstratin'."

"That's it, is it?" Brennan walked to his horse and mounted.

The old man was a picture of innocence, too realistic to be true. From his hip pocket he drew a plug of tobacco and bit off a chew.

With a touch of spur, Brennan put his horse to a lope. He rode straight toward the live-oaks. The other two followed.

Brennan pulled up within a few feet of the cowboys.

"I've come to take that man Smith to town," he said. "Get this right, boys. You're in Mexico now. I'm a colonel in the new army. You'll get yourselves into a hell of a lot of trouble if you interfere with me. Understand? I can bring a thousand men along with me just as well as I can a dozen."

"What do you want Smith for?" Ritter asked. "He ain't done anything he shouldn't."

"The law will decide that, Stan. You keep out of it."

Jim Yell tried suave argument. "Now see here, Ranse. You know us. We've bunked with you an' ridden the range alongside of you. We've eat Lazy R beef an' swapped lies over the camp-fire. What's eatin' you? You know doggoned well we ain't huntin' trouble with you. Let's talk this thing over friendly."

"There's nothing to talk over. I want Smith. I'm going to take him. See?"

116

"Sho, Ranse! You're a white man, same as we-all are. You don't aim to throw down on us for this here spiggetty rebellion. Why, you couldn't ever come back to the States if you did that. If you want to join up with these birds, that's all right, but lay off your friends."

"When did this fellow Smith come to be my friend, Yell?" Brennan demanded. "I hated him and he hated me as soon as we set eyes on each other. You can't talk me outa this, any of you. What do I owe the Lazy R anyhow but a grudge? Kicked out by a squirt of a girl who tried to kill me. Me, Ranse Brennan! Do you claim *she's* my friend, treating me that way after all I did for her? I told her not to get hell in her neck, but she knew so much and wouldn't listen to reason. All right. Before I'm through with her, she'll listen. I'm telling you. She won't be so high-headed."

Unexpectedly Stumpy, the insignificant, lost dog of the outfit, took for the first time in his life a speaking part. "Don't you dass threaten Miss Lee," he stammered, fists clenched. "We won't stand for it a minute. No, siree!"

Brennan looked at him and laughed scornfully. Stumpy always had been a joke. The next words of the ex-foreman ignored him completely.

"Are you going to disarm Smith and turn him over to me, missie? Or shall I have my men do it?"

Jack Hadley had been standing a little back from the group, a rifle in his hands.

"Have your men do it," he suggested coolly. "If they feel lucky this afternoon."

"You're figuring on these boys defending you, eh?" Brennan sneered. "If they do, they'll be outa luck."

"Guess again, Brennan. These boys aren't in this. Miss Reynolds isn't in it. This is between you and me."

"Meaning what?"

Hadley's eyes, ice-cold, looked into those of his enemy.

"Meaning that you'll not take me to Palo Duro today alive or dead."

"How will you prevent it, fellow?"

About one hundred and fifty yards away an ace of spades had been tracked to a tree as a target. Hadley raised his rifle, seemed scarcely to take aim, and fired.

"Get that card, Stumpy," he said.

The bow-legged little puncher ran to bring it.

"Grandstanding, eh?" Brennan scoffed.

"Get this," the young man answered. "I'm playing a lone hand. Miss Reynolds discharged me this morning. I aim to leave here tonight. I'm going into the bunk-house to pack my roll. If you want me, you can find me there. But if you come looking for me, Brennan, come a-fighting."

"You don't think you can stand off a dozen men, do you? What you got up your sleeve?"

Lee's fascinated eyes were on this youth who challenged with such cool aplomb the man who had come to arrest him. He had lied when he had said he was no longer an employee of the Lazy R. Of course he had done it to keep her skirts clear of trouble. But she would not be saved at such a price. If he tried to defend himself, against this squad of soldiers, he would be

118

killed. How could she prevent it? What could she do to aid him?

Stumpy came back with the card. He offered it to Hadley, whose white teeth showed in a sardonic smile as he declined it.

"With my compliments to Colonel Brennan," he said.

Brennan took the card. A bullet had gone through the exact center of the pip.

"A regular Buffalo Bill, ain't you?" he said.

Daggett offered information. "He can do it twelve times out of twelve, Ranse."

"I've just been hearing you are not in this, Dunc," retorted Brennan. "If you're out, like he claims, stay out. You'll live longer."

"Good medicine, Dunc," agreed Hadley. "Superfluous information, anyhow. For if Colonel Brennan means business, he'll soon find out for himself how straight my bullets go."

"You're threatening me, an officer of the patriot army!" Brennan flung back savagely. "I'll show you! *Muy pronto!* Fire a shot at me or one of my men and you'll go to hell on a shutter right now. I don't waste time capturing a lobo wolf. I kill it."

"Yes, I expect you're quite a killer, when there's no danger in it," the young man drawled, his narrowed eyes on the horseman. "I wonder if I'd get to town alive if I surrendered. Probably not. Killed while attempting to escape."

Standing by Brennan's horse, her nerves tense, her slender body taut and straight, Lee knew a crisis was approaching. It was curious that just then a fugitive recollection, apparently totally irrelevant, flashed to her mind. It had to do with the horse of her former foreman. It came. It was gone. Her whole being was absorbed in this drama skirting so close to tragedy. Was it true, what her rider charged, that his enemy would find an excuse to kill him somewhere out in the hills?

"Fellow, you're monkeying with dynamite," Brennan said.

"There was Jack Hadley, for instance." The searching eyes of the man who called himself Smith bored in like steel drills. "The man you betrayed and killed in the Sierras at the Isabella Mine when you were one of Francisco's gang."

The bulbous eyes of Brennan seemed fairly to pop out. They stared at his accuser, as though fascinated. Who was this man? How did he know that secret out of a dead and buried past? Where had that familiar face . . .

Recognition leaped at Brennan. It was the face of Jack Hadley himself, the murdered man come to life. But that wasn't possible. A firing squad had put an end to him. His son, of course. The little brat that had come to camp the day Hadley had given him his time.

A fire, compound of fear and hate, seared through Brennan. Now. Better do it now and be done with it. He dragged from its holster the revolver by his side and fired. Once, twice . . .

His horse went into the air like a skyrocket, came down, whirled around and went up, landed humpbacked, all four feet stiff as piles. Totally unprepared, the rider shot sideways and struck the ground. His revolver went flying against a tree.

Hadley did not cover the man. He watched him, the rifle held loosely in his hands.

"Dog my cats!" shrilled Daggett, all excitement. "Tequila got him a man."

Brennan rose and faced the group, snarling. It was to Lee he spoke. "I saw you, missie. I won't forget it. One more I owe you."

Jack Hadley did not understand what he meant until Daggett flung his old hat to the ground joyously with a yelp and an explanation.

"Whoopee! She's the doggonedest girl I ever did see. Think of her remembering that Tequila always bucks when any one puts a hand onexpected on his nose."

Brennan straddled away, motioning his men to come forward.

"What are you going to do?" Lee asked of her rider breathlessly. She felt the life ebbing out of her heart. Did he mean to fight all these men, to let them kill him.

The smile on his brown face flashed, warm and reassuring. "Don't worry, *muchacha*. I won't start trouble for you. *Adios* — till later. All of you."

He ran to the bunk-house and slammed the door. Lee made as though to follow. Dagget seized her arm.

"Don't you, Miss Lee. He's got his play all figured out. Trust that boy an' don't gum up the works."

They caught a glimpse of him jamming a mattress against one of the windows of the bunk-house. The girl was pale to the lips.

121

"Don't you see! He's going to stay and fight it out," she pleaded.

"He ain't either. Didn't he tell you he wouldn't start trouble for you. Give him credit for horse-sense."

Brennan deployed his men in a half-circle. They moved forward slowly. "Come out and surrender, fellow!" Brennan cried. "You're bucked out."

There was no answer. The Mexicans sent a volley crashing into the adobe walls of the bunk-house.

The muscles of the girl's throat tightened. "I can't stand it, Dunc. Don't let them kill him," she begged.

"They ain't a-goin' to kill him. Not none. They can't if he ain't there."

"But —"

"There's a window in the back of the bunk-house. A limber lad like Jack could go through it an' light a-runnin'. He'd find hisself in a li'l' arroyo that don't show from here. If he hasn't hot-footed it up that draw to a horse waitin' saddled in the willows, I'm plumb disapp'inted in that boy."

When the attackers could bring themselves to the point of storming the fortress, they found their quarry gone. He had left a note on the table addressed to "Ranse Brennan, Killer." It said:

You'll have to wait to get me. An important engagement in the hills. Don't shoot from the saddle next time.

Brennan cursed, fluently and fervently. He took an installment of his revenge out on Lee. Instead of cutting twenty-five steers from the herd, he took fifty.

122

He did not get a chance to taunt her with it. She had disappeared into the house after the fiasco of the attack upon the bunk-house. By Daggett he sent her a message. It was to the effect that she might consider him a steady customer, since he intended to bleed her dry.

Lee was writing letters when the foreman knocked at the door and came in at her invitation.

"Workin' kinda late for a li'l' girl, ain't you?" he suggested. "It's 'most twelve o'clock."

"I don't feel sleepy. Probably I'm nervous about the way things are breaking, Dunc. I don't see what's to prevent Ranse from stripping me of all my stock, cattle and horses both."

Through the slitted lids the old man's faded eyes looked venomous. "Wisht I could get a crack at that buzzard from the bush with a scatter-gun. Dawged if I wouldn't make a vacancy in this spiggetty army. Colonel Brennan! Hmp!" Dunc fired a center shot of tobacco juice at a log in the fireplace.

"I ought to be happy that Jack got away," the girl went on. "I am, of course. You don't think they'll catch him, do you?"

"They ain't caught him yet."

She looked quickly at him. "How do you know?"

"Leastways they hadn't five minutes ago. He's waitin' out there at the corral now."

"Waiting?" Her star-bright eyes searched his. She could feel the beating of her heart against her forearms.

"To have a powwow with you."

She rose. "Let's go."

As Lee drew near the corral, a long lithe figure came out of the shadowy night to meet her, and at sight of it she knew joy.

"Your bad penny turned up again," the voice she loved best on earth called gayly.

Her two hands went out to his, then she steadied herself, to say quietly as her arms dropped, "I wish my penny wouldn't have so many adventures. I was worried about it this afternoon."

"Did you think I would start gunfanning and bring Megares's army down on you?"

"I was thinking about you," she said simply.

"When you put your hand on that bronc's nose?" he asked.

"Yes. That is, I wanted to shake his aim."

"You knew Tequila would start pitching?"

"He was in a circus once and learned the trick there.

"Lucky for me you remembered that." Then, with studied lightness, "I'll not forget," he added.

"Is it safe for you to be here? Oughtn't you to be riding for the border? Alone, you might get across."

"As safe for me as for you."

Daggett had discreetly vanished. They turned and walked into deep shadows of the live-oak grove. Lee caught herself wondering at her emotion — a world remade, and all because a man was walking beside her.

"Why isn't it safe for me?" she asked.

He did not beat about the bush as he would have done with Doris. He told her his thought, sure that she would have the courage to face any danger that threatened.

"Brennan won't stop until he has ruined you — unless we can prevent him."

"Take my stock, you mean?"

"That, anyhow." He left the answer vague, unless it was more definitive to say, "He's a bad *hombre*, and he hates you."

"Not as much as he does you now."

"I don't know. The point is you're within his reach. He'll put you in the wrong if he can. How can we prevent it?"

She loved that "we." He had identified himself with her. He had taken over her troubles for his own. All her life she had been mistress of the little kingdom about her except during school-days in the East. She had liked the sense of power, the assurance that she was first and her will was law. Freedom had been second nature to her. Often she had exulted because she was her own woman with none to say her nay. She could ride into endless miles of sun and wind fancy free, a part of the untamed life stretching all around her.

Now it came to her, thrillingly, almost as a shock, that freedom was a dubious gift. She did not want to lead, to give orders to others. She no longer wanted even to manage her own life. A strange new humility flooded her with delight. She wished now to be told what to do, and then to do it without question; to be owned, to be absorbed into the life current of this man whose voice set her pulses strumming. He might or might not make her happy. That was beside the question. Out of a world of men he was the mate her soul longed for.

With that assurance beating wildly in her heart went such a shyness as she had never known. If he knew how she yearned for him, how entirely she had surrendered without conditions, he might be repelled and withdraw even from the dear friendship she had won. She was just a woman to him, not *the* woman.

He did not want her love. Even Doris was more to him than she. He had saved Doris from dreadful disaster. He had spent long hours under the stars alone with her and had felt the lure of her loveliness, the smile adorable and provocative, the warmth of her gracious body as she sat beside him. Lee knew with the sure instinct of a lover that his lips had kissed the seductive mouth lifted to his, and the certainty of it was like a dagger thrust. Couldn't Doris, to whom all men paid tribute, leave this one alone for her?

"Ranse hates us both," she said, talking of the surface thing in her mind. "It's queer he could work for us so long and keep his real nature covered. I knew he was harsh and overbearing, but I didn't realize he was bad. Did Dunc tell you he took fifty of our best steers with him?"

"Yes . . . He's driving through tonight?"

"He told his men he expected to make it beyond the pass before daybreak."

"Chances are he'll stay with the bunch till they are over the pass and then ride on to Palo Duro ahead of his men." He hesitated before telling what he had

126

planned. "I wish I had met Megares and knew what he was like personally."

"Why?"

"He's a queer compound, they say. Vain and foppish, with a good deal of play at being the gentleman, but really as callous as an Indian. That's what I've been told. If he's as ambitious as they say he is, probably he wants to make a good impression just now on our government in order to give no excuse for intervention. What I'm getting at is this: Why not appeal to Megares over Brennan's head? It might do some good. If he gave an order, Brennan's hands would be tied."

"How would we reach Megares?"

"Go in and see him. Put our case before him."

"I'd have to go myself, of course."

"I'd drive you in tonight. We'd see him as soon as we could in the morning and get our facts in before Brennan reports his version of the story."

"But you couldn't go to Palo Duro," she objected. "It's the very thing we've been trying to avoid."

He grinned. "John Theocritus Smith, cowboy, couldn't go, maybe, without being put in the hoosegow, but Jack Hadley, millionaire oil man of California, wouldn't have any trouble."

Lee opened her eyes wide. "Are you a millionaire oil man?"

"Something like that. No credit to me. I'm rather ashamed of it. Other men found it and sunk the wells and pump it out of my land. All I do is collect the royalties. If there's any justice in that, I don't see it. But I don't complain. It's convenient for me."

"I should think it might be," she said.

But the fact distressed her. As a rich man he was farther from her than as a Lazy R cowpuncher hiding in the hills. Though she had plenty of assets, somewhat encumbered, she felt for the moment like Cinderella.

"I'll put on my glad rags and never be suspected. I was wearing my cowboy togs last time I went to Palo Duro."

"You're wearing the same face and it's still scarred from the fight."

"It's almost back to normalcy. The very fellows I mixed with would never guess I was the same man. Flannels, white shirt, sport shoes, panama hat. You've no idea how respectable I can look."

"I'd be afraid you'd be recognized. Dunc can go with me."

He shook his head. "Dunc would carry no weight. He's only your employee. I'd take credentials along that Megares might respect."

"Might," she repeated. "That's just it."

"Would," he corrected. His smile was persuasive. "Come. Be a sport, *muchacha*."

It would be an adventure, one to be shared with him. They would drive together through the soft velvety night just as he and Doris had done. In the morning they would face together any danger there might be. She longed to accept his offer. After all, would there be much chance of a recognition?

"Why should you do this for me?" she demurred. "It was different before —"

128

"Before you knew I was John D. Rockefeller," he finished for her. "Can't I have any fun, just because some company happened to drill in one of my pastures?"

"I know, but —"

"We'll start in just fifteen minutes," he said decisively. "I want to get across the pass before Brennan."

"If anything happened to you because of this, I'd never forgive myself," she told him. "You oughtn't to go. I know that. It's selfish of me to let you."

"Was it selfish of you to spoil Brennan's aim and increase his enmity at you? What's the big idea, young lady? Can't any one but you do any of the giving?"

"Oh, that was nothing. I just happened to remember about Tequila."

"You didn't happen to remember, though, that the bronc might have pounded right down on you. Now you listen to me. Go and get ready for a drive. Take a heavy coat. It'll be cold in the hills. You've got just ten minutes to meet me at the garage. That plain?"

"Yes, my lord."

She curtsied, turned, and ran lightly toward the house.

CHAPTER
EIGHT

Lee's room was on the second floor, and it adjoined that of Doris. As silently as possible she made her preparations for the trip to town. She did not want to waken her friend. Dunc could tell Mrs. Silver in the morning where she had gone.

The suit she chose was a russet silk knitted one, with a close-fitting little hat of the same shade. When she was dressed, she blew out the lamp and tiptoed out to the piazza. She was going to the adventure as excited and as doubtful as a sub-deb on the way to her first grown-up party.

During the first hour of that rush through the night, they talked little. She was content to sit bside him, to know that he was near. His gaze was intent on the road, and she could steal little glances at him unobserved. He had a face not easy to read, sometimes hard and cold, often mocking. Most men she had found obvious, but not this one. Many women, it was easy to guess, must have looked for something in it that eluded them, must have wondered with a kind of despair what weapons they had to penetrate the mask. That the spirit back of it was reckless and bold Lee knew. One might find anything there but weakness. He would go on, head up, with that air of victory regardless of the issue.

It thrilled her to know there was one thing he had given her not offered many. That was comradeship. It implied a meeting of their souls on a common ground. Between Doris and him such a relationship would be impossible. Mrs. Silver offered men the more subtle and exciting appeal of sex.

Two or three times he stopped the car to listen. What he wanted to hear and what at last did come to them on the night breeze was the bawling of restless cattle on the move. He was driving without lights, and he detoured slowly to pass the drive without being observed.

The wheels bumped over the rough ground for what seemed an interminable distance. Jack nosed expertly through narrow lanes fenced by cactus and mesquite. Time and again he backed to find another passage. Once he got out to see if the sand of a dry wash was negotiable. At last, after a tortuous circuit, the car came back to the road well ahead of the Brennan party.

Before they reached the pass, Jack turned on the lights. There was a straight run ahead of them now with no likelihood of interruption until they reached the outskirts of the town.

After a time they dropped down from the hills into a great gray desert beginning to take form in the dim morning light. They could see rimrock castles rising above the plain, freakish effects of erosion of countless years. A sheep corral with long flat sheds appeared by the roadside and was left behind.

Jack drew out into the chaparral and stopped the engine.

"Can't reach town at two or three o'clock in the morning," he said. "Might as well stay here as anywhere. Better try for some sleep on the back seat."

She curled up there and presently did fall asleep. The sun was up when he awakened her. They followed the road into Palo Duro. As they approached, a bunch of distant firecrackers exploded.

Lee looked to her companion quickly for an explanation.

"I judge the rebels haven't captured the barracks yet," he said. "The Federal commander retreated there after the row broke. I suppose he's hoping to be relieved by government troops."

From the hill which looked down into the town, they could see troops in the plaza. The road was guarded by soldiers. They were stopped and arrested.

Hadley spoke in Spanish to the officer. "You are of the patriot army?" he asked.

"Yes. Who are you?" the man replied.

He, too, used the same language.

Jack gave their names, and added that they had come to see General Megares on important business.

"I don't know whether he'll see you," the Mexican said. "He's pretty busy. What is your business?"

The American's smile was disarming. "If you don't mind, Captain, I'll tell it to the General."

"He's asleep now after being up nearly all night."

"We'll wait," Hadley said.

They spent five hours without breakfast, in an adobe hut adjacent to the General's headquarters. There was a bench inside the room, but no chairs. Two soldiers guarded them. Jack did business with the more intelligent. He had already sugared the palm of the captain, but he did not want to run any risk of having Megares go about his affairs without having been informed of their presence. The guard kept his eyes open. Five dollars in good United States currency did not come his way every day.

"The General will see you," he announced at last.

Lee and Hadley were led into the government building, along a corridor, and into an office where a man sat at a desk. He wore a uniform with the insignia of a general. A stenographer sat near taking dictation. Other men came in, saluted, gave messages, received orders, and departed.

The man behind the desk was slim and trimly built. His uniform fitted him excellently. The boots he wore were small and highly polished. For a Mexican he was light in color, and he would have been handsome except for a scar disfiguring the alert face. The black, beady eyes told no stories. It was the set of the mouth beneath the small brush mustache that backed the stories current about the callous cruelty of the man.

When he took time to look at his visitors, at sight of Lee he rose and bowed from the hips. "A thousand pardons, *señorita*," he said, and the voice which had been cold and curt grew almost mellifluous. "Pray accept the apology of a busy man. I did not look."

His English was perfect, with no trace of an accent. To deny him grace would have been folly. Lee had never seen a man whose movement seemed to flow with such rhythm.

Lee's head inclined to forgive his exaggerated discourtesy. Hadley introduced her and himself. He handed to the Mexican his passport and other papers to establish his identity.

Megares looked them over and glanced up at Jack.

"You are the John Hadley connected with the Visalia Oil Company?" he asked.

"Yes, General."

"I have heard of your fairy tale of good fortune. Let me congratulate you, sir."

"Luck out of a clear sky," Jack said, with a shrug. "Those who like General Megares carve out their own fortune with the sword are much more to be congratulated, I think."

Susceptible to flattery, Megares took this with a smile.

"*Gracias, señor.* Who knows? Mexico needs her Washington and her Bolívar," he purred.

The ego in the man almost startled Hadley. He had not realized that this bandit's ambition leaped so high, but he did not hesitate to play on it. "And will, I am sure, find him," he said, admiration in the look fixed upon the Mexican.

"I hope I have not kept you waiting. It is unfortunate. I did not retire until after dawn. Personally I directed the attack upon the troops of the tyrant government. The defending officer will surrender before night."

"Our wait does not matter, since we have the pleasure of seeing you now," Jack assured him. "By the way, General, we are not quite sure whether we are to regard ourselves as prisoners. We have been rather sedulously guarded."

"In no way treated with disrespect, I hope?"

"Not at all." Jack smiled. "I am not making a complaint, but raising a question."

"Consider yourselves my guests while here. In such times, with cut-throat riffraff floating about, it is necessary to protect neutrals. You will understand that, I am sure."

His gaze rested upon the young woman. Her brown beauty he found good to look at. The silk knitted suit set off to advantage her slender curves. There was something gallant about her poise, about the lift of the spirited young head. He guessed why had she come to see him, and though he did not intend to be moved too much by her charm, he was willing it should be a factor in the situation. A similar smoldering heat in his eyes she recognized. Megares was fond of women. There had been times when they had brought him to the verge of ruin, he had more than once admitted. A truer statement would be that he had let the passion for them burn him too fiercely.

"And thank you for it, General," Lee assented.

"We have come to see you, General Megares, about Miss Reynold's cattle. She brought them to the Costillo Rancho by arrangement with the then existing government. She comes to you in person because she desires to have a cordial understanding with the new régime."

"That is well." Megares shifted his gaze back to Lee. "I feel sure Miss Reynolds and I can work together. There will be among my people a prejudice against her as a foreigner, but I, Manuel Megares, know how to tame the unruly . . . You will lunch with me, while we discuss such little matters as are necessary."

Lee's glance fluttered to her friend and back to the Mexican. She did not altogether like the look in those bold black eyes, but she had to take the man as he was.

"That will be a pleasure," she said.

"If you don't mind Spanish cooking."

"I'm very fond of it, General."

She could have done justice to a much worse luncheon than the one to which she sat down. The *cabrillo*, fresh from the Gulf, was delicious, and the *frijoles* were excellently cooked. Lee was a healthy young animal, and she tucked in to make up for lost time.

"You have saved two starving tourists, General," she told him, not too seriously.

"I pay a debt, *señorita*, for you, I understand, desire to help save our patriot army from possible hunger," he answered.

The strong white teeth of the girl showed in a smile. "I want to do only a reasonable amount of saving, General. An army can get so hungry. It could gobble me out of my little herd so quickly."

"We mustn't permit that," Megares assured her. "We must find a way, you and I, to prevent it. Eh, *Señor* Hadley?"

"I'm sure Miss Reynolds can rely on your sense of justice," the American replied evenly.

"Indeed, yes! My sense of justice!" The bandit chief laughed, seeming to relish the flavor of the phrase as applied to him. "But justice is a cold word, one not to be used among friends. You would be surprised, señor, but there are those — enemies to the people's cause, of course — who have felt that justice would be served by putting Manuel Megares before a firing squad. Let us find some other word, a kinder one, Miss Reynolds, for use between you and me."

Lee was not looking for words to define a relationship between her and this man. Already his manner made her uneasy. It had a suggestion of the significant rather than the casual. She reverted to the business that had brought her here. In a dozen sentences she sketched the situation, the enmity of her ex-foreman, his determination to ruin her.

Megares watched her. He liked the fit of the rust-colored silk dress. He liked the unconscious pride with which she carried the lissom young body, and the way the color beat through the tan of her cheek. She was a charming young thing, full of clean courage and fire. "Colonel Brennan is a diamond in the rough," he admitted, with a sweep of the hand that disposed of that officer. "It will be better for us to settle our little matters together, you and I, Miss Reynolds."

"I want to be reasonable," she said. "But that is not what Ranse Brennan wants. He came to get twenty-five beef steers. He grew annoyed and took fifty. By my foreman he sent word to me that I was to herd the rest and he would get them at his leisure. Is that fair?"

"War is war, my dear," he said, shrugging his shoulders. "It is well to have a friend at court. I give assurance you have one. We must put a curb on Colonel Brennan, I think."

The soldier waiting on table poured wine into the glasses. The host apologized for it. "Native. Officers on active service must take what they can get. But such as it is, let us drink to the success of the revolution and to many pleasant meetings."

The guests drank the toast, with mental reservations. Lee was thinking that she would prefer to avoid meeting him. Some sure instinct warned her that the man was not safe. Jack, watching with cool masked regard this bland villain who was half savage and half pseudo-gentleman, wondered whether he was one of the outlaws who had taken part in the murder of his father. Old Dunc Daggett had mentioned a Mexican with a scar. Scores of Mexicans carried scars on their faces. Still . . .

"The revolution goes well?" Hadley asked.

"I think so." Megares smiled pleasantly. "If it does not, that will be just too bad, as you say across the line, for one poor general who has the honor of being your host today."

An orderly came into the room, and saluted. "Colonel Brennan returned, General."

★ ★ ★

"Tell Colonel Brennan to wait until I'm through lunch," Megares said carelessly.

The orderly hesitated. In a lower voice he made an addition to his message. "Colonel Brennan spoke about being in haste, General. He told me to say . . ."

Megares looked at the man, and a chill ran down the spine of the soldier. The sentence he was speaking died on his lips. Jack could see fear jump to the eyes of the messenger as he tried to divert the menace of that look.

"I'll tell him, General," he said, hurriedly and humbly.

The insurgent leader turned again to his guests, all suavity. It would have been impossible for any one who had not seen it to guess that only an instant before the savage in him had leaped out. Slight though it was, the incident gave Lee a shock, a queer little tremor of fear. She began to understand how Megares had earned his sinister reputation.

During the cigarettes Megares broached again the business that had brought them. He suggested that she sell to the insurgent government a few cattle in order to satisfy public opinion. Unfortunately, he could not pay cash, but would give a promissory note on the treasury.

Lee agreed. "I'll be frank, General. I can't afford to be generous. Would twenty-five beef steers be enough?"

"Quite." The rebel chief turned to the soldier waiting on them. "Tell Colonel Brennan I will see him now."

Lee had her back to the door. She could not see Ranse as he strode into the room, but at his first words she knew he was black as a thundercloud.

"I've been up all night getting supplies for your rabble," he stormed. "I've had no food today. As soon as I got here I came to eat with you, and —"

"Probably my error, Colonel, but I don't remember having invited you."

"Invited me? Hell's hinges! Haven't we eaten fifty times at the same camp-fire? Haven't I —"

"You forget that you're in the army now, Colonel," the Mexican cut in sharply. "Have you something to report to me?"

"Report to you?"

Brennan's anger, about to break out, found itself checked. His eyes had fallen on Jack Hadley and his surprising garb. He stared. His hairy hand shot out, forefinger pointing at him. Fury mapped his face. "That man!" he cried.

"My guest you refer to, Colonel?" Megares asked silkily.

"Your guest? Do you know who he is? He claims his name's Smith. It's a lie. He's tricking you. If you knew —"

"Can I be wrong?" The eyes of the bandit chief flashed warning at Brennan. "Isn't this Mr. John Hadley, president of the Visalia Oil Products Company?"

"I don't know anything about that. He's the son of that Jack Hadley who — who — was killed at the Isabella Mine fifteen years ago."

"Regrettable, I'm sure, though I am not acquainted with the circumstances and never had the pleasure of meeting your father, Mr. Hadley." The black eyes of Megares met the gaze of his guest steadily. "I judge,

140

from what Colonel Brennan says, rather abruptly, that he is better informed than I."

Jack looked at Brennan. "This man worked for my father at one time. He betrayed him to his death by bringing Francisco and his gang to hold up the mine payroll."

"Ah! A bad man that Francisco. Indeed, yes. He was a devil from hell — and I sent him back to the father of all devils." Megares stroked his little brush of a mustache and smiled at Hadley. "He was a ruffian feared by very many, but he made a mistake. He got in my way, and so —"

The Mexican moved a hand gracefully for a few inches to indicate that Francisco had therefore been obliterated.

Lee looked at the man. She found herself caught up into the drama of it, fascinated by the starkness of life so raw and insecure.

"You — punished him?"

"Exactly, Miss Reynolds. I executed him, because he became a nuisance to me — for his crimes, of course. Perhaps Mr. Hadley owes me a slight debt for that."

Jack bowed, his face impassive. "I shall try to repay my debt to you, General. I acknowledge it a great one."

Brennan had made another discovery. The lady with her back to him was his former boss. He broke out bitterly.

"Is this a party to my enemies, Megares? Did you invite them here to —"

The rebel leader struck the table with his knuckles. "You forget yourself, Colonel. As I mentioned before, you are in the army now. My title is General. I am your superior officer. Remember that."

Brennan struggled with his rage and choked down the expression of it. He would have liked to fling out a defiance, but he knew his man too well. Megares had served notice that the days of equality were past.

"All right — General, if that's what you want," he said sulkily. "But as an officer I've got my rights. This woman shot me — tried to kill me — less than a month ago. She made trouble yesterday when I went for the cattle. Even though she's your guest, I'm going to tell you that she's against us."

"Against us? Or against you, Colonel?" Megares asked, almost in a murmur. He was enjoying himself. Brennan was inclined to forget that he was a subordinate. It would be well to teach him now.

"It's the same thing," the big man retorted.

"I wonder," Megares mused aloud.

"And this man — this Hadley. He's the fellow came to town and raised a riot three or four days ago, the one who sent Juan Perez and two others to the hospital."

Megares raised his eyebrows. "Is he raving, Mr. Hadley?"

"Unfortunately, no, General. Soldiers will be a little rough when they have been drinking. You understand that, of course. They enticed a young lady who was with me into the house and carried her upstairs. The lady is a guest of Miss Reynolds, the wife of a prominent capitalist in Philadelphia. Perhaps you have heard of him — Harold Silver. I went in and explained to the men that it wouldn't do. Of course, I did not know they were of your party, General. I didn't even know they were soldiers. Some of them got a little excited, and we pushed each other around. A rail broke on the balcony, and two or three fell and got hurt. I regret it greatly. It would be a pleasure to me to pay all bills and plaster all hurt feelings with poultices of greenbacks."

"And when I went out to the Costillo Hacienda, yesterday, he refused to let me arrest him!" Brennan cried.

"You had troops with you," Megares reminded him.

"Not at the moment. He ran to a bunk-house and barricaded it, then slipped out of a back window."

"After Colonel Brennan had shot at me twice. I didn't dare trust my life with him, General. I preferred to come in and see you in person."

"You shot at him, Colonel? Why?"

"I told you why. He wouldn't surrender."

"That's not why," Lee corrected. "He shot at Mr. Hadley after he accused Brennan of killing his father."

"Are you going to listen to these people against me?" Ranse demanded.

"I'm going to listen to them and you too," Megares said, and his grin was ironic as he told why. "My well-known sense of justice demands that."

"Your what?" asked Brennan bluntly.

"I said my sense of justice. Are you hard of hearing, Colonel?"

"No. I thought maybe I didn't get you right."

"You — have an opinion on the subject, perhaps, Colonel?"

"You bet I have. But what's the use of beefing, Megares. The point is —"

"General. Don't let me have to mention that again, Colonel."

Brennan glared at his chief, purpling with rage. It seemed once more that his anger would break bounds, but again he managed to restrain himself.

"I'm trying to tell you that this woman shot me. Got jealous because I had been out riding with her friend. She's against us. Refused to sell me any cattle. Lemme see you alone."

"You didn't bring any cattle, then?"

"I brought fifty. Now, listen. This wildcat girl here and this *hombre* Hadley are with the enemy. They're against you, same as they are against me. I can tell you all about both of 'em."

"Fifty? I told you twenty-five."

The big man ripped out an oath, his patience gone at last. He swung his quirt and brought it down heavily on a small service table. "You trying to ride me, Megares?" he roared.

The insurgent commander touched a bell. An orderly appeared. "Bring a sergeant and a guard," he said in Spanish.

"What's the big idea?" Brennan asked belligerently.

"The idea is, *señor*, that you are going to cool your heels in jail," Megares answered. "I'll show you who commands here, my gringo friend."

"You can't do that to me, Megares," the other threatened.

"No? Let us see."

Six men filed into the room. Megares gave orders for the arrest of Brennan.

The Colonel drew back, snarling. His hand moved toward the butt of the revolver at his side, but he thought better of it. He was in Mexico, among revolutionists. He might kill Megares and some of these men, but in the end he would be destroyed.

"Don't touch me!" he warned. "I'm a friend of General José Barela and an officer in the army."

"Ah! You are a friend of Barela, eh?" The black eyes of Megares were narrowed to shining slits of light. "But General Barela does not command here. I, Manuel Megares, lead this army. Think of that, Mr. Brennan, while you look through the bars." Then, in Spanish, he added abruptly: "Disarm the man. Arrest him."

Brennan surrendered his revolver. "I'll remember this," he promised the bandit chief.

"You'll have nothing else to think of until you change your tune," Megares flung back.

After Brennan had been taken away, the Mexican general turned to Lee. "Twenty-five of your cattle will be returned to you, Miss Reynolds. This man will drive them back himself. And I — I shall give myself the pleasure of calling in person to make sure they have safely arrived in good condition." He bowed urbanely, full of smiles which were not reassuring.

"You are very kind, General," Lee said.

"But it is you who are kind, dear lady. I am a rough soldier, in camp, far from home. To be entertained at your hacienda by one so charming will be delightful. I do not say good-bye, but *au revoir*."

He held her fingers, and his eyes grew sultry as they looked into hers. With a flourish he stooped and kissed her hand.

"As for you, Mr. Hadley, let us, *for the present*, forget your little difficulty in this city with my naughty boys. I wish you and Miss Reynolds a pleasant journey back to the rancho. Command me when I can be of service."

Jack made the proper acknowledgments. Ten minutes later, he and Lee were driving out of the city.

"What did he mean when he said to forget *for the present* your trouble here?" Lee asked.

"He meant I was on good behavior; that he'd forget it if I didn't get in his way."

"How could you get in his way?"

Even as she asked the question, she knew the answer.

"We've got to watch our step," he said. "Megares is dangerous. He'll stop at nothing to get what he wants."

"What does he want?" Lee wanted to know.

Their eyes met.

"I don't know. Nothing yet, probably. Hope he's kept too busy to come to the ranch."

"Yes." Lee added, doubtfully, what was in her mind: "He's a man I could be afraid of. There's something ruthless about him."

"He's a bad egg," Jack admitted lightly. "But he'll likely have troubles enough of his own without worrying us. The President of Mexico is a strong man. He's backed by powerful forces. General Luna, in chief command of the government troops, is an able general.

146

I expect to see the insurgents defeated. It can't be too soon to suit me."

"Nor me. Weren't you surprised at the quarrel between him and Ranse? There didn't seem to be cause enough for it."

"It had been simmering before this came up. Megares was just waiting for a chance to clamp down on him."

"What will he do to Ranse?"

"Not much, if Brennan eats humble pie. They seem to be old companions. Did you notice how Brennan looked when he said I was the son of Jack Hadley of the Isabella Mine. He was warning Megares. I believe the Mexican was with Francisco the night he killed my father."

"Maybe." Though the sun was warm, Lee felt drenched by a cold shower of dread. "I wish we were all out of this country."

"Oh, well, we'll get out one of these days. If Megares comes to the ranch, we mustn't let him see Doris Silver."

"No," she said quietly, not looking at him.

A pang of jealousy stabbed her. It was so much more important to him, then, that Doris should be safe than she.

"She wouldn't realize how dangerous her smiles would be."

"They're always dangerous, aren't they?" Lee wanted to know. "To men, I mean. We women survive them."

"Do all men succumb?" he countered lightly.

"All I've ever noticed." She laughed as her eyes slanted toward him. "Do you want to take an exception?"

"Maybe I'd better not boast."

"I wouldn't. Anyhow, we'll try to save her from this bold bad man."

She wondered if she had given herself away.

CHAPTER
NINE

Megares was as good as his word. Twenty-five Lazy R steers, thirsty and hard-driven, came bawling over the hill to the gates of the Rancho Costillo. They were driven by two Mexican *vaqueros* and a very sullen gringo. Juan carried a message to his mistress which brought her to the *patio* porch.

She found Brennan waiting there. Inside, he was a caldron of boiling poison. His rage was comprehensive. It extended to the whole world, but was more intensive toward those who were factors in the humiliation he was undergoing. Two days had been spent by him in a filthy calaboose with drunken riffraff before he had been able to bend his pride to ask pardon of Megares. He had gone through the form, but only because he had made up his mind to betray the fellow to the government that had put a price on his head. So much for Megares. After him, this fool high-heeled girl and his enemy Hadley.

Brennan scowled at the young woman. Her clean remoteness, the light, quick step and the lifted head, stirred resentment in him. He was no more to her than the peons waiting outside with the cattle. One day he would shake her pride yet.

"Compliments of General Megares," he jeered, parroting his piece. "Your cattle are at the door. The General will call himself this evening to pay his respects if other duties permit."

Lee had an impulse to placate the man's hostility. It seemed so useless and so wrong.

"Let's call it quits, Ranse. There's no sense in hating. It never gets anywhere."

"We'll see if it doesn't," he snarled. "If you think you can shoot me and kick me out and have me flung into a bull-pen with drunks, and get away with it — well, you've got another guess coming, you little hellcat. Go ahead. String along with Megares. You think he's your friend. All right. See how safe that is. I'm not good enough for you, but a dirty greaser cut-throat suits you fine."

Lee did not answer. She turned on her heel and walked into the house. Contact with a mind capable of such a venomous outburst degraded her.

Hadley and Doris were sitting in a sunny window nook. He was plaiting a horsehair band for her hat and she was taking a vivid interest in the process, one that necessitated her fingers touching his occasionally as he intertwined the strands.

"We're to have a guest this evening — General Megares," Lee told them.

Jack looked up. "Who says so?"

"He sent a message with Ranse along with the cattle."

"Hurrah!" Doris cried. "At last. I have not lived in vain."

"You're not going to see him, my dear," Lee told her.

"Not see him! Of course I'll see him. Why shouldn't I see him?"

"Because he isn't a safe playmate for little girls."

"Oh! So I'm to be sent to bed while you play with him!"

"The damage is done as far as I'm concerned — and, anyhow, I'm not Doris Silver. Ask Jack what he thinks."

"I think that the less either of you see of him the better," Hadley said bluntly. "He's a dangerous man."

"Is he? I like dangerous men." The eyes of the blonde beauty sparkled.

"When Jack says dangerous, he doesn't mean fascinating, Doris. He means not safe for a woman like you to meet, in a place like this, where he is just now a dictator."

"Isn't that a little absurd, Lee? You said yourself he was very friendly to you. He has shown this by sending back your stock. I think he has behaved very well."

Jack decided to mention a story he had heard. A young Mexican had hidden Megares in his home while the outlaw was being hunted. A week later, the pretty girl-wife of the host disappeared. She had gone into the hills with Megares. The affair had a tragic ending when the girl commited suicide.

"I'll promise not to run away with him," Doris said. "If he's one of the reason why girls leave home, I'm all the more anxious to see him."

"One version of the story is that this young wife didn't leave home of her own accord, that he abducted her," Jack explained.

"Not likely," Doris demurred. "Men don't want to be bothered with women who scream for another man and scratch their eyes out. I think I'll not believe that version."

"You're not in Philadelphia now, Doris. You had a reminder of that the other day. Terrible things happen in this country during these revolutions. I'm responsible for your safety. I don't want this Megares to see you. Maybe it would be all right. Maybe it wouldn't. There's no need taking risks not necessary."

Lee gave her opinion like a Supreme Court decision, Doris thought resentfully. After all, she was not a little girl. She had a right to do as she pleased.

From her window she watched Megares drive up in a high-powered car just before dinner-time. Unexpectedly he had come early.

Doris did not waste a moment. Presently Lee would get word to her that the ogre had arrived and that her dinner would be served in the bedroom. She flew to the dresser and very swiftly used a lipstick, touched her soft cheeks with rouge, and patted her golden hair here and there. Slipping downstairs, she opened the door of the living-room and walked demurely in.

Her surprised consternation at sight of the gold-laced officer was perfect. Lee gave her credit, though she knew it was acting.

"Oh!" Doris stopped near the door. "I didn't know. Please excuse me."

152

Megares had risen instantly. He stood staring at this vision of shy blonde loveliness. His blood began to quicken.

"Ah-h!" he purred. "But you do not intrude, señorita. Far from it. Pray introduce me, Miss Reynolds."

Lee went through the formula. She watched Doris unmask her devastating smile, watched her let her innocent eyes grow big with admiration.

"If this is for business —" Doris began, and stopped to ask the question with her most childlike look. "If I ought not to be here —"

"No, no, madam," Megares replied quickly. "I come for pleasure. I am a thousand times repaid. You will remain, I beg."

He offered her a chair, bowing from the hips in the exaggerated graceful manner he had, a picture of raffish impudence posing for an effect. Doris floated down into the chair and the Mexican sat down in another, drawing it closer to her. His bold eyes devoured her.

Dinner was announced. Lee planned the exit from the room in such a way that the men had to go first. She fell in beside the other woman and her strong fingers tightened on the soft white flesh of Mrs. Silver's arm.

"You little liar!" she murmured. "You saw him when he came."

Her friend's grin was impish. "What a suspicious mind you have, darling!" she reproached, also in a whisper. "But I don't blame you for trying to save him for yourself. He's a darb."

153

At dinner Megares did not pretend to keep his gaze from Doris. His conversation was directed at her. He had to remind himself occasionally that his hostess was not a piece of furniture.

Doris was at her adorable and provocative best. She knew she was amusing Jack and annoying Lee, and this lent an edge to her enjoyment. She guessed she was playing with fire that might prove a devouring flame if she could not control it. But she could. It was a part of her equipment as a coquette to know how to side-step adroitly and successfully. The faint, far whiff of danger was enough to excite without disturbing her.

"Are you as bad as your reputation, General?" she asked, following a lead he had given. Her eyes lifted with shy audacity to his.

Megares was delighted. It was part of his vanity that he was always willing to discuss himself with a charming woman.

"But how bad do they say I am? And who says it?" he smiled, stroking his little brush mustache as he ogled her.

She threw up her hands. "Everybody. You're the bogy man of the border. Mothers frighten their little girls to be good by saying you will get them."

"Ah-h!" He lifted an inquiring finger. "How old are these little girls?"

She laughed. "Quite little. The older ones — I think they are curious as well as afraid. They would perhaps like to see what Bluebeard looks like."

"But I am not Bluebeard, my dear young lady. Not at all. I have not seven wives."

"It would be inconvenient to have so many nowadays."

"And against the law," he assured. "But let us not talk of wives and husbands. I do not feel domestic tonight. Romance is in my heart. We are young — all of us." He lifted a wineglass. "Let us drink, my friends, to one of my two gods — Love."

That business finished, Hadley offered a diversion.

"Your other god, General, I guess to be Ambition," he said.

"Correct, Mr. Hadley. I do not worship war. It is a necessary evil which I use for my own ends. Money, merely a convenience except for sordid souls. But power, which is ambition achieved — a great man would wade through blood for it. He would take his fortune in his hand, and risk it — and his life — and all he has — to reach the summit where men can fear and envy him."

Jack offered no opinion upon this philosophy of life, but sardonically suggested the alternative. "Or to be dragged down and destroyed while climbing."

Megares shrugged. "Perhaps. I am a fatalist. What is to be will be. But I would not want to live a week if I had to exist like the insenstitive rabble I command."

"The patriot army," Jack offered with an ironic smile.

"Exactly. The claptrap of politicians. We live in the richness of our sensations. I enjoy today the more because tomorrow I may be extinguished. Danger is the breath of life, Mr. Hadley. And unless I miss my guess, you know it."

"And morality, General? The good of others, the sense of justice, which I think we mentioned before."

"Words. I live for myself — once only — for a few years. I am a fool if I am strong enough to take what I want and do not do so."

Doris protested. This was her own philosophy, ruthlessly phrased and applied, carried to its logical conclusion and not left vaguely in the air. But she did not recognize it in the harsh clothes it wore.

"Oh, I don't think you ought to say that, General. I'm sure you don't really mean it. We can't take *everything* we want."

His little black eyes fastened on her. "Can't we?"

"No. How could we? It wouldn't work. Civilization, and that sort of thing, you know. Of course I want what I want. Still —"

"I'm not concerned with civilization, but with Manuel Megares," he told her.

"But if you wanted something you ought not to have?"

"That's just the point, Mrs. Silver. I ought to have anything I want, if I'm strong enough to get it."

He was smiling as he watched her, but that smile sent up and down her spine the little cold feet of mice. It made her very conscious of being a woman, and one stripped of all the protections which society has built up since cave-man days. Here was a stark savage force she could not brush aside by coquetry. Her glance fluttered to Lee for help and found none there. It passed to Hadley. That young man's eyes had gone cold and grim. He knew trouble when he saw it coming.

One diversion he had already tried, but Megares had made of it a road which led back to Doris, a medium for making clear his intention. Jack tried another.

"I've noticed that ambitions go to wreck, even those of big men, because of weaknesses which trap them," he said casually. "Indolence, perhaps, or wine, or most often . . . women."

"Yes?" the Mexican inquired with thin politeness.

"Not the fact itself so much as a lack of judgment at the critical time when the whole attention should be on the great ambition. One president of your country went to wreck, for instance, because he did not cultivate the friendship of the President of the United States."

"Ah-h!" A ferocious gleam showed in the black eyes. "That big bully Uncle Sam must always be placated, eh?"

Hadley poured himself a glass of wine and looked speculatively at the rich color of it. "None of us dare forget facts because of our prejudices, General. If we do, we lose the great throw. A big bully, perhaps, but not to be ignored. And that reminds me. We might be able to help your cause at Washington. Mrs. Silver's husband went to college with the President. They belong to the same fraternity. Silver was very active in securing his nomination. Can't we make that count on your behalf? I suppose diplomacy is part of the game and all wires must be pulled."

A bull's-eye shot. Jack knew it at once. This man might hate gringos, but he knew that north of the line was a crouched lion that might leap and destroy him as it had Huerta while Wilson was President.

157

"Indeed! A friend of the President!" The Mexican turned to Doris. "I have forgotten for the moment what college," he said.

By good fortune Doris remembered what college the President had attended. She named it, and Hadley breathed again.

Megares stroked his mustache reflectively. Perhaps he had better go a little slow.

As they were rising from the table, Lee referred to Megares's victory at Palo Duro.

"You captured the barracks and the Federal forces there, didn't you, General?"

"As I told you I would. The day you lunched with me, Miss Reynolds."

To make conversation, she asked carelessly, "Are you holding the men prisoners?"

"No. They joined the patriot army."

"The commander, too?"

Megares smiled blandly. "No, Miss Reynolds. He did not join us — and we are not holding him prisoner."

"You let him go?" Doris said, surprised.

"Have another guess, Mrs. Silver," he said suavely. Looking at him, she did not need to guess.

Doris rode with Lee and Hadley to help them drift a bunch of cows into the hill country north of the rancho. Stumpy was the fourth member of the party. The men carried rifles in addition to their revolvers. Bands of roving guerrillas, attached loosely to the rebel cause, were said to be in the district, though none had been sighted near the Costillo place.

158

Lee had nominated Stumpy to go along because she thought it would please him. He was a lost dog who wagged his tail at the least friendliness from her. Well aware of the state of his feelings, she usually did not encourage him. But he was congenitally a victim of lack of confidence, and there were times when she patted him on the back to make him buck up.

This morning she rode beside him. Hadley and Doris were in front. While she chatted with Stumpy, Lee watched the others, the straight-backed man she loved who sat a horse with such a perfect seat and the golden girl who appropriated as a matter of course the attentions of every desirable man she knew. Lee had known other girls with the same selfish vanity that had to be fed constantly with admiration, but most of them lacked the compelling charm of Doris — the warm, slow grace of body, the silken lashes drooping over appealing baby-blue eyes, the color and animation that made her a miracle of loveliness. She did not blame Jack for his capitulation to Doris. Why should she? Nor did she hate Doris for capturing him. She was what she was.

It was a day of warm and pleasant sunshine. A coma of peace rested over the drowsy land. It was hard to believe that war filled the minds of thousands of men within a few score of miles.

Hard to believe one moment. The next it leaped out at them.

A score of riders rode lazily around the shoulder of the hill above. One of them caught sight of the Americans, gave a shout, and spurred toward them.

The others followed. A long line of loping horses pounded down the slope.

Hadley did not wait to ask questions. He rounded up his party and turned heel. If these men were on a raid for cattle, they might be contented to take the herd.

"Head for the patch of timber away down there to the left," he ordered. "Use your quirts! We've got to move fast!"

He looked at Lee, searchingly. She nodded. "I'm all right. Take care of Doris."

Jack glanced back. The first of the pursuers had rounded the herd and were still coming. His heart chilled. It was to be a fight or a surrender. He dared not turn these women over to such riffraff as this. The guerrillas were the scum of the country. Would it be possible to stand off so many? He rode alongside Doris and grinned at her. "Another adventure, lady."

She did not smile. Her lips were white and trembling. "Save me, Jack!" she begged pitifully.

A bullet plumped into the sand a dozen yards away. From Doris's throat there broke a moan. She swayed in the saddle. Jack's hand went out to steady her.

"It's all right, little girl. They couldn't hit a barn. Not shooting from the saddle. Steady-o!"

Another spurt of dirt jumped up in front of them. Five or six shots sounded.

Doris leaned forward, slumping down. Jack ranged closer and leaned over. He dragged her from the saddle and bundled her between himself and the horn. Her eyes were closed. She had fainted.

"They're getting nearer!" Stumpy shouted to Hadley. "Think I better turn an' take a crack at 'em?"

"No. Ride hell-for-leather. And look after Lee."

"Y'betcha!"

The riderless horse still pounded beside them toward the timber: Jack measured the distance with his eye and that between them and the enemy.

"We'll make it," he called to Lee. "Through the timber and into the gulch beyond."

But he was not so sure of it. One Mexican, leaning far forward in the saddle, was driving his mount on like a racer. Jack shifted the weight in his arms and drew a revolver from its holster. He could hear the thudding of the hoofs at the heels of his sorrel, could see the rider over his shoulder drawing closer as the gap closed.

The man yelled something at him, at the same time shifting the rifle in his hands. When Jack fired, the galloping horses were almost neck and neck. The shot of the Mexican went wild. The bay was rushing on alone. The other horse had plunged off at a tangent when the rider slid from its back.

Lee and Stumpy had reached the live-oaks and were pushing through to the gulch.

Over her shoulder Lee flung a question.

"All right? Not hurt?"

"All right!" Jack shouted back. "Keep going!"

They reached the mouth of the cañon.

"Do we make a stand here?" Stumpy asked.

"Not yet. Near the head of it."

Jack saw that the guerrillas were coming through the timber, but at no headlong pace. One had been shot down because he was in too big a hurry. The rest did not care to make that mistake. They would drive their prey through the gulch into the open country above and close in on them there safely.

The horse of Doris had left them in the timber. The others clattered into the dry rocky bed of what was apparently a creek in rainy seasons. The cañon was steep. In places big boulders filled the channel and the cow-ponies had to work their way around them. The muscles of the animals stood out as they clambered catlike up the rough and precipitous waterway. The crack of the rifles behind them came booming up the narrow gorge like the roar of cannons. A bullet struck a flat rock close to Lee and went ricocheting into the brush.

Jack turned in the saddle. He could see three or four of the Mexicans, not more than a hundred and fifty yards away. One had dismounted and was taking aim across his saddle.

That would not do. It had to be discouraged. Jack looked at Doris. She lay in his arm, her fear-filled eyes turned to his.

"It's going to be all right," he promised. "Can you ride alone for a little while?"

"No, no! Do not leave me!" she begged.

He neither argued nor explained. She was in physical collapse and would listen to no reason. Riding close to Stumpy, he passed the woman to the cowboy as he would have transferred a sack of flour. On the bow-legged little man's face there was a sickly grin.

"What's the matter?" Hadley asked sharply. His first thought was that the man was frightened.

"One of 'em plugged me in the back," the *vaquero* answered. " 'S'all right. I'll keep going."

"Stick it, Stumpy, till you reach the rimrock above the falls. See? Where the big tree leans out. Wait for me there."

Jack slipped from the saddle and handed the bridle rein of his horse to Lee. "What are you going to do?" she asked.

Their eyes met.

"Going to hold them back a bit. Don't worry. I'll be with you at the rimrock in no time. If I'm not there in five minutes, light out for the ranch, all three of you."

"No," she told him.

"Do as I say."

"Let me stay with you."

"No. You've got to take care of the others. Stumpy's shot. Doris is crazy with fear. It's up to you to save them."

Inside, she was a reservoir of woe. He would stay, and they would kill him. But she had to leave him there alone. Her duty was to to go with the others, to do as he told her.

She turned the head of her mount to follow Stumpy.

Jack had slipped the rifle from its scabbard alongside the saddle. He ducked behind a large boulder. A bullet zipped past his ear. Without taking aim, he flung a shot toward the dismounted man below. His intent was to protect Lee's retreat.

163

The challenge had its effect. He saw a couple of other men scrambling from their horses and scooting for cover. Swiftly he fired again. One of the men stopped, as though startled, then went limping into the brush.

Jack turned his attention to the man firing from back of the horse. He raised his hat above the rock on a dead stick. Instantly two guns roared. Not a split second later, he had taken sight around a corner of the rock and fired. The bullet struck the saddle and the animal went plunging down the creek bed. The man who had been taking cover behind it dropped down among the rocks.

Other horsemen of the banditti were moving closer. Jack picked out a rock forty feet above him and raced for it. He heard the whistle of a bullet and the crash of exploding guns echoing up the gulch. But he reached his boulder and threw himself down back of it. Looking up, he could see that Lee was vanishing above the rimrock.

Another moment, and he was on his feet again dodging in and out of the brush which fringed the bed of the creek. The guns boomed and reverberated like giant firecrackers flung into a narrow alley between tall buildings. He kept going and presently came to a clump of wild cherries. Into these he dived, wriggling forward under cover of the heavy foliage. The rifles were still sounding, but he knew that only a chance shot could find him. A minute later, he was among the boulders along the edge of the dam.

164

"You're not hurt?" Lee asked quickly as he emerged from them above the rimrock. She was busy trying to give first aid to Stumpy. Doris leaned against a rock, lacing and unlacing her fingers as she wailed in terror.

Jack examined the wound of the cowpuncher. The bullet had struck the small of the back and ploughed through the vitals. Already the little man was almost green in the pallor of his face.

"I hate to — to be so much trouble, Miss Lee," he said weakly. "Seems like I — I'm thataway."

Lee wiped the beads of anguish from his face. "You poor boy," she murmured.

Briefly Hadley outlined their plan of action. He spoke to Lee. "You and Doris must ride fast to the ranch. Get help and send it to us. We'll hold the rimrock, Stumpy and I. You can save us if you hurry. They can't easily get at us. Now, go."

He lifted Doris to the saddle. "I'm afraid," she moaned. "I — I —"

"Don't be a fool! I'll hold them here. Ride with Lee and you'll be all right."

Lee looked at him and gulped. Would she ever see him again alive? Without a word she swung to the saddle and led the way up the opening gulch to the mesa above.

Jack picked a spot for his defense where the rocks protected him, but left a loophole through which he could fire. He shot once, as a warning to the huddle of men below that he was on guard, then laid down the rifle. He knew they would not rush his position immediately. They would talk over the best way to drive

165

out the defenders and they would then inch their way forward through such chaparral as there was in the cañon.

He did what could be done to relieve the wounded man. It was not much. To Jack it was apparent that he would not live many hours.

"Wisht I had some water," Stumpy groaned. "I'm burnin' up inside."

Water could not be had, unfortunately. There was no external flow of blood. All Jack could do was to prop the unfortunate man up in a position less painful to him.

"Don't you worry none about me," the cowboy said. "I'll make out. You go back an' tend to them greasers."

Jack returned to his post. The Mexicans had separated in order to offer a less conspicuous mark. But the cañon was not wide and it was not possible for all of them to find cover that concealed them entirely. The agitation of thick brush showed the defender where men were creeping up the gulch. He dropped a bullet into the moving foliage and the quivering of branches stopped.

"Get one of 'em?" Stumpy asked.

He had crept to the edge of the rimrock, rifle in hand.

"You lie quiet, Stumpy. I'll do this job," Jack told him.

"Lemme help. It won't hurt me any . . . now. I got mine."

"In much pain?"

"Not so much." After a moment the wounded man plumped out a request, boyishly. "You tell Miss Lee I was game, Smith."

"Game as any one I ever knew, Stumpy." Jack fired at a man dodging across the creek into the cherries. The fellow gave a howl and vanished among the tangle of young trees. "I'll certainly tell her, though she knows it already."

Jack was no sentimentalist, but he felt a queer little tug at his sympathies. This poor lost dog of a *vaquero*, who all his life had been cuffed from pillar to post, had evidently given his heart in dumb devotion to his mistress. He had never amounted to anything. He had always been a failure and conscious of it. Around camp-fires and in the bunk-house he had been the butt of practical jokes. Even in the business of punching cows he did not qualify as a top hand, since he was a poor roper and only a fair rider. But none the less his inarticulate soul had ached with hopeless love and dreamed its moments of heroic glory.

The sniping of the attackers varied in intensity. At times it would amount almost to a fusillade, then would die down to an occasional shot. But the net was drawing tighter. Jack had not been firing to kill, since the first minute of the defense when his revolver had saved him from the charging man on horseback. He had wounded two without stopping the Mexicans. The circle was closer. He could see a slim figure creeping out from the wild cherries to the rocks above.

Stumpy's rifle cracked. Jack fired at the fellow emerging from the cherry thicket, missed him, fired again as he broke into a run, and dropped him.

Bullets came pinging against the rimrock and whistled over the heads of the Americans. From somewhere in the boulders not far below the dam, a sharpshooter was sniping. Intermittently Jack turned his attention to him. He could not watch for him, since his gaze had to sweep constantly the whole battle zone.

A flame seared Jack's shoulder. He had been hit, by the sharpshooter among the boulders. Jack caught a glimpse of a wide Mexican sombrero above a rock. He did not take the bait, but lay crouched ready to fire. Presently the hat disappeared and a head was very cautiously lifted above an edge of out-cropping quartz. Jack blazed at the forehead above the peering eyes. There was a rattle of slithering shale. A body pitched into the open and somersaulted into the sharp boulders below.

The attackers had had enough. Cautiously they gathered their casualties, crept down the cañon with them, and disappeared around a bend.

When Dunc Daggett and the Lazy R riders arrived thirty minutes later, guided by Lee, they found the two on the rimrock holding the battlefield alone.

Lee slipped from Nuggett and ran forward to Jack. "You've been hurt!" she cried.

"A flesh wound," he told her. Then, in a lower voice, "Stumpy is dying. Forget me and think of him."

Lee knelt down beside the lad. She could see he had not many minutes to live. He smiled feebly.

"I'm gonna take . . . the long trail," he murmured.

"Can I do anything for you, dear Stumpy?" she begged. "Anything — anything at all. Have you any father or mother?"

"I ain't got no one . . . if you'd sing for me, it'd kinda ease me over the bumps." He got it out a word at a time, gasping for breath.

"Yes. What shall I sing?"

"Sing . . . the Cowboy's . . . Dream, ma'am, if — if —"

Lee sang to him, her arm under his head, her face close to his so that as he slipped away he might hear.

> Last night, as I lay on the prairie,
> And looked at the stars in the sky,
> I wondered if ever a cowboy
> Would drift to that sweet by and by.

"Yes, ma'am. I'm a . . . heap . . . of trouble. Do you . . . reckon . . . maybe —"

"I know it, Stumpy, dear boy. You're going home — to that sweet by and by — where there's no more trouble and pain."

"I . . . ain't . . . ever . . . been . . . any . . . account."

She stooped and kissed him. A smile, happy as that of a pleased child, lit his pale face. The body stiffened and then relaxed, sinking down. Stumpy had gone to the land where the wicked cease from troubling and the weary are at rest.

CHAPTER
TEN

Immaculate and trim in the uniform of a general officer, Megares smiled at Lee with all the benevolence of the cat which has swallowed the canary.

"I am desolated to learn of the atrocious attack upon you by murderous bandits. After our cause has triumphed, it shall be my pleasure to scour the country of such vermin. Meanwhile, dear lady, I must protect you. The district is restless and unsettled. Bands of ruffians commit offenses and discredit the patriot cause. I, Manuel Megares, will look after you — and your charming friend, Mrs. Silver."

"That is kind of you, General," Lee replied, and wondered just what he had in mind. She was uneasily aware of some intention not yet fully expressed.

"These scoundrels, with no regard for law or property or human life, give it out that they are of my army," Megares went on, virtuously indignant. "They ambush you, take your cattle, murder your *vaqueros*, and wound your friends. By the way, how is *Señor* Hadley?"

"Doing very nicely. He is up and about, though we think he should remain quiet and rest."

"They greatly frighten you and our mutual friend, Mrs. Silver. I will not have it. I shudder to think of what might have happened to you. No. I shall establish a headquarters here as well as at Palo Duro. I shall be what you call a commuter."

"But is it necessary that we should trouble you so, General?" Lee protested. "Now that we are warned, we can look after ourselves. We shall stay close to the rancho in future."

"Don't say another word, my friend," he urged paternally. "My duty and my inclination run hand in hand. I shall make of this a pleasure."

"But —"

"It is decided. If any evil should befall you or Mrs. Silver, I would not only be grieved myself beyond measure, but I would be held responsible by your government. So I forestall this evil. I make you — and Mrs. Silver — my personal wards. From today I am a guest of the rancho. Let me hope, a welcome one."

He knew how welcome he was, and he let his appreciation of it show in his grin. Whether she wanted him or not was the least of his worries. Though he pretended ironically to be a guest, he let her know within a few hours that his suggestions were to be considered commands. They were, too, enforceable. A company of his soldiers were camped just outside the gates. An aide-de-camp and a corporal's guard lived in the servants' quarters.

He had taken over the establishment, though he apologized elaborately for the trouble he was causing Lee.

Megares was usually away during the day. He rose early, breakfasted alone, and drove to Palo Duro. No decisive battles had as yet been fought, but Hadley gathered from what he could pick up that the rebellion was not making headway. Locally the revolutionists were in control, but their numbers were not increasing fast and the forces of the government were being consolidated for a decisive campaign. That Megares was worried could be guessed from his manner. As often as possible he ate dinner at the rancho with the Americans. At times the veneer of his courtesy wore thin. The irritation that leaped out of him was a reflection of his troubles.

His intentions regarding Doris he scarcely took the trouble to veil. There was a feline streak in the man. He had jumped to the conclusion that Hadley was in love with Mrs. Silver, and he took delight in making love to her before the younger man. Somehow he had learned of Brennan's feeling toward her, and he brought Ranse out to the rancho several times for the pleasure of seeing the man's curbed rage when he purred over her and stroked the soft flesh with the velvet paw that had such terrible claws.

It did not take Lee long to discover her status in the house. She and Hadley were stopped by a guard as they were starting for the corral where the Lazy R riders were calf-branding.

In Spanish, Hadley asked the man by whose orders they were detained. He learned that the General had given instructions. This was about a week after Megares had fastened himself upon them.

"He's drawing the net closer," Hadley commented to Lee when they were alone.

"Yes." Her troubled eyes turned to him. "He's getting impossible. I'm awf'ly uneasy about . . . Doris."

"So am I."

"He's trying to tempt you to interfere. I can see that. He doesn't like you, and he wants an excuse to — to —"

Hadley nodded. He had known that for several days and he had restrained himself deliberately. He did not want to make futile protest. When the time came, he must strike effectively if possible.

"What are we to do, Jack?" she asked.

"There's one thing we could do . . . maybe, if we got the breaks. Slip away — the three of us and your riders — and push for the north."

"But we couldn't get across the line, could we?"

"I don't know. But if we could reach Barela, we could throw ourselves on his protection. He wouldn't like it. He'd be embarrassed because he can hardly dare to offend Megares. But he is a gentleman and he is no fool. He would know he couldn't send us back to this bandit. What he would probably do would be to turn his back while we escaped to Arizona."

"If we only could reach him, Jack."

"We'll have to try. It won't be easy to get away, but it might be done, perhaps."

At dinner that night Lee asked Megares if they were prisoners. She put her question smilingly, with a touch of gayety, as though the thought of it were absurd.

"But no, dear lady. Why do you ask?" the General replied.

"One of the men you left — it was silly of him, of course — wouldn't let me and Mr. Hadley out to check the calf-branding. He said you gave him orders we were to stay inside."

Megares appeared to be distressed at this interpretation of the incident. "Absurd, Miss Reynolds. Why should you be my prisoner, since we are all good friends? No, no. You are my charming hostess, and I am your indebted guest. But you are too daring. You would venture out and perhaps get shot. I must protect you against these assassin guerrillas. You are safer at home."

The General had brought Brennan to dinner with him. The big man laughed, unpleasantly. Megares glared at him.

"You are amused, Colonel?" he inquired suavely.

Brennan looked at his chief with a murderous eye. "I laughed at the way the guard misunderstood you," he growled. "Do I have to explain to you when I laugh?"

Her own nerves a bit on edge, Doris made petulant complaint. "Good gracious, what's the matter with everybody? I haven't seen a real smile or heard a laugh for a week. I wish you'd take your old revolution off somewhere and bury it, General."

"If you would help me to forget it, lovely lady, I would be enchanted. Up Eros, down Mars!" He leered across the table at her and spoke in a stage whisper. "I will walk with you in the *patio* after dinner and discuss that, *chiquita*, if you will so far honor a rough soldier."

174

It was while he and Doris were smoking together in the *patio* that Lee approached Brennan.

"Why did you laugh when General Megares said he must protect us from the guerrillas? What made you look so queer?" she asked.

"Have I got to tell you, too, why I laugh?" he snapped.

"You don't have to explain, but I thought you might want to."

His eyes narrowed. "You thought we were such good friends I'd naturally want to confide in you."

"I think you hate Megares and perhaps know something about him."

"I know he is a murdering wolf," he broke out savagely. "Tell him I said so if you like."

"Why should I tell him? Is he a friend of mine?"

"You know what he's up to, don't you? You know what the dirty greaser wants and means to get. He's going slow because he doesn't want our government riding him if the rebels win. But I know him. He's a wolf, I tell you. He'll leap and pull her down when he's ready . . . Since you want to know, I'll tell you why I laughed."

"Yes?"

His eyes jeered her. "Who do you reckon the scalawags were that killed Stumpy?"

"I don't know. Riffraff of some sort. Outlaws, I suppose." As she looked at him, the suggestion he had offered grew in her mind. "Do you mean that Megares — ?"

"I'm not saying so. Figure it out for yourself. You claim to be smart as a whip. You know it all. If he wanted to move in, wouldn't he want to give a good excuse? And what could be a better one than that it wasn't safe for you-all to stay here without him to protect you?"

"But —"

"All right. Suit yourself. But remember, I'm telling you. The damned wolf had you attacked to give him a plausible reason. I don't reckon it would have hurt his feelings if that yap Hadley had been bumped off during the rumpus — or you either for that matter. He wants one thing, I tell you, and he aims to get it. If you weren't blind, you'd see."

"Suppose I do see. Is there anything I can do about it? We're helpless here — prisoners. He as good as told us so tonight."

"The hellhound!"

Lee heard the edges of his teeth grind. "Are you speaking of your friend?" she asked.

"Friend! To hell with him! I'd gun that *hombre* in a minute if —"

"If you weren't afraid to," she finished for him.

"I'm not afraid of any man alive!" he boasted. "But I'm no fool. They'd tear me to pieces in five minutes. What's in your mind, girl? You can't use me for a cat's paw if that's what you're figuring on. I won't lift a hand for you after the way you've treated me."

"Nor for Doris either," she said.

He had nothing to say about that, but the look in his smoldering eyes told her that he was burning with jealousy.

"He's out in the *patio* now forcing his attentions upon her," Lee went on, watching him.

"Does he have to force them on her?" he demanded. "The little fool hasn't got any more sense than to flirt with him. Why, a baby might just as well play with a tiger."

It was true that Doris flirted with Megares. She was afraid of him and yet was fascinated by the very danger of such a relationship. Having observed the two together, Lee was not sure that she agreed with Brennan as to the folly of her friend's course. For Doris to turn her back upon the bandit general would be to raise an instant issue. Was it not better with such a man to play for time, to lead on with vague hints that quickened hope of a surrender due to his personal charms? The question was as to how long she could evade payment. Not long, Lee's heavy heart told her.

Hadley was at the piano playing soft music.

"Shall we go into the *patio?*" she asked.

The young man rose. There was a tacit understanding that when possible Megares must not be left alone with Doris too long. Interruptions annoyed him, but they diverted his mind from Mrs. Silver.

Hadley rattled the handle of the door and opened it. He followed Lee to the porch. Megares confronted them angrily. He had evidently whirled around when he heard them coming.

"What do you want?' he demanded.

Doris was standing in the shadows back of him. Her eyes flashed gratitude to Lee. Automatically she patted her disheveled hair into place.

Lee played up the demands of the situation. "If we only knew, General. Do you men? None of us women do. We think we want one thing and all the time it is something else." She laughed lightly. "Tonight, in the *patio* here, with the fountain splashing and such a moon, I'm almost convinced I want romance. But who knows? Probably if I had it, I'd be wondering what the quotation is today for beef in Kansas City."

Slowly the Mexican relaxed. He had been prepared to issue an order, but the girl's persiflage took the wind out of his sails. He suspected she had come out to interrupt his love-making, but he was not convinced of it.

"You have a saying, you Yankees, that three makes a crowd," he told her. "A moon loses its luster when it looks down on more than two. I, Manuel Megares, tell you so out of my experience. A man, a maid, and a moon. That is a perfect combination. Try, it, my dear hostess. One man, no more." His black eyes quested from Hadley to Brennan and back again, then maliciously he fired a double-barreled thrust. "From the advantage of his years, the Colonel perhaps smiles wisely at such follies of hot-blooded youth, but surely Mr. Hadley could be persuaded to play Romeo to so charming a Juliet."

A warm color beat through the tan of Lee's cheeks. She knew she was blushing and was grateful for the dim light of night. That she could muster a laugh pleased her.

"Mr. Hadley has not your Latin temperament, General. He probably couldn't be persuaded that the world would be well lost for love."

"Oh, couldn't he?" Doris murmured.

"At least he'd want to choose his own Juliet," Lee added.

"We've all been heard from except Mr. Hadley himself," the Mexican said. "I'm sure Mrs. Silver is right. Come, Mr. Hadley. Are you one of those prosaic Yankee business men who find the romance of life in the price of pork?"

"Not quite, General," he said carelessly. "But Romeo is a little out of my line. Mercutio always seemed to me a better bet. Still, I'm teachable, though young and inexperienced."

"Listen to the epistle of John, but remember that it isn't gospel," Doris contributed, and tilted a mocking smile of reminder at Hadley. She was moving with supple grace into the house, and except Jack himself only Lee caught the look.

Inside the lighted room, Doris turned to Lee, all animation. "What do you think, dear? General Megares has brought our mail out from Palo Duro, where it has been lying ever since the war began. Where is it, General?"

Megares turned to Brennan. "Will you get my brief-bag, Colonel?"

Brennan looked as though he would like to tell him to go to the devil, but he contented himself with the ugly glare of resentment. Reluctantly he walked out of the room.

Presently he returned with a bag stuffed with letters and magazines. Megares distributed them. Those belonging to the Lazy R riders Lee put to one side.

One of the letters was addressed to John T. Smith. The Mexican looked at the address and grinned.

"Have you a *vaquero* by that name, Miss Reynolds?" he asked.

"I had, General, but I had to discharge him. I'll see it reaches him."

"Please do."

He handed her the letter and she flipped it over to Hadley. Jack ripped open the envelope and ran his eye through the contents.

"Is it an important letter, Mr. Smith-Hadley?" asked Brennan, speaking the name with a sneer.

Jack looked at him, with a strange cold fire in his eyes. "You'd be surprised to know how important it is, Mr. Brennan," he answered, almost spacing his words in their low distinctness.

The looks of the two men clashed. Brennan did not understand what the letter had to do with the antagonism between them, but he knew that some day he must meet the challenge of this man's vengeance.

Deep in one of her letters, Doris gave a little cry of surprise. "Harold is coming West! Why, he must be here now — in Arizona, I mean."

Megares brushed his mustache with finger-tips. The mocking smile was scarcely concealed. "So near and yet so far," he murmured.

180

"But I must meet him," Doris said. "Can't you arrange it, General? If we could get a pass to cross the line!"

"Impossible. The troubled state of the country — roving bands of outlaws. I couldn't consider it."

"But if you sent a guard with us —"

"I have no men to spare," he answered curtly.

"It would be rather a sporting thing for us to try it alone — just the Lazy R outfit," Jack suggested, to see the effect.

"No. You'll stay here." Megares spoke with sharp decision.

"I want to see my husband," Doris said wistfully.

The eyes of the Mexican, hard as jet beads, did not waver. In the hinterlands of his mind, back of that masked smiling face, not even an optimist could have expected to find unselfish kindness.

"We must try to make up to you, *corazón*," he said, in the low voice that could be so dulcet. "I, myself, am very much at your service. Husbands, after all, are not indispensable. For myself, I have often found them annoyances. Let us bear ourselves with resignation in his absence. The moon will still shine — for you and for me."

"But Harold —"

"Is in Arizona and must stay there. Come, come, *chatita*. Husbands are forever, lovers but for a day. Let us forget your good, dull, money-making Harold just now. It will make him more ardent to fret for you."

Daunted, Doris looked at Jack, urgent appeal in her eyes. All her life she had shuffled and dealt the cards.

Now her wishes did not count. The dread of imminent disaster chilled her.

Jack knew better than she did how great was her danger. If the revolution gave promise of success, the peril might be delayed, but as soon as Megares knew he was doomed to failure, fear of the United States would no longer be a factor in his calculations. He would probably seize Doris and take her into the mountains with him, there to lead a fly-by-night existence, harried from one fastness to another, as the Federal troops pursued the outlaws. Doris would have to endure hunger, cold, hardship, neglect, and probably cruelty. For such a woman as she, life under such conditions would be hell.

The young man smiled cheerfully at her. "What must be must, Doris. After all, General Megares has given his word that all will be well. Some day, when he is the great man of this country, we shall look back on these days and remember how exciting they were."

"Yes, indeed, dear lady, and you will visit me in Mexico City and we will talk of moons and old memories," Megares purred. Doris forgot her fears and began to smile.

Doris never appeared until nearly noon. She ate breakfast in bed and spent a great deal of time dawdling over her toilet. As usual, Lee and Jack were alone at the morning meal on the day succeeding the one when their mail had been delivered. Long since Megares had left for Palo Duro. This hour was the best in the day for Lee. She loved its intimacy.

182

"Dunc tells me that each of my riders has to report at night," Lee said, pouring coffee for her guest. "They are to take care of the stock during the day, but if they don't show up to report, they'll be treated as spies. That was made very clear to them. And if one disappears, the others will be held responsible."

"Megares doesn't intend we shall have any communication with the other side of the line," Hadley commented. "He doesn't leave us in any doubt about that."

"No. From now on Dunc is to talk with me only once a day to get orders. Just after breakfast. We're only prisoners."

"I had guessed that," he said, with his sardonic smile.

Her clear eyes looked into his. "What will he do to us when he sees the revolt is failing — if it comes to that?"

"He'll probably let us go."

"And Doris?"

"He won't let her go," he answered slowly.

"We must save her, Jack! We must find a way!" she cried.

"I don't see how," he admitted. "Megares is wily. He knows we'll escape if we can. That's one reason he commandeered your car for revolutionary services. He doesn't mean to give us a chance."

"No. But — what are we to do? We've got to save Doris somehow."

"I've been wondering if Brennan might not help us. He hates his chief. He's jealous. Of course he hates us, too, but at the moment his feeling is more virulent toward Megares. And he isn't easy in his mind. He's afraid of him. So would I be in his place. He can't dissimulate. The Mexican knows how he feels and finds joy in feeding his jealousy. But, after all, he's not a tame cat, but a tiger. Megares, I mean. Any day he might get tired of Brennan and strike him down."

"Yes."

"By the way, the letter I got last night was from the nurse in Los Angeles." There was, she noticed, a cold glitter in his eyes. "She writes me that the name her patient gave as one of the murderers of my father was the one I had asked her about in a letter."

"Ranse?" she asked.

"Yes."

She waited a moment before she put her next question.

"What do you mean to do?"

"Nothing, at present. The important thing now is to get out of here safely. My personal business must wait. Can we get hold of Brennan and use him to help us escape?"

"We might, after what he told me last night. But I'm not sure he could do much. Megares doesn't trust him. If he helped us, he'd have to go with us to save himself."

"Probably. I'll take some more toast, please."

A rap on the door interrupted them. At Lee's invitation Dunc Daggett came into the room.

"Good-morning, Dunc," his mistress said. "Will you have a cup of coffee?"

"Yes, ma'am. I been chasin' a *ladino* beef, an' I'm some tuckered. Well, I got news for you, Miss Lee.

Rusty came in from the big pasture half an hour ago lickity split. He bumped into some surprise an' b'lieve me he drug it for the ranch to spill it. Down in the hollow of the hills there he found an aeroplane. It landed just before daybreak. There's two men in it. One of 'em said he was Miz Silver's husband."

"Harold Silver — in our pasture?"

Lee's whole being was quick with excitement.

"Yes, ma'am. I told him to keep his trap shut. We don't want all the boys stringin' down there an' puttin' these spigotties wise to what's there. I got an idea. Maybe you can make out to slip down there an' he can scout you over to Douglas or Tucson."

"He must have come here to get Doris," said Lee to Hadley.

"Perhaps he can take both of you. We'll have to get you out of the house somehow," Hadley replied.

"And you — what will you do?" she asked. "And the men I brought with me?"

"Don't worry about us, Miss Lee. We'll make out all right," Dunc told her cheerfully. "Point is to get you an' Miz Silver away."

"The point is to get *her* away, not me," Lee corrected. "I'm not going to walk out on you after bringing you here. How can we get her out of the house?"

"Her an' you, too," Dunc insisted stoutly. "What kind of birds do you reckon we are, Miss Lee? You come first with us. Now we got a chance to send you home, you can bet yore boots you're going."

"Yes," agreed Hadley quietly.

"We won't waste time arguing now. How can we get to the pasture?" Lee asked. She knew she must appear to give way.

"We might make a break an' fight our way there," Dunc proposed. "Kinda take 'em by surprise. There ain't more'n forty or fifty of 'em around."

"No," vetoed Lee. "That won't do at all. It would mean that those left would be sacrificed to Megares's vengeance. We must use strategy."

"Why can't you and Doris dress up as Mexican girls?" Hadley wanted to know. "There are three or four of them around the hacienda, and others have dropped in from the village to see Ysela or to meet Megares's men. The guard would probably let you pass, unless he stopped you to flirt with him and recognized you. You'd have to do the talking, Lee, and the less you said the better."

"We could do it, and get by with it, I think," Lee assented at once. "Both of us were in theatricals at school. Ysela will give us clothes. Doris would have to play shy and not talk, keeping most of her face covered with a shawl. I believe it will work."

"Fine. Hop to it." He relapsed into bitter self-justification. "I done told you-all Mexicans were p'ison an' you steamed me all up with talk about how nice an' law-abidin' they are. Y'betcha! They're as friendly as rattlesnakes. Me, if I owned Mexico an' Hell, I'd sell Mexico an' go live in the other place. Tha's how much I think of it."

"You're prejudiced, Dunc. Why should we hate all Mexicans because we know one bad hombre among them? Well, I'll get Doris up and we'll get ready for our big scene. Of course Rusty warned Harold Silver to lie quiet until he heard from us?"

"So he claims. Get a jump on you, girl. I'll be plumb worried till I see that big bumble-bee p'inted north for the good old U.S.A."

Swiftly Lee departed. Daggett left for the stables. Jack waited in the living-room. He was glad that Lee had consented to go, though he was a little surprised that she had yielded so readily. As soon as the plane got into the air, he meant to make a break for the corral. Dunc would have a horse saddled and waiting for him. They would round up the other Lazy R riders and strike into the hills. The odds were against them, but at least they would have a run for their money. If they remained on the ground, with both women gone, Megares would almost certainly have them butchered.

Jack looked at his watch impatiently every few minutes. He wished they would hurry. At any moment the Mexican troops might discover the concealed plane and wreck the chance of escape. The young man smiled grimly. He was in love, for the first time in his life. This girl, so direct, so honest, whose slender body moved with such fluent grace, had stepped into his life and filled it with gladness as no other woman had ever done. He had been thought hard, but he was not hard with her. She had, by merely being herself, worked some chemical change in him. That she was a perfect comrade he knew, and no less certainly that she would be a perfect lover.

Two Mexican girls came into the room. One was shy and retiring. The other smiled and flung a provocative tag of Spanish at him.

"You'll do," he prophesied. "*Adios,* my dears. Luck with you."

Doris came up and kissed him good-bye. It was her habit to scatter casual kisses as she did smiles. They did not mean very much. But Lee offered only her hand in farewell. His heart registered a little pang. She might have kissed him once . . . just once. It was likely that if she escaped, he would fall a victim to the rage of Megares. She might have remembered that.

But she did not. She smiled at him and said, "I'm going to see you again — soon."

"I'll never forget you, Jack." Doris promised, facile tears in her big eyes.

He smiled, the cynical smile that disturbed women because they did not understand it.

CHAPTER
ELEVEN

Lee and Doris went out by the servants' gate. A soldier was doing sentry duty there. He stopped them.

"Where did you girls come from?" he asked in Spanish.

In the same tongue Lee answered, "From the house, you stupid donkey. Did you think we flew down from Heaven? We spent the night with Ysela."

"Oh! I hadn't seen you go in. Are you sure it was with Ysela?" He chucked Lee under the chin.

Her bright eyes flashed at him. "Does General Megares pay you to insult us village girls?"

"He hasn't paid me at all," the man chuckled. "When he does I'll spend my pay on you, *chatita*. Come. A kiss, and I'll let you pass."

Lee offered her cheek pertly, and as he leaned forward for his reward swung the palm of her hand smartly against his face. She laughed, merrily, and fled, Doris at her heels.

"Ho, ho!" she called back. "That for you, pig!"

The man laughed. "I'll comb the village for you tonight, spitfire."

Other soldiers were in sight, five or six of them at the stable, two or three at the corral, others in front of the house. None of them paid any attention to the girls except one, who shouted an invitation to come and help him wash his clothes. They moved into the orchard, passed through it, and slipped between two strands of a barbed-wire fence into the pasture.

Daggett had given directions to find the aeroplane, but Lee did not at first head straight for it. They might be seen and followed by a pair of amorous soldiers. It was better to drop into a deep arroyo and follow it until they were out of sight, then cut across at an oblique angle.

They moved through the chaparral into the arroyo and along its tortuous course. After a time they clambered up the bank, wound through a thicket of mesquite on the shoulder of a hill, and dropped into the valley below. It was a small saucer-shaped park, level at the base. Into it the plane had dropped for a safe landing. Not a hundred yards from the girls it could be seen.

Two men were tinkering with the machinery. At sight of the women, one of the men moved toward them, at first uncertainly.

Doris gave a little cry of joy and ran forward. He dropped the monkey-wrench in his hand and came swiftly to meet her. She went straight into his arms. Hungrily he kissed her. She had been away from him for months. Fear had ridden him, since he had known she was cut off in a land ravaged by war. What Rusty had told him had quickened his anxiety. And now he had found her alive and well.

190

Lee waited for recognition, smiling at their ardor. Harold had rowed on his college crew many years before. But he was developing avoirdupois. He was getting quite bald. Big business takes its toll of the trim, athletic figure. He was not exactly a figure of romance, yet there was a sturdy manliness about him quite attractive.

He came up and shook hands with Lee.

"I've got a good pilot here," he said, after the greetings were over. "You girls will be quite safe with him. He'll have you back in Arizona in a couple of hours."

Lee made no comment on that. Instead, she asked a question. "How many will the plane hold?"

"Three."

"You mean you'll stay here?"

"Of course. Jackson will come back for me."

"And will he find you?"

"Certainly he'll find me. Why not?"

"Because, as soon as the plane rises, the soldiers of Megares will make a search and will probably capture you."

He shrugged his shoulders. His fine steel-barred gray eyes met hers.

"I'll have to take my chance of that."

"Oh, no, Harold," Doris cried. "You crowd in too. He's a terrible man, this Megares. You don't understand."

"Sorry, sweetheart. Can't be done. The plane will carry only three. Don't worry. He won't hurt me."

"He happens to have fallen in love with Doris," Lee said quietly. "We've been worried, all of us. You haven't come any too soon."

"He wouldn't have dared to touch her," Silver said.

Lee corrected him. "He'd dare anything. One of his officers called him a wolf the other day. That's a good word for him. He's a murderous ruffian, without the least sense of morality. If Doris escapes from him, some one is going to have to pay for it."

"We'll see about that. The United States Government would have him by the throat if he hurt me."

"Provided it could catch him," Lee explained. "You don't understand, Harold. You wouldn't, since you haven't been here. If he's defeated — and we think he will be — he'll be an outlaw, anyhow. What does he care about our government? What did Villa care when we hunted him?"

"Then I'll have to hide in these hills till Jackson comes back for me. After all, since I've got to stay, there isn't any argument."

"But you're not going to stay. You're going along with Doris."

Again he explained that the plane could not possibly carry four. "But I'm not going," Lee told him.

"Of course you're going! Do you think I mean to leave you here after I've come for you?"

"You're not leaving me here. I'm staying of my own accord. I'm not going. That's all there's to it."

"But why?"

"Because my place is here. The riders I brought with me are here, and so is Jack Hadley, who is a friend of

192

ours. If I go, Megares will kill some of them. I can't desert them. Don't you see that? As long as I stay, my presence here is a kind of protection for them."

"You've just told me some one would have to pay if Doris goes. How do I know it wouldn't be you?"

Her answer was not candid, but she made it seem so. "Because I'm a woman."

"As Doris is. But you said —"

"He isn't passionately in love with me as he is with Doris. That makes all the difference."

"I don't see it, Lee. The simple fact is that I'm a man and you're a woman. If one of us has to stick it — and one of us has — it has got to be the man. I couldn't hold my head up afterward in case anything happened to you."

"Not if you intended to desert me. But you could get a bigger plane and come back for us all. I'm not going now, Harold. That's all there's to it. You may talk till you're black in the face. I brought my friends down here, and I won't leave them to that tiger Megares. As long as I stay, they have a chance. When I go, their chance goes too. So that's that, old dear."

And it was. He argued, pleaded, threatened, and got nowhere. She was as firm as Ailsa Craig, and in the end she had her way. He was to go with Doris back to Arizona, pick up a large plane at Tucson or Los Angeles, and make a try to rescue the Lazy R party.

Doris flung herself into the arms of Lee. "Dearest, dearest, I hate to leave you here," she wailed. "You've been so good to me. I love you — and — and I'm afraid that —"

"I'm not," Lee told her.

And, oddly enough, she was not. A queer exaltation, akin to joy, flooded her. She was staying to face danger beside the man she loved. She would not have wanted it to be any other way. They might go down to death together, but for one hour of hours she would know keen happiness.

"I'll be back," Silver promised. "Have your party all ready when you see me coming. I'll circle around in the air before we land, to give you time. Come on the run and pile in. I'll have a machine gun, and we'll try to stand off this Megares crowd till we take off again. Where had I better land?"

"On the mesa in front of the house. There's a flat place along the road about a mile from the main rancho. We'll reach you if we can. You'll know our party because I'll wear a red dress. If we don't show up within half an hour, you'll know there's no chance and you must take off before the soldiers get to you."

"Right-o, Lee. Good-bye — if you're sure you won't go."

"Good-bye — and good luck."

The girls clung to each other and kissed. The eyes of Doris were filled with tears as her husband led her to the plane.

Lee watched the plane rise from the ground, sweep around in a half-circle, and go droning into the north. She walked quickly back to the arroyo, followed its bed, and came to the orchard. As she neared the house, she realized that the aeroplane had stirred up a lot of

194

excitement among the soldiers. They had come together in little huddles, buzzing like bees.

The girl slipped around the house to the servants' entrance. The sentry stationed there had deserted his post. She could see him thirty or forty yards away jabbering and gesticulating with two other men. At sight of her he ran toward the gate and shouted for her to stop.

Lee flung at him a mocking kiss, cried in Spanish, "Farewell — until tonight," and vanished into the house.

She found Jack in the living-room. He was looking out of the window. Hearing some one come into the room, he turned toward the door. At sight of her he gave a cry of astonishment.

After the girls, metamorphosed into dusky young Mexican maidens, had left the house on their way to the plane, Jack waited in a stress of anxiety the result of their adventure. He did not pace the floor or make any display of his worry, but his excitement was none the less keen-edged.

He knew that Daggett was already gathering in the Lazy R riders. As soon as they were sure the women had escaped, the men would strike for the hills. There would be a fight. The chances were that some would be wounded or killed. The others would be followed. The pursuit would be close and continuous. Jack admitted to himself that the likelihood of a getaway for any of the Americans was very slight. But it was better to take a fighting forlorn hope than to wait tamely for Megares's vengeance to fall upon them.

Jack looked at his watch. Lee and Doris had been gone only five minutes. But they must have passed the guard at the door, for they had not been brought back into the house. By this time, if they were free of the soldiers, they must be passing through the orchard. He found himself checking their progress. They ought now to be halfway throught it . . . They should have reached the pasture . . . They must be in the arroyo . . . Nine minutes. What was it Shakespeare had written about time dragging?

He examined his revolver. It was a part of Megares's mocking gesture that he had not disarmed them. But he had taken good care to leave plenty of men to watch they did not escape. Soon, now, if the plan of the women to reach the plane did not miscarry, the Lazy R riders would be starting on a long journey. How long a one would it be? As long as the one Stumpy had taken? How many of them would live to tell the story of that desperate break to escape the firing squad?

Fourteen minutes. If all was well, the girls should be clambering out of the arroyo and slipping through the chaparral. He went to the south window and looked out of it, though from it one could see only a small sector of the pasture and not that part of it where the plane was resting. Soon now. Surely they could not be far from the landing-place. Presently the big dragon-fly would go zooming into the sky and he would hear its droning flight . . . Curious that none of them had heard it when it came. The pilot must have kept well away from the ranch house.

Why didn't the plane start? Had Lee and Doris been detected and caught? Were they now in the hands of the jeering soldiers? If so, their plight would be more desperate than before. The attempt at flight would quicken Megares into action . . . Twenty-one minutes . . . Maybe the plane wouldn't take off. Some of the machinery might have gone wrong. Perhaps the landing-place wasn't level enough.

He heard the distant roar of the plane. He caught a glimpse of it driving northward. The dread lifted from his heart. He gave a boyish whoop of joy, restrained decorously for personal audition only. They had made it. They were headed for safety at last. In a couple of hours they would be looking down on brown Arizona. If they got across the line, Megares could do his worst.

Jack intended to allow half an hour after the hop-off, on the chance that Lee and Doris had failed to make connections. But in his mind he did not doubt in the least that they were gone. Silver would not leave without his passengers.

Frequently he consulted his watch . . . Ten minutes . . . A quarter of an hour . . . Eighteen minutes . . . Just a little while now and the band would begin to play. He had to fight his way out of the house and to the corral. Daggett and his riders would be there to help. Well, it was on the knees of the gods.

Then the door of the room opened — and Lee walked in to meet him.

From his throat leaped a cry of amazed distress.

197

"You failed?"

"No, we succeeded. Doris got away."

"But you?"

The eyes of the girl were starlike. "There wasn't room for me."

"Not room for you! Did Silver go and leave you here?"

"He wanted to stay. I wouldn't let him. He urged and begged me to take his place."

"Then why didn't you?"

"Did you think I'd go and leave you here alone — you and my waddies — for Megares to take vengeance on — after I'd brought you all here?"

He caught her by the shoulders. "My God, girl, do you realize what you've done?"

"With me here you'll have a better chance," she said simply.

"At your expense!" he burst out. "Don't you see, Lee? He'll make you pay, too, for what we've done."

"Why shouldn't I, if it has to be?" she cried softly. "Why should you suffer alone? I couldn't go, Jack — I couldn't — I couldn't — and leave you here."

He saw in her eyes the fire which is lit for only one man, and it struck a spark to the banked passion within him. He had ached to take her in his arms, this fine brave young creature who had so grown into his life. He snatched her close, and body clung to body in mad sweet intimacy. Her lips, lifted to his, gave him the keys to the city of her soul.

They forgot time, forgot the desperate plight in which they were. One certainty stood out, in a situation that made for many doubts. They had found each other. No sinister fate could rob them of that.

"Before I met you I used to think I must be the kind of woman who couldn't love," she confessed. "I met men, and each one was just another man. But when I met you, the very first time, something queer happened inside me, and I knew it was different this time. I knew you were the man I wanted. So I was afraid of you, and I tried not to like you."

Looking down into her shining amber eyes, he laughed, her soft, strong body in his arms.

"And I, do you think I wanted love — this kind of love, that possesses one? I was hard as nails. I knew all about women. I expected to lead a life of intelligent selfishness — that side of me, at least. A sort of Megares inside the law, one fitted to the social system — that is about what I intended, to play my hand first and last."

Her fingers tightened on the muscles of his arm. (And even in that moment a fugitive subconscious joy raced in her at the feel of the flowing, rippling muscles which gave the motions of his body such a tigerish litheness.) That he loved her was still almost too precious to believe.

"I was all for myself, too," she admitted. "I had to be first. Everybody had to know that I was boss. And now . . . I am all yours. What are you going to do with me?"

He came to earth. "First, I'm going to save you if I can. We were going to make a break to get away. But with you here —"

"That doesn't matter," she told him. "Oh! I haven't told you yet. Harold is coming back with a big passenger plane to try to pick us up."

"When?"

"He doesn't know. He may have to have it sent from San Diego or Los Angeles. But he's very efficient. He gets things done in a hurry. By tomorrow he'll very likely get back."

It occurred to Jack that tomorrow might be too late, but he did not say so. Too late for him, but very likely not too late for her and her riders.

"He's going to bring a machine gun," she explained. "I told him to make a landing on the mesa. We're to try to reach the plane."

Swiftly his mind swept over the problem. With Silver and his machine gun, and five or six good fighting men by his side, the chance of escape would be far better than to try to make a run for it now. That is, if Megares left the cowboys free and did not take their arms. The trouble was that Megares would very likely round them all up as prisoners. For himself, Jack knew that he would be very lucky to be a prisoner. The savage impulse of the bandit would be to put him before a firing squad, though he might compromise by having him killed by accident.

"We'll wait," Jack decided. "I'll get a note to Dunc by Ysela telling him the war's off for today. It was a pretty bad bet at the best. We'll give Silver a chance."

Ysela carried the note and brought back a verbal message that the boys would stick around and be ready for a loose blanket stampede when Hadley gave the word. She got Daggett's peculiar verbiage a little mixed in transmission, but the two in the house got the drift of it.

Another plan suggested itself to Hadley. If Lee, in her Mexican garb, could get out of the house again, she might wait in the hills back of the mesa until Silver's plane arrived. She would have a cold, lonely night of it, but this would be better than remaining in the power of the insurgent chief. Lee objected, instantly and with energy. She gave various specious reasons, but the one she did not voice was that she could not desert her lover. Staying, she would divide the blame and perhaps the punishment. If she went, too, the vengeance of the bandit would fall on Jack alone, except so far as her riders might be swept into the orbit of his rage.

They argued the matter. Into the discussion walked the officer in charge of the soldiers at the rancho.

He gave his name as Lieutenant Rodriguez, and he was as full of suspicions as the *dueña* of a soft-eyed, flirtatious *señorita*. At sight of Lee in the costume of a native girl, his doubts became certainties.

"Where is *Señora* Silver?" he asked in Spanish.

Lee answered, smiling at him. "We don't know."

"What do you mean you don't know?"

She, too, spoke in Spanish. "Mr. Silver arrived in an aeroplane and she has gone back with him in it to Arizona. She is in the air somewhere between there and here."

Rodriguez stared at her, aghast and shocked. The General had left her in his charge, had told him plainly that he was responsible for her safe-keeping. If he had let her get away — But he would not believe it. They were making a fool of him, these gringos.

He called in soldiers and searched the house. They found Mrs. Silver's clothes, but they did not find the lady. Rodriguez was in a panic. He did not dare to think of what his punishment would be. The best he could do now was to lock the stable door after the horse was gone. He put Hadley and Lee in a locked room and guarded both door and windows, after he had first disarmed the male prisoner. A messenger was sent post haste to Megares with the news of the escape. Soldiers were dispatched to comb the chaparral on the chance that Doris was still in the neighborhood.

The situation of the two prisoners was precarious, but there was no despair in their hearts. If they were locked in a prison, at least the rest of the world was locked outside. Lee should have been a prey to dreadful anxiety, and there were moments when she looked at her lover and the bottom dropped out of her vitals. But for the most part she could not believe doom was hanging over him and perhaps over her. They had found each other. No gods could be jealous enough of their joy to destroy them now. To see the strong and poised energy of this splendid animal she loved, to feel the gay charm of the gallant soul so dear to her — a gayety that had its birth in consummate daring — was to draw from him courage as from a reservoir, and not alone the courage which endures, but that which overcomes, which finds in the very breath of peril a zest to lift the spirit. From the hours of that long summer day came memories she had never forgotten. It was as

202

though they drank in the fine rare air of the high hills. All the fogs of the little swamps and marshlands lay below them.

Her heart exulted. "I've climbed the mountain with you today," she told him. "I can't ever be quite the same again, can I?"

In the afternoon there broke upon them the sound of thunder. They listened.

"The big guns are booming," Jack said. "Must be a battle on. It has been due several days. Luna has been massing government troops. He ought to win, unless he is attacking prematurely. Even though Megares drives him back, I don't see how the insurgents can win eventually. Their only chance lay in surprise — swift overthrow of the government before it could assemble its strength. And they didn't pull that off."

All the rest of the day they could hear the far, faint roar of cannon. At times it would die down for a few minutes, but always to be renewed. The sound of the great guns so far away sent a thrill through Hadley's veins and through Lee's. Upon the issue of the battle being fought might lie not only the fate of the government, but life or death for him and for her happiness or disaster.

Through the windows they observed the restlessness of the soldiers. They were uneasy as quicksilver. They could not sit still, but gathered in groups to talk excitedly and to gesture with the abandon of Parisian cab-drivers.

Even the coming of darkness did not bring a cessation of the artillery fire. It became apparent that this was no skirmish, but a major battle.

Juan lit the lamps and afterward brought in food for the prisoners. He let them know that Ysela had prepared the meal with much care because of her fondness for the *señorita* and that she was offering prayers to the blessed Mother Mary.

"Ysela is a dear," Lee said. She took from her throat a jade necklace the Mexican girl had admired. "Will you give her this, Juan, for her birthday from me with wishes for many happy returns? Friday is the day, but perhaps I had better not wait until then."

"*Gracias, señorita,*" the old man said. "I brought you a bottle of wine from the Costilla vineyards. It warms the heart."

Lee thanked him and added with a smile that their hearts were already warm.

Juan shook his head, looked around fearfully, and lowered his voice. "He is one devil straight from hell, this Megares."

Rodriguez came in before they had finished eating to tell them of his dispositions for the night. They were to be in adjoining rooms. The place would be well guarded and if they attempted to escape they would be shot. The officer treated them courteously, but with a manner of hurt resentment. He seemed to feel that their connivance in Mrs. Silver's escape had been with deliberate intent to injure him. When he referred to it, his voice quavered. His mind had lively pictures of swift and terrible punishment for his carelessness.

Jack poured him a glass of wine.

"Drink with us, Lieutenant," he invited. "Happy days."

As they lifted their glasses, the eyes of the lovers plumbed each into those of the other. They were drinking a pledge to the brave adventure that was to stretch down the years for them.

The Mexican officer drank, but there was no joy for him in the toast. He knew Megares too well — and yet not well enough. He was a pockmarked little man who had been a tailor before his vanity had led him to accept a commission in the rebel forces. Devoutly he wished himself in his shop again. What would Megares do to him? If he only knew! Had he better desert and hide himself in the hills? To be caught after that would be certain death. Yet if he stayed to meet the furious eyes of that terrible man . . .

The room swam dizzily before him.

"I am afraid," he confessed miserably.

Jack had realized this. "Of what use?" he asked. "What is to be will be, unless by foresight and boldness you can avert it."

"I have a wife and a baby."

They were speaking in Spanish. "That is too bad," Jack told him gently. "I am sorry. We must do our best. Sometimes to walk hardily through danger is to brush it aside. But if not — if it overwhelms —" He shrugged his shoulders and quoted in English Sir

Walter Raleigh's memorable lines written the night before his execution:

> Cowards fear to die,
> But courage stout
> Rather than live in snuff
> Will be put out.

"I do not know your English, sir. All I know is that fear melts the tallow on my bones. I am not brave. No. I am timid. And I think of my family left alone." He stopped to listen to the faint booming of the big guns. "War is not for men like me. Oh, no! I am kind and have many friends. I do not want to kill."

"Why don't you slip away and go over to the Federals? General Luna will win. Go now, while there is time. Take us with you. Miss Reynolds's *vaqueros* will ride with us as an armed guard. We will protect you."

The little man was tempted. It was not loyalty, but fear, that made him hesitate. If he took any steps to make his men doubt him, they would certainly arrest and hold him.

"No. No, I cannot!" he cried, and he wiped little beads of perspiration from his forehead. "My men would not let me go."

A heavy footstep sounded in the corridor outside the room. The door opened, and a swarthy, heavy-set Mexican in the uniform of a major stood at the entrance. He was dusty and grimy and disheveled.

"The General has sent me to take command here," he announced in a harsh, decisive voice. "You are under arrest, Lieutenant Rodriguez."

The little man shut his eyes. He swayed on his feet.

"I — I beg you to believe that I did not mean any harm, Major," he gulped.

"That is not my affair. The General will be the judge of that."

The Major turned opaque eyes on him. "The General is just now busy elsewhere, sir."

"A big battle is being fought, I think. How does it go?"

"The cause of the patriots will prevail."

"Is General Luna attacking?"

"Yes."

"With a large force?"

"I do not know the size of his army, sir."

"We've heard the big guns for six or seven hours. It's a major battle?"

The Major frowned at him. This gringo was a prisoner and ought to be treated as such. But he had a pleasant manner — and the Major was bursting with news of events at the front.

"A great battle. We have repelled General Luna's forces many times. They come back. They pour into the streets. We drive them back. They are lodged in one end of the town. Many have been killed and wounded. The end is not yet."

"Your forces are entrenched in the town and the barracks?"

"Very strongly entrenched, sir. And General Megares is a lion in the field. He inspires all his men. He risks his life with the greatest boldness."

Jack nodded. "I'd expect that of him. He looks like a first-class soldier, and he's playing for big stakes."

"For a free Mexico," the Major said sententiously.

"And incidentally for his life," Jack added dryly.

"Do you expect him here tonight?" Lee asked the officer.

"Not tonight. He will not leave the field until the enemy is defeated and our army safe . . . Meanwhile I, Pablo Marcos, command here. You are prisoners. I shall take precautions to see you do not escape."

"Why are we prisoners?" Jack inquired.

"Because General Megares says so."

"He didn't give a reason?"

"I do not ask for reasons. I obey orders. We will not discuss it. When the General arrives, he will if he chooses answer your questions."

"I am afraid the General may be a little annoyed at me," the American said.

Four men filed into the room.

"The lady will remain here," the officer told the corporal in charge. "You will take the gringo prisoner to the room at the end of the corridor. Lieutenant Rodriguez will be put in a tent outside. See that both are well guarded. The vaqueros of the señorita will be kept in the bunk-house, also under guard. You will have the bunk-house searched for weapons. The General has ordered a very strict watch over all prisoners."

Marcos stepped aside to make way for the soldiers to leave the room with their prisoners.

"May I speak with Miss Reynolds?" Jack asked.

"You may speak with her, in Spanish, before me."

Jack took her hands in his. The smile he gave her was cheerful and warm. "Don't be afraid, little comrade," he said. "It's going to be all right, and I'll still be with you here — in spirit."

She nodded. "I'll remember. I won't be afraid . . . much."

"When you need me I'll be near."

"Yes, Jack."

The young man turned to the officer. "Ready, Major."

A moment later Lee heard the tramping of feet as they passed down the corridor.

The Major closed the door behind him and locked it.

She sat beside the window as the darkness gathered. A pair of sentries paced a beat below. At times when they met there drifted to her the soft liquid Spanish speech of the words they interchanged. The light of the camp-fires of the soldiers faintly tinted the sky. Sometimes she heard laughter and once the twanging of a guitar.

Her mind was busy recapitulating the events of the day. It had been the most memorable one in her life. She had found her love, had known a joy which had throbbed through her whole being vehemently. In the hour of peril they had come together so closely that it seemed to her their entities had mingled and poured as one stream down the current of life. She was his and he

209

was hers in spirit. Nothing could change that. No matter what Megares did, he could not rob them of each other. Somewhere, in this world or another, their love would find completion.

She was sure of it, not by theological reasoning, but by the sure instinct of a lover's ego.

He was her man — and such a man! She loved the gay charm which could not conceal, which was indeed a product of the stark courage of his dare-devil soul. He would never wince . . . never. He would hold his head up, with that characteristic gay effrontery, and mock at the murderous bandit while they led him to his death.

But from that conclusion her mind shied with a shudder. It wouldn't come to that. It couldn't. After all, what harm had he done to Megares? And he was an American, with the flag of his country back of him.

Her thought was of Jack rather than herself, though in the penumbra of her mind she guessed that Megares would find a sadistic pleasure in substituting her for Doris. If it came to the worst, she would sacrifice herself instantly to save the man she loved.

Still, at intervals, there came on the night breezes the far explosions of the big guns. As long as they lasted, she might hope. Manuel Megares might be killed. He might be captured. He might be driven away in another direction and the rancho be relieved by Federal troops.

The artillery was still sounding when at last, long after midnight, she fell into troubled sleep.

210

CHAPTER
TWELVE

A ball of fire was just tiptoeing over the jagged hills of the horizon line when a car drove up to the rancho. Looking out of his window, Jack saw five men descend from it. They passed out of his sight, headed apparently for the house.

When the soldier brought him food ten minutes later, Jack offered casual conversation. "The General has arrived?"

"Yes. After a glorious victory."

"Luna was defeated, then?"

"He is flying south with his broken army. The patriots will control the government very soon, and the oppressors will be shot or driven out, God be praised."

"Your information is sure?"

"Would General Megares leave the army if the despots had not been crushed?"

A few minutes later, a guard of armed men came for Hadley. They led him to the big living-room. Megares sat at a table flanked by other officers. Brennan was one of them, Major Marcos another. All of them looked haggard and worn. None of them had been shaved except Marcos. A bloodstained bandage was tied around the head of Megares.

As Jack entered the room, Lee was led in by another door. He smiled at her and bowed. Megares did not rise. His suave urbanity had been sloughed. He looked harsh and sullen. It struck Hadley that his manner was hardly that of a general who had just won a decisive victory over the enemy.

"So!" he cried savagely, and brought his fist down on the table. "While I am fighting my country's battles, you dare to make a fool of me — of me, Manuel Megares. We shall see. We shall find out how safe it is for a pig of a gringo to make mock of me . . . Ha! Rodriguez! Very good. The lesser first. We will waste no time with tailors."

The unfortunate Rodriguez had just been brought into the room. He dropped on his knees before the General.

"Mercy! She was disguised and the soldier on guard let her pass. Mercy, I beg, my General."

Megares turned to the officer sitting beside him. "Find the man. Give him a hundred lashes and throw him into the guard-house." The officer saluted and left the room.

"Now for the tailor. He betrays his trust. He lets a valuable prisoner escape. What do you say, gentlemen? Shall it be death?"

"He might be flogged," some one suggested.

The General exploded a violent "No!" And added an abrupt sentence. "Let him be shot tomorrow at dawn."

212

Rodriguez tried to babble a frantic protest. Megares leaped to his feet, snatched a quirt from the table, and lashed it across the face of the protesting lieutenant.

"You complain, eh? While better men than you are dying, you stay in safety and let prisoners escape! Away with him!"

The condemned man was dragged from the room.

Megares turned once more to the young American. It was plain that he was trying to control himself, just as it was evident from the furious eyes stabbing at Hadley that he found it difficult to keep from raving at him.

"We will hear you, Mr. Hadley. You will tell us, if you please, about the escape of Mrs. Silver and your part in it."

"Not much to tell, General. Her husband knew she was here and dropped down in a plane. Naturally she wanted to go back with him. So she went. She would, of course, have asked your permission if you had been here, but since you weren't . . ."

"Ah! She would have asked my permission? And you advised her, no doubt, to go?"

"She didn't really ask for my advice."

"Or for yours, *señorita?*" Megares demanded, turning abruptly to Lee.

"No. Doris tires easily and likes a change. I think she was hungering to get back home to teas and theaters and bridge, General."

"You aided her. You disguised yourself. You poor fool, do you think you can talk me out of what I know?"

"She was so anxious to get home, General. I'm sure if you had been here —"

He interrupted rudely. "And you. Are you anxious to get home, too? Will you not stay with us, señorita, and console us for the loss of Mrs. Silver?"

She could not miss the cruel exultation in his voice. He did not need to put more clearly into words his meaning. She looked at him steadily, in silence, pale to the lips. Her lover, she believed, was very close to death, and she herself to dishonor. There was no logic in such reasoning. But what had logic to do with such a man as this bandit?

Her anxious eyes passed to Brennan, to Marcos, to the other officers present, and found no hope in their faces. Their general was a despot and would have his way. Any protest they made would be only a formal one. And yet — surely he could not destroy two Americans of standing without an excuse that would pass muster.

His excuse was offered with a grin of cynical malice. "You are charged, both of you, with having attacked peaceful citizens of the country, friends to the revolution, and with having murdered two of them and wounded three others. We are returned from battle, from the defense of our country against traitors who have sold it to greedy foreigners exploiting its natural wealth. None of us have slept. We have scarcely eaten. Time presses. But we are just. You shall have a fair trial before you are executed."

"A fair trial," Jack repeated. "And you have convicted us already. I protest. We are citizens of the United

States. You have no authority to try us by court-martial. I demand to see our consul."

"Refused. You will be tried by this court — now."

Hadley's cold, steelbarred eyes met the crouched ferocity ready to leap like a wild beast out of the black balls glaring at him.

"Very well. Try me if you want a victim. Miss Reynolds was not armed the day we were attacked. That can easily be proved. Confine the trial to me."

"We will try you both. If she is innocent, let her convince the court."

"I advise you to be careful — all of you," Jack said, speaking to the others. "I will make you a promise. Listen to it well. If you do this girl any injury, my government will hunt you down like wolves. None of you will escape. None of you!"

"Gringos all boast!" Megares cried. "They boast even while they are robbing us of our oil and our ore. But what did you Yankee pigs do to Villa? Did he not laugh at the army you sent down to capture him? And so I laugh."

One of the officers, a small, lean man with a face pitted by smallpox, shrugged his shoulders in approval. "All gringos are pigs," he summed up. "The General says well."

Jack looked from one to another of the members of the court. Brennan was an enemy to both the prisoners. Marcos looked like an honest man. The rest had been hand-picked by Megares. Probably they had been members of his outlaw band, ruffians ready for any crime. His gorge rose at them. Undoubtedly there were in the insurgent forces thousands of good citizens. Many of them were officers. But this bandit leader had passed over all of them to choose men who had lived for years in defiance of law and order.

Megares knew very little about courts-martial. The trial was in any case only a form, but he might as well make a pretense of fairness.

"We shall proceed at once. One of these officers will represent you as counsel," he said.

Hadley looked the men over scornfully. "No thanks."

"You don't want a counsel?"

"I'll represent myself."

"And you?" Megares asked, turning to Lee.

It was in her mind to say that Hadley would represent her, but some instinct stopped the words. Ranse Brennan hated her. But she had read in his face a sullen reluctance at taking part in the proceedings. He was, after all, an American. He had known her since she had been a little girl. No matter how great the grudge he held against her, he could not want to see her destroyed by this villian.

"I choose Colonel Brennan," she said impulsively.

Hadley looked at her in astonishment, but his surprise was no greater than that of her ex-foreman. Brennan's choleric face flushed. "Me! You want me to defend you?" he burst out.

Her eyes held to his bravely, but her lips were tremulous. "If you will, please."

He stared at her, so slender and boyish, yet so gallantly poised. Perhaps his memory bridged the years to the old days when there had been kindness between her and him, to that summer when he had been to the girl home from school a hero to be admired.

"Why pick me?" he demanded roughly. "You know I'm against you all the way."

"I know you. I don't know the others. You can tell them it isn't true, what General Megares wants them to believe."

"All right," he said gruffly. "It's all cut-and-dried, anyhow."

"Not meaning any reflection on the court, I hope, Colonel," Megares suggested, his eyes narrowed to shining slits.

Brennan met the challenge angrily. In the battle yesterday he had fought with signal courage. He was about fed up with this bandit's treatment of him. His hatred of the man had become a banked volcano within him. If he had luck — if his plans didn't miscarry — he would pay all debts in full within twenty-four hours.

"What do you want me to say — that you're aiming to give these folks justice?" he blurted out.

"That's exactly what I expect you to say, Colonel!"

The eyes of the two clashed. There were reasons in the back of Brennan's mind why he did not want to force an issue. He gave way, sulkily.

"All right. I'll say it," he growled. "Let's get on with this business."

Witnesses were called. The first ones were Mexicans who testified that, while they were riding peaceably through the hills, they had been attacked by four or five Americans and two women. Taken by surprise, they had defended themselves after two had been killed and three wounded. Jack and Lee were identified as two of the assailants. It was quite clear that they were parroting a tale they had learned by rote, but neither Hadley nor Brennan was able to shake their testimony.

In rebuttal the defense brought in Juan, Ysela, Dunc Daggett, and one of the Lazy R riders who had been present when Lee and Doris rode in to get help. All of them testified that neither of the women was armed. The riders who went to the rescue of the besieged men swore that they found Hadley and Stumpy in a position of defense above the rimrock and that those scattered in the cañon below must have been, from their position, the attackers.

Megares had craftily selected Major Marcos as the prosecutor. He was not sure enough of Marcos to give him a vote as one of the judges. Therefore, he had assigned him the position of court advocate.

The Major showed no animosity toward the prisoners. He examined the witnesses fairly enough, though Megares frequently broke in with leading questions designed to influence the testimony of those on the stand. Even the statement made by Marcos in summing up had a judicial tone. He asked the officers sitting on the bench to weigh the evidence and if they found the prisoners guilty to assess such punishment as seemed to them just. His own opinion he did not give in the case of Hadley. As to Lee, he said he felt it only fair to say that he had great doubt as to her participation in the fight. He was inclined to believe that she had not been armed.

Brennan spoke bluntly and briefly in fluent but faulty Spanish. His emotions were mixed. He did not understand them himself. He had sworn to get even with this girl for the way she had treated him. Now he had his chance, and he discovered that his anger against her had evaporated. She was an American girl in trouble. It was up to him to support her.

"I've known her since she was so high," he said, measuring a space from the floor with the palm of his hand. "You're crazy with the heat if you don't let her go. She's straight. The worst I know of her is that she's got mixed up with this fellow Hadley here. I don't care what you do to him. Give him the limit. But don't convict this girl. I tell you she's all right. She didn't have a gun with her. She never harmed any one in her life. Some of you may have daughters of your own. Maybe —"

"One moment, Colonel," Megares interrupted, with the grin of a Mephistopheles. "This lady is so harmless — yes? Did she not once shoot you?"

Brennan was flung off his stride. The men sitting as judges had heard him tell how he intended to get even with her, and the kindest name he had had for her was wildcat.

"Maybeso. We ain't trying her for that, are we?" Brennan demanded.

"Not at all, Colonel. I'm just wondering how she can be so harmless now and could have been such a little demon then."

"She's a hellion enough right now," Brennan flung back. "I ain't claiming she hasn't got a temper and is as bossy as a lone bull in a herd. What I'm saying is that she's just a spoiled girl. You wouldn't shoot her for that, would you? Why, this thing don't bear talking about. You can't do a thing like this. You couldn't do it and ever look a woman in the face again. It's just one of those things men can't do."

He sat down abruptly, mopping his face with a handkerchief. Nothing could have surprised him more than the glow of anger surging through him at the outrage under way. He ought to have been satisfied. He had promised out of a bitter heart to ruin her, to drag her pride through the dust. Well, here was his chance. All he had to do was to stand aside and watch complete disaster fall upon her. But he couldn't do it. Somewhere inside his callous being there burned a spark of decency that was being fanned to a flame. He wasn't going to stand for any lousy Mexican outlaw hurting her to feed a grudge.

Jack did not talk long. He addressed what he had to say, not to Megares, but to the other officers. That they would find him guilty he knew. No use wasting time trying to save himself. He spoke for Lee, with a crouched and forceful directness. She was an American lady, wealthy, well known, with hosts of powerful friends. If they did the thing Megares wanted them to do, if they convicted her against the evidence and contrary to all sense of justice, her country would demand vengeance. The revolution would be doomed, and the men responsible for the crime would be dragged from their holes and executed. He urged them to remember that. He begged them as officers and gentlemen to release her and to send her in safety across the border. As for himself, he was innocent of this charge. Their party had been attacked, probably on orders given by General Megares. But if a victim was needed, let him alone pay the penalty.

The prisoners were removed. At the door of the room while being led away to await the verdict, Lee and Jack came face to face.

"Courage, little comrade," he said, smiling at her.

She mustered an answering smile, but it was wan. "It's for you I'm afraid, Jack. They won't . . . do much . . . to me."

"I don't think they will. The fear of Uncle Sam is in their hearts."

"But you — surely they can't find you guilty on such a trumped-up charge. But, oh, Jack, they will — they will!" She broke down and wailed the last words in a little cry of fear.

The guards pushed her through the door and led her along the corridor to the stairs. Following her, Jack watched the girl, woe in his heart. She was a fine brave young thing, sensitive and strong and eager for life. What an evil trick Fate had played on her! He would have given all he had to save her, and he could do nothing. His strength was of no avail, any more than his youth or his wealth. The amber eyes that had looked love at him, the eyes sometimes filled with laughter and sometimes overflowing with tenderness, would know only sorrow and grief. There would be no more sunshine for her; nothing but the gloom and the shadows of the night.

She would probably escape with her life. Even the riffraff sitting as judges with Megares would hardly dare to kill her. The consequences would be too dangerous. But even if they let her go, he knew the bandit general would step in and make life hell for her. He had as good as said so when he asked her ironically if she would not stay and console them for the departure of Doris. He had used the plural, but he meant the singular.

The man intended to be her lover. Jack was sure of it, and he writhed at the thought.

And there was nothing that he could for her. Nothing.

CHAPTER
THIRTEEN

Lee waited in her room, all her being submerged in dread. She could read the handwriting on the wall. Megares had written it so that a fool could have guessed what the verdict would be. It did not matter about her. She did not know what they would decide. But as to Jack — had not Megares told the result before they had gone through the farce of trying him? They would take him away to his doom. He would go, with that light, easy stride of his, head up, smiling ironically, to meet the death they were even now voting for him. It couldn't be! She would wake up and find it was a ghastly dream. It wasn't reasonable to think of death in connection with one so quick with life, so strong, so valiant. He was inextinguishable. All that vitality couldn't be put out. God would not permit it.

She prayed — wildly — desperately. She made promises. If He would only spare Jack for her, she would be a changed woman. Give her his life and take hers, or put on her any punishment no matter how great. But save him — save him . . .

A guard opened the door. She looked up at the brown, immobile face in swift appeal. The man knew only that she was to be brought back to the courtroom.

As she entered, she saw the judges sitting at the table. Megares was telling some jest and laughing at it. Jack came in a few seconds after her. The prisoners stood side by side. Jack's hand caught her cold fingers. His heart smote him because she was so pale and tired and shaken.

She looked up at him, grateful for the warm grip. At the contact life seemed to flow from him to her. The pressure of that warm palm was like a song of hope. It gave her a vision of his soul, still strong and undefeated. For a moment only. Then the weight, cold and heavy as lead, settled again on her heart. Of what use hope and courage when she could see the shadow creeping toward him? A gay and dauntless spirit could not avert his doom. All it could do was to give fortitude. What were those verses he had quoted to Rodriguez? Courage stout . . . rather than live in snuff will be put out . . .

The voice of Megares, a soft feline purr, came to her as from a long distance. He was speaking in Spanish.

". . . and in spite of weighty affairs pressing upon us, we have taken valuable time to give you a fair and impartial trial. Only after mature deliberation have the findings of the court been reached."

He broke off, holding the verdict back, to gloat over them as a cat does over a mouse before the kill. His black eyes searched Hadley's face. He wanted to quench that sardonic smile, to bring fear into the cool, contemptuous gaze. And if a certain guess of his was correct, he thought he knew a way to break that insolent gringo spirit. Time would tell.

His rhetoric flowed on. A cynical grin belied the unctuous periods. "The members of this court, ever inclined to mercy, regret the necessity of trying this case, but we have been driven by an urge higher than personal considerations. Only the good of the country has been in our thoughts. The verdict has been forced upon us by overwhelming evidence. One of the accused has threatened us with the vengeance of a great and greedy power if we do our duty, but we are not to be deterred through fear of our individual safety."

Suddenly, grown tired of his own verbiage, Megares flung away indirection. His body straightened. Words came with the sharp snap of a whip lash. "As to the prisoner John Hadley — guilty. The sentence of the court is that he be taken at sunset to the west wall and there shot to death. As to the prisoner Lee Reynolds — guilty. The sentence of the court is that she, too, be shot to death, but the time and place of the execution of this sentence is left at the discretion of the general commanding the patriot armies in this district."

Lee swayed. Her head drooped. ". . . taken at sunset to the west wall and . . ." The world had ended with that sentence. She did not even know what they had determined in her case.

Later, she thought she must have swooned for a moment on her feet. When her mind picked up again the scene, Jack's arm was around her shoulders. He was looking into her eyes.

225

"Courage stout," he whispered.

"Today," she quavered. "At sunset."

"But the sun is still high."

"It can't be. There must be some way ... some way ..."

Megares watched them, black beads smoldering behind the narrowed lids. He was confirming a suspicion.

Jack held her slack body close. Once more the contact drove back the chill and brought to her warmth and some faint reflection of his intrepidity.

"We must ... find a way."

"There's many a slip," he told her.

"You won't leave me today. You'll stay with me," she begged.

Jack looked at Megares. "Unfortunately, impossible," the bandit chief answered. "Remove the prisoners."

Lee clung to Jack, despairingly. "Oh, no — no — no!" she cried.

Jack asked one favor. "May we see each other again before —"

Megares shrugged. "Very well. For the last half-hour. And be comforted, Mr. Hadley. Your friend will not be alone all the time. Busy though I am, I shall see her. Perhaps I may bring her comfort. Who knows? Life is full of partings, alas! We must make the best of it. Mrs. Silver goes, Miss Reynolds stays. You go, I stay. So the world wags."

"You endure with philosophic resignation the tragedies of others, General," Jack told him, an edge of scorn to his voice.

"Why not? If the cards had fallen differently, I don't flatter myself you would have been inconsolable at my leaving the world. We are all so full of ego, so important in the scheme. So we think. But are we? You, for instance, Mr. Hadley! You leave perhaps a friend, a lover." His sarcastic gaze shifted to Lee. "Will she die of grief? Not at all. If she is a wise woman, she will dry her eyes and busk up for the approval of another man. Not romantic, perhaps. But the way of life."

"Give them the day together, Megares," broke in Brennan abruptly.

"You will not interfere, Colonel," his chief told his curtly. "Take away the prisoners."

Brennan glared at him, but said no more. Megares was riding a high horse, but soon he would come a cropper — if a certain message he had sent through to Luna reached that officer in time.

"I can't let you go, Jack," Lee sobbed. "I can't. It's too . . . awful."

Jack kissed her. "We're to see each other again. You must be brave."

"I know, but —"

He held her for a moment tight, then gently passed her to the waiting guard. When she tried to break away to get back to him, he was walking from the room between two armed men.

Jack looked around as the door opened and a man walked into the room. He did not rise. He did not speak. The man was Megares.

"I hope you're comfortable," the Mexican said.

He moved forward, raffish and graceful, to take a chair.

"What do you want?" Jack asked.

"You are so direct. It is the way of your countrymen. I think your favorite words must be 'Yes' and 'No' and 'Now.' With us it is so different. We lack your energy, so bustling and so practical. A national fault perhaps, still —"

"Did you come here to discuss the traits of our peoples?"

"You are so impatient, Mr. Hadley," the bandit general demurred gently.

"You may remember, perhaps, that I have not much time," Jack answered grimly.

"That is true. And as you thought, but out of politeness did not say, you are particular with whom you spend it. Not so?"

"Yes."

Megares relaxed in the chair and leaned back, his fingers laced back of his head. "I wonder why I came to see you. I'm devilish busy. And yet my business is not important. The truth is that our game is up, Hadley. We've lost our big throw."

"Didn't you defeat Luna yesterday?"

"We did, and we didn't. He failed to drive us out of Palo Duro and drew back for reënforcements. But that's exactly the point. He can get fresh forces — plenty of troops and ammunition — and we can't. I don't mind telling you because — well, you're not likely to talk about it."

"No," agreed Jack.

228

"I'm telling you this so that you may understand my position," the rebel purred. "I'll imitate your charming frankness. If we were going to win, I'd have to walk softly in this little matter of you and your friend. I'd hardly dare to have you shot, because as you mentioned that big bully up north might jump on me. But since the cards have fallen the way they have, I don't have to worry about that. I'm going back to the hills. Have you ever been a hunted outlaw, Mr. Hadley? No? You've missed a thrill."

"It's not your plan to have Miss Reynolds shot," Jack ventured quietly.

The outlaw brushed his mustache with two fingers. "I think not. I have other uses for the lady. The fact is, I propose to suggest myself as your successor."

Jack felt a turmoil in his blood. He said, in an even voice, "You're a cold-blooded villain."

"Oh, yes! Deep-dyed, and all that sort of thing."

"You'd drive a girl desperate, and take advantage of her fears."

"That's a point of view, Mr. Hadley. Aren't you just a little prejudiced in this case? A woman is to be won. All's fair in love, you know."

"You devil!"

"But you're an extremist. All women since Eve have wanted to be loved, though some of them never found it out. They want to be stormed and taken possession of. Which brings us back to that point I mentioned — our clamorous egos. Each of us wants to believe that he is the man, that the eye brightens and the cheek flushes for him alone. Alas, propinquity! You pass on to —

wherever you are going. I am no theologist. I remain, the available man. The lady prefers you. She hates me. But a curious psychology is at work. It produces a chemical change in her emotions. There is truth in the reversal of the old saying that love is akin to hate."

Jack knew the man was taunting him, that he was airing his cynical philosophy for the same reason that an Apache might have driven a burning splinter into the flesh of a victim. He wanted to see him writhe. But even as Hadley fought down the rage that boiled in him, he was aware of a subconscious amazement at the fellow. He knew that Megares was the son of a wealthy Mexican family, that he had spent many years at school in the United States and abroad. Yet it seemed strange that a man who was acquainted with art and literature could have assimilated culture, externally at least, and remained at heart a savage untouched by civilization. No arguments that might have availed with an ordinary man would touch him. He would live for himself alone. When he died, the world died with him. That was his pragmatic philosophy.

"I wonder," Jack said, as though he were musing aloud. He had a proposal to make, and he felt his way toward it carefully. "You may be right, though I'd bet heavily against it. I suppose that even you have standards. For one thing, a sporting pride in your skill at playing the game of love. You wouldn't, I judge, take a woman against her will."

"Wouldn't I?" The eyes of the bandit smouldered. "That's more of your chivalry stuff. I thought you knew me better. There is what you gringos call a kick in dealing with a woman whose little fists clench and whose bosom pants with fury. Come, Hadley, you prefer to ride a horse with spirit, one that fights for the mastery. It's a triumph to break the will of any thoroughbred animal. To know that I am the lord of creation satisfies my vanity.

> 'A woman, a dog, and a walnut tree,
> The more you beat 'em the better they be.' "

Hadley did not pursue that line. He tried another.

"I'm going to surprise you, General," he said. "It's in my mind to make you one of my heirs."

The black, beady eyes gleamed. Megares relished this.

"I knew you were fond of me, but I hadn't realized your affection went so far," he jeered. "What are you thinking of willing me — in addition to one of your friends?"

"I was thinking of a hundred thousand dollars," Jack said.

"Good. Shall I send for a lawyer?"

"There is a condition attached."

"I thought so. In exchange for your life, perhaps."

"For Miss Reynolds's freedom."

"You have the money with you? In your pocketbook?"

"It could be got. A letter to my agents would be sufficient."

"I'm afraid not, Mr. Hadley. There would be a slight difficulty in collecting. The situation would be unusual. If I appeared in person, some one would be unkind enough to arrest me and communicate with Luna or some one on this side not quite friendly to me. And explanations by mail would be a little complicated. Perhaps I'm too suspicious, but I fear that when I told him I had been compelled regretfully to terminate your career because you had interfered in my affairs, your agent might refuse payment."

"He might. There's an alternative," Jack suggested. "Hold me a prisoner to a hundred-thousand-dollar ransom. Send Miss Reynolds with the order signed by me. After the money comes, if you still feel bloodthirsty, I could be shot as well then as now."

"Why send Miss Reynolds? It's a long journey, dangerous in the present state of the country. One of her *vaqueros* could carry the message."

"I don't think so," Jack disagreed. "That's the nub of it — that Miss Reynolds is to go free."

"After which I'm to take my chance of getting the money. No, thank you. Fact is, I've tried this ransom game. It didn't work. You may recall the Faraday case. His friends tied up with my enemies and tried to trap me."

"Whereupon you shot Faraday."

"What else could I do? I played fair, but his side didn't. Sorry. I could use a hundred thousand American dollars. But the catch is — as you Yankees say — that I wouldn't get it. For one thing, I expect to be very transitory in my places of residence. A hunted man has to move rapidly and often. Offer declined."

"You wouldn't take my word to go to Los Angeles, get the money, and bring it back to you?"

232

Megares lifted an inquiring eyebrow. "Miss Reynolds to go with you?"

"Of course."

"Do I look like that particular kind of a fool, Mr. Hadley?"

There was a commotion at the door, the sound of voices in argument. One of them was high and squeaky.

"Dog my cats! Ain't I sayin' it's your general I want to see? What's eatin' you, fellow?"

Megares rose and walked to the door. He threw it open, but Jack noticed that his hand was on the butt of his revolver.

"Who is it? What does he want?" the bandit general demanded of the guard.

"He wants to see you, General."

"That's right," Daggett assented. "I want to have a talk with you."

Megares stood aside. "Come in. Talk. But be very brief. What do you want?"

"I got a proposition to make," the old-timer said. "Here's its shape. What's the sense in foolin' with this young squirt an' Miss Lee, General? They're just kids. If you've got to stand some one up against a wall, what's the matter with me?"

"You would like to be shot?" Megares asked, with a polite, cold smile.

"No such thing. I'd hate it. But sho! I've lived my three-score years an' ten, an' then some. Some of these young barbers that ride for me an' claim they're cowpunchers give it out that I'm two years older than God. Well, I ain't. I'm spry as any of them. Fact is, I've

233

kinda took a smile to these young folks. You let them go, an' bump me off instead."

"No."

"But why not?"

"Because I do not choose."

Daggett's voice grew higher and more excited. "You got no business shootin' these young folks. Nobody but a devil right straight from hell would do it. I've had an elegant sufficiency of you. Think I don't recognize you, eh? Well, I do. You're the moke that shot me when Francisco killed this boy's dad. If I had a gun here, I'd go to fannin' right here an' now."

"Get out!" ordered the rebel chief.

"You're nothin' but a dirty greaser murderer. I ain't scared of you. Pull that six-shooter if you've a mind to and plug me, you rat. I've got your number. You figure this boy knows you was in with Francisco an' Brennan on that raid when his dad was killed, an' you want to get rid of him while you can."

The words of the old man shrilled to a scream. He trembled with excitement. His pale eyes blazed.

Hadley spoke sharply. "That's enough, Dunc. You're not in this. You've no business here. All you're doing is making trouble for yourself when you ought to be thinking how you can help Miss Lee after I've gone."

"But they're gonna kill her, too," the foreman wailed.

"I don't think so. General Megares says not. But she'll need all the help you can give her. It's up to you and the other boys to look after her."

234

"Not at all. I'm going to do that," the Mexican disagreed. Then savagely his temper broke. "Get out of here, you old fool, or I'll send you to hell, too."

"Don't get on the prod, Megares. I'll go when I'm good an' ready. I came here to make you a fair offer, an' I've made it. All I got to say is, if you hurt Miss Lee any, I'll . . . I'll —"

Megares ordered a soldier to throw Daggett into the guard-house. With a revolver in the small of his back, the old man departed with voluble protest.

"You were with Francisco, then, when he murdered my father," Jack said to the bandit.

"Perhaps. I do not remember all the little raids I have been in. But the old fool may be right. I dare say he is." The outlaw watched the prisoner closely, with smiling lips and eyes hard as jade.

"You know it. That's another reason why you want me dead. It will be safer for you."

"So I am afraid of you? I, Manuel Megares, who never feared man or devil!"

"I think so. That's why you're having me killed."

The outlaw's vanity was stung. "What have you ever done to make me afraid of you, Yankee pig? I wipe you out because you dared to interfere, to take from me the woman I wanted. Because you thought you could make a monkey out of me. You have learned better now." He glanced out of the window. "The sun is halfway down. You have about three hours, my friend. Meanwhile I shall go and have a little talk with that charming lady who is just now so inconsolable. *Adios.*"

Megares turned and walked out of the room.

CHAPTER
FOURTEEN

The verdict at the court-martial had been a shock to Ranse Brennan. He had expected an acquittal for Lee. Major Marcos had in effect asked for one. Her conviction could have been due only to the pressure of Megares upon the other members of the court.

Brennan realized that only a thin veil of pretense stood between him and his chief to prevent open hostilities, and he knew that Megares would sacrifice him without the least hesitation if need be. But he was a bull-headed man, and he had plenty of what in the West is called guts.

As soon as he could free himself of routine duty, he went to the General.

"What's the idea, Megares?" he demanded. "I'll not stand for having that girl shot. You can't get away with it. She's done nothing, and you know it. For that matter you had no right to try either her or Hadley. You know well as I do it was self-defense. But it's all right with me about Hadley. I've got no kick coming there. But I have about Lee Reynolds. You made those yellow dogs convict her. Think I don't know that?"

The black eyes of the Mexican narrowed. "One thing at a time, Brennan. You've said a lot that'll have to be explained before I'm satisfied. But we'll take the last first. I made them vote guilty. You're right."

"Why? What deviltry are you up to? What's your game?"

"Suppose you leave the young lady to me."

"What for?" Brennan asked harshly. "Do you mean to put her up against a wall? Is that it?"

"You're insolent, my friend. But let that go for the moment. I don't intend to have her shot. I never did."

"What's in your mind, then? Out with it."

"You forget yourself, Brennan. I command here. What do you mean telling me what I can and can't get away with?"

"Command, hell! The insurrection is shot, and you know it. In three or four days you'll be flying through the hills same as I will unless I can sneak across the line."

"Perhaps. In three or four days. But just now I'm God in this army. Don't forget it for a moment. If I lift a hand, you'll go to the wall yourself."

Brennan evaded that. "I'm asking you a question, Megares. What's your idea about the girl?"

"And I'm telling you if you're wise you'll mind your own business."

"I'm making it my business. What do you mean to do with her?"

"You're getting in my way damnably," the Mexican warned.

The big man scowled at him. "Think I don't get you, fellow? You're going to use the sentence to scare her to death and get what you want. You're a dirty dog,

237

Megares. But I won't have it. I've known her too long, and anyhow she's an American. Keep your hands off her."

Ranse turned and strode out of the room. He knew his words might turn out to be a death sentence for him. Just now he was beyond caring for that. The anger in him had become so explosive that an outbreak had been necessary.

But as he hurried away, the danger of his situation grew on him. At any moment Megares might give the signal for his arrest. After that his execution would follow very rapidly. All he needed was time, provided Luna had received his message. But how much time would Megares give him? Had he better saddle a horse, shoot down the bandit leader, and try to ride hell-for-leather from the camp? They would get him probably. Too many armed men were on guard duty.

First he must see Lee if possible.

Brennan was not given to introspection. It was his way to ram-stam through difficulties by sheer force. He had no imagination, and he had the driving power that usually carried him to success. But he had now a queer prescience of impending doom. A bell of warning tolled within him. He pushed the presentiment from his mind. It returned, and its presence affected what he said and did. He was not his usual self, and the fact was disturbing. Often he was a bully and frequently a ruffian. For the moral code he had scant regard. As he had told Doris once, he thought a man a fool who did not play his own hand selfishly for all it was worth.

Yet now he was walking into great danger for this girl who had flung him aside like a worn-out shoe. He was passing up his chance for revenge. He no longer wanted her to be broken on the rack. Emotions surged in him because of her desperate plight. Ranse did not understand himself. What in Mexico was the matter with him? He was not responsible for her. Why not stand back and let Megares do as he pleased?

But he knew he could not. There was something in him stronger than the habit of his life. He set his teeth with grim determination to balk Megares if he could.

In his pocket was a pass Megares had written for him the day the revolution broke. It had been given him to show to any insurrectionists who might doubt the gringo's good faith.

Brennan walked across the patio, up the stairs, and along the corridor leading to the room where Lee was imprisoned.

Curtly he nodded to the guard outside the door. "Miss Reynolds inside?"

"*Sí señor*, but the General has given orders none are to be admitted save him."

"The General does not mean me. I am his friend and an officer in the patriot army."

"I know, but —"

"Don't argue with me, fellow. I'm your officer."

The man poured out a flood of protesting Spanish. He was a good soldier. He obeyed orders. It was all right, of course. Still, his captain had told him that the General's orders were . . .

Brennan pulled from his pocket the pass and showed it. Certainly it told all good patriots to let Colonel Brennan go wherever he wished. The man moved aside. The big cowman opened the door and walked in.

Lee turned a stricken face toward him.

"You — Ranse!" she cried.

"Listen. Megares doesn't mean to have you shot. It's a bluff. He wants you, and his play is to scare you."

"And he isn't going to shoot Jack?"

"You bet he is. I ain't interested in him. I'm talking about you. I'll balk that devil Megares if I can. There's help coming. Never mind from where. Promise if you must. But stall — play for time — kid him along the way Doris did."

She scarcely heard him. "Save Jack. Save him, Ranse. Don't bother about me."

"No chance. I couldn't if I would, and I wouldn't if I could. Megares isn't going to let him live. He's going to put Hadley against a wall the way he and Francisco did his father. The young guy blames me for what they did to his dad. I hadn't a thing to do with it. I couldn't help it any more than I can help him now with Megares. Even if I wanted to . . . But you. I'm talking about you. Play your cards close. Stall for time. Act like you're just being coy. If you do —"

"I don't care about myself, Ranse," the girl broke in. "It doesn't matter about me. We've got to save Jack. That's the only thing. Don't you understand? I love him. If he dies . . ."

"Can't be helped. I said, no chance. Well, there's a chance for him, but a mightly slim one. It depends on when that help comes — if it comes at all. What I came to tell you is that I'll be sticking around. When you need me I'll be there."

"If you really want to help me, Ranse —"

"Nothing doing. I've got to drag it, girl. It wouldn't do for me to be caught here. I've already had one run-in with Megares about you. So-long."

She cried out against his leaving. Her mind was still full of Jack's danger, and she wanted to plead with her ex-foreman for him.

But the door closed behind Brennan and left her alone.

Despairingly she wrung her hands. She paced the floor. She sat down and jumped up again instantly driven by her unhappiness to a wretched and futile restlessness.

To look out the window drove a knife into her heart. For the sun was sinking toward the horizon. At sunset, Megares had said. Never again would she look at the declining sun without horror.

But there must be something she could do. There must be some way she could save him. If only she could think . . .

After Brennan had stormed out of the room with that explosive "Keep your hands off her," Megares stood for a minute in deep thought stroking with finger-tips the black mustache. Had he better put an end to this blustering fool before he did any harm? Or had he better give him more rope?

There were objections to putting Brennan before a firing squad. The other officers would not like it. They had no particular fondness for the Colonel, but they would naturally resent the execution of one of their number. It would be too suggestive and would arouse suspicious. Even as things were now, Megares realized that he was in no enviable position. The government had put a high price on his head. One of his own subordinates could win immunity and the nest egg of a fortune by betraying him. He did not want to give them any added inducement.

Of course he could have Brennan assassinated. That would take a little time to arrange, but perhaps it would be the better way. He could put his finger on a private who would be glad to do it for fifty dollars Mex.

For an hour he was busy over various matters. There were letters to dictate, orders to give, telephoning to do. He got Palo Duro over the wire and talked with the officer whom he had left in command. All was quiet at the front. Megares said he would stay at the rancho until morning and then would drive to town.

He hung up, stretched himself, smiled, lighted a cigarette, and walked briskly out of the room. Like Brennan, he crossed the patio, took the stairs to the second floor, and moved along the corridor to the room where Lee Reynolds was under guard.

Opening the door, he walked in and bowed to his prisoner.

"*Buenos tardes, señorita,*" he said.

242

"Tell me you will save his life!" she cried.

He moved forward, smiling at her. "Whose life, dear lady? Let us not talk of others. Let us have this one hour alone."

"You can't mean to kill Jack Hadley! You are trying to frighten me. Well, you have won. I am frightened. Now you will save him, will you not?"

The sad eyes beneath the long silken lashes pleaded with him to be pitiful.

"But I cannot save him. He was convicted by court-martial. It is out of my hands. I must not interfere. All my concern is with you, *niña*. I am grieved that you must so soon pass out of the sunshine. So young, so fair — and so soon the firing squad. It is most touching."

"Let me die tonight — with him — if he must die. I beg that of you with all my heart."

He was taken aback. He had come prepared to bargain with her for her life, to grant it at a price. And she preferred to die with her lover. He reflected that all women are fools sentimentally. Yet this was annoying, since what he had to offer was something she did not value.

"You do not want to live," he said.

"Why do you say one thing and mean another? Why don't you tell the truth? I'm not afraid for myself. You do not mean to kill me. Before those other men would find me guilty, you had to promise to pardon me. Any one could see that. But if you must have a life, take mine and spare Jack Hadley."

243

A second time he was surprised. How had she guessed this? Had any one told her? Could Hadley or Brennan have got a note to her through the guard?

"So you are quite sure I mean to pardon you. Don't be so certain. I may, if you are reasonable. You shall bargain for your life, my dear."

"For his," she substituted.

"For your own. Look at the picture. On one side swift death — oblivion; on the other love and sunshine, pleasant days and ecstatic nights, all the good years ahead. What will you pay to make the latter come true?"

"It could come true only if Jack was alive. I'll give you everything I have in the world to let him go. My ranch — all my cattle — what money I have."

"Not feasible. I am wanted in your United States just as I am here. Your government would not permit me to enjoy these good things. Have you nothing else to offer — for your own life, not for his?"

"Nothing."

He moved a little closer, graceful and raffish and debonair. "Think, *chiquita*. Moonlight and music, wine and song, the whispers of a lover. Shining eyes that look into yours. Kisses that thrill the blood. Hours of madness and merriment. Are these worth nothing?"

She looked bleakly at him. "Are you God? Can you work a miracle? The joy in me will be stricken dead if . . . if you kill Jack Hadley. There's nothing else I want but his life. Give me that, and I'll bless you forever."

244

Irritation flashed from him. "Wake up, you fool! I give the word and you will walk out to death. Think. Worms will eat your body. I can save you — I alone."

"You can save me for long years of sorrow and grief. That is all."

He put an arm around her and dragged her slender body close to his. His hot black eyes blazed into her amber ones and lit no answering fire there. She made no resistance. She was inert and lifeless, unmoved by his anger and his passion.

"You Puritan Yankees!" he cried. "None of you know what love is! It is hot lava in the blood! It is desire storming through the veins! It is passion crying for its own! But I will teach you! I, Manuel Megares, will change that water in your arteries to red and rushing fire! From me you will learn how a Spaniard loves."

"I will learn only how to hate you as a cruel savage animal."

"We shall see. But whether you love or hate, you shall be mine. You and that blundering fool Hadley came between me and the woman I had chosen. I swore then you should take her place. If I have to hide in the hills, you shall go with me. From one gorge to another I will drag you as we are being hunted."

Into her mind a dark thought came. He had spoken of a bargain. Since she was lost, anyhow, why not get something out of the wreck? She offered a compromise, hating herself and him.

"I will go with you. I will pay the debt I owe. What you teach me I shall learn. But you will give me something in exchange? You will spare my friend and let him go? If I am to . . . to be yours . . . you must be generous. You must give me this one thing I ask."

All the young life had been stricken out of her. The big eyes had lost their luster. The cheeks were pale and cold. The body in his arms was flaccid. She looked a bride fit for death. But he knew that youth is resilient. His hour would come, he told himself.

His wily brain busied itself planning deception. He could pretend to give way, could promise her Hadley's life, and even let her see the man starting for the line. Then he could have him seized and secretly killed. Why not? She would not learn for weeks how he had fooled her. By that time it would not matter.

He laughed. "You are persistent, my dear. Very well. You win. The Yankee shall live, and you shall go with me — willingly — and he shall be nothing to you and I shall be everything."

"Yes," she answered, in a small dead voice.

He kissed her eyelids and her lips, ravenously, and she stood there in his arms, a lax, dead thing, and wondered how life could go on in the days to come when she would be paying forfeit. "You will free him at once," she said.

"At once. Let him go back to his oil wells. The sooner he is out of our lives, the better."

"I may see him before he goes?"

"Why not?" He smiled at her, with the diabolic malice that was a part of his nature. "Tell him that a better man has won. And he will wish you joy, no doubt, in the life to which you are looking forward so eagerly."

The door opened abruptly, and Brennan stood at the entrance to the room glowering at them.

The arms of the Mexican fell away from the girl. His lids narrowed, but his words were ironically suave.

"You are a trifle abrupt, my friend, in interrupting our love making. Malapropos is the word. You will wish, perhaps, to apologize and retire."

Brusquely Brennan brushed aside the man's grim foolery. "I told you I was declaring myself in on this play. I'm going to look out for the girl. She's going to get a square deal."

"Ah! Isn't she getting it?"

The eyes of each man were fastened on those of the other. Not once did either relax for an instant the rigor of his steady regard. For both knew, by that sixth sense which warns men who have faced danger often, that the quarrel between them was about to come to tragic issue. The harsh, imperious temper of the big man had crashed the barriers of caution at last. He had made one stipulation with his recklessness and only one. Just outside the *patio* a fast horse stood saddled, tied to a post by a slip-knot. That much chance he had given himself.

"No. I know you, fellow. You've always been a double-crossing wolf. I wouldn't trust you as far as I can throw a bull yearling by the tail. What story have you been stringing her with now?"

"He's going to save Jack!" Lee cried. "We've made a bargain. He's going to free him and let him go home."

"That's a lie. He's not going to do anything of the sort."

"Take care," Megares warned.

The Mexican was watching him intently, every nerve wary, every muscle alert. It would be soon now, he was thinking.

"I've watched your smoke, you crook. If you're pretending to let Hadley go, you're aiming to have him bushwhacked. Haven't I known you twenty years? The girl's to pay the price while you fool her. That's to be the way of it, eh? That would hand you a great laugh, wouldn't it? Well, you don't get by with it."

"You threaten me?"

"I'm telling you. Made a bargain with her, did you? She's to give you her good clean body in exchange for your damned lies. No. I'll send you to hell first."

The brown fingers of the Mexican swept up to the revolver butt above the holster. Even then, in that fraction of a second before the guns blazed, Brennan knew he had let his anger trick him. Lee was standing back of Megares almost in the line of fire. The knowledge of this disturbed the aim of the big man.

While the revolvers roared, Lee crowded close to the wall. She saw stabbing spurts of flame, two distorted faces wreathed in smoke, bodies tensed and crouched like those of wild beasts about to spring. She heard an oath, a gasp, the crash of a table as it went over from the impact of a staggering weight.

Ranse was on the floor, trying desperately to raise his weapon, and Megares was flinging bullets into the prone figure.

248

Lee screamed out a protest and ran forward. She threw herself beside the body of her former employee. He was dead before she could even lift the head.

She looked up into the twisted face looking down with such fiendish hate. At sight of it she shuddered.

Already men were pouring into the room.

"He threatened me and attacked me," Megares explained. "I call this woman to witness. Look at his gun. It has been fired two or three times. The man was a traitor. He deserved death."

"Are you wounded?" a soldier asked.

"No. I was too quick for him." The killer was recovering his surface aplomb. "The assassin drew and fired before I got my revolver out. By the grace of God, he missed me."

"The gringo dog!" A soldier muttered. "He was always a bully."

"Take out the traitor's body and bury it," Megares ordered.

Lee sank into a chair and covered her face with her hands.

The bandit chief looked down at her for a moment, smiled cruelly, then turned and walked from the room. He was going to be busy for a short time explaining what had occurred to his subordinate officer. It was just as well the official report of Brennan's death should bear the color he wished.

CHAPTER
FIFTEEN

Jack looked out of the window and saw the sun sinking into a crotch of the jagged hills. His heart was leaden. He could count the remaining span of his life by minutes. He would never look into another sunset. He would never see again any of the thousand pictures that had gone to make this panorama of his life — cattle grazing in a meadow, shadows on a slope, antelope slipping through the sage. Never again would he hear the rustle of the wind through trees on a starlit night far up in the mountains. He was done with all the lovely things that had been so much a matter of course.

And the loveliest thing of all, the joy that had blossomed in him with a promise of such wonderful fruition — this, too, was to be destroyed. It was such a cursed ironic tragedy, to have found the one woman he wanted and to lose her merely to satisfy the malice of a savage. Such frustration was so useless. It had no meaning. Was that the answer, after all, to the riddle of life — that it was all haphazard chance, with no aim, no purpose, no intent?

He was to be wiped out and his lover's fine pride dragged in the dust to sate the urge of a murderer's whims. There was no reason in it. No logic in it. Yet it was an inexorable fact. All the lusty life in him resented it. Fear swept through him in waves, but greater than the fear was a cold, implacable anger at an exit so absurd and yet so tragic.

The voices of the men moving to and fro outside came to him. A horse nickered. Ysela went to the well with a bucket, drew water, and returned with it . . . All the homely little details of existence would go on as usual. But he would not be here to see and share in them.

It was going to be a ghastly business for Lee. To let his mind travel along that road was torture. That he whom she loved must die was in itself terrible enough, but she could have survived that. Time assuages such wounds mercifully. What she could never recover was the zest for living born of youth's fine unconscious pride. When Megares had finished with her, she would be a draggled and a beaten creature. If she went on, it would be as a poor pitiful soul shamed and hopeless. All the splendor that gave a lilt to her voice and music to her walk would be blotted out. He ached with his pity for her. It was almost better to go as he was going, still young and strong and unconquered.

The sound of shots shattered the quiet, the crash of revolvers pumping bullets fast and furious. The firing came, he guessed, from a room farther down the corridor. From Lee's room, perhaps. His pulses quickened with apprehension. He walked to the door and beat upon it, demanding to know what was wrong.

Nobody paid any attention to him. Excited voices were raised. Men raced along the passage, rushed up

251

and down the stairs, called to one another. Some one, he gathered, had been killed. A man. A gringo. Presently he could hear the shuffing of feet and the giving of orders. They were carrying out the body. Whose? Had old Dunc Daggett flung away caution and attempted to do something foolish for Lee? Had he paid the penalty of his rashness? If so, what effect would it have on Lee's fate?

The noise quieted. Death had come and gone, just as in a few minutes it would come and go again . . .

Guards came into the room and tied his hands behind him.

"I am to see the *señorita?*" he asked.

"Yes," the corporal said. "For ten minutes. No more."

"Alone. But if you try any monkey shines, it will be the worse for you, Yankee. There will be guards outside the window and in the hall."

"Who has been killed?"

"Ho! What do you care? A gringo pig. You will join him soon. You can ask the devil who came down to hell just before you."

The guards led him along the corridor, opened the door of a room, pushed him inside, and closed it.

Lee turned as he entered. A little choking sound came from her throat. She stretched her arms toward him and he moved forward. Her hands caught and clung to him above the elbows, and even as she kissed him she broke into sobs.

"He killed Ranse . . . here . . . just a little while ago."

"Who — Megares?"

"Yes. Ranse stood up for me. They quarreled. He shot Ranse to death . . . But he has promised me to let you go."

His daze searched her. "Has he? You sure?"

He did not believe it. Yet his heart leaped, as though it were something in him not a part of him.

"He promised me. Does he mean it, Jack? Ranse told him he was lying to me, that — that —"

"Probably he doesn't mean it. He's vindictive and full of tricks. Have you a pair of scissors? Can you cut the cord around my wrists?"

"No. Not here."

"You'll find a pocket knife in my trousers. Open it."

She sawed through the cords. He took her in his arms.

"Has he told you what he means to do with you?"

She hesitated. "Yes," she said at last in a small voice.

He did not ask her what it was. He did not need to ask her. They held each other tightly, as though by physical closeness they could escape the fates appointed for them.

"Why is he going to let me go? I mean, why did he say he was?"

"I begged your life of him. He said you might have it and that I could meet you this once to say good-bye."

Jack held her at arms' length and looked into her soul. "You made a bargain. You sold yourself to save me," he charged.

"Does it matter? I am lost, anyhow. If he will let you go, that is something gained, isn't it?"

"I won't have it. You can't save me at that price," he said hoarsely.

"But, Jack — don't you see? — I'm in his power. It doesn't matter to me what I say or don't say."

"Don't surrender. Fight as long as you can against him. Brennan was right. He isn't going to let me go. It's a trap for you. That's all."

"But he promised me," she insisted. "He said I could watch you go. He said the sooner you went, the better it suited him. Maybe he'll let you go. Why shouldn't he? You haven't done him any harm."

"He thinks I planned it to get Doris away. His vanity demands revenge. But that isn't all. He knows I know he murdered my father. He's not going to lose this chance to wipe the slate clean. No. He's lying to you. It's just the sort of thing that would please him — to get rid of me quietly and let you find it out later, after he didn't care whether you knew or not."

"Can he be as dreadful as that!" she cried. "It doesn't seem possible."

"Evade him. Use all your wits. Play for time. Perhaps you'll get a break. His promise means nothing. I can see that now . . . clearly. It was given only to drive you to him."

"But if he meant it, dearest, if —"

"He didn't. Don't fool yourself. He's full of lies. He never meant for a moment to let me go."

She broke down. "I can't bear it! You're the only man I've ever loved. It's so terrible! I get to thinking it must be a dream. What are we to do, Jack?"

254

He could give her no comfort. He could find none for himself. All they could do was to cling to each other, desperate young lovers who could find no way of escape.

A knock sounded. It struck on their hearts like the toll of a knell. Their time was up. They had come to get him.

Megares walked in, the embodiment of suave and sinister malice.

"Enter the villain," he said, and showed his teeth in a smile one might have mistaken for benevolence.

"Not yet!" Lee cried. "You promised us a half an hour."

"But events have crowded so, *chiquita*. Alas, the course of true love never did run smooth. Your Shakespeare was an amazing writer, Mr. Hadley. We have none like him in our language. He hits off human nature, profoundly and at the same time lightly, from a thousand different angles. Not so?"

Jack looked at him, not answering. The river of woe that had been running through him was now frozen to ice. His eyes were like cold steel.

"You've promised me his life," Lee reminded the Mexican wildly.

"Yes. As a special favor to you, heart of my heart. He shall ride north, out of our lives. And we, in the joy of our honeymoon, will forget him and his crimes. We will even hope that he may live to repent of them. The king is dead! Long live the king! When I say dead, you will understand, Mr. Hadley, that I mean metaphorically speaking."

"I understand you," Jack said quietly.

The bandit's black eyes mocked him. "Indeed! When you meet Mrs. Silver, will you give her my best regards — I should say *our* best regards, little one — and tell her how through her abrupt departure the blue bird of happiness came to sing its song to two loving hearts!"

"You yellow wolf!" Jack said, not raising his voice.

"No gratitude." Megares sighed. "It's the way of the world. We must comfort ourselves, *corazón*, in knowing that to do good is its own reward."

"I am free?" Jack asked bluntly.

The bandit glanced at the cut rope on the floor. "Are you not?"

"I may leave here whenever I please?"

"We shall be sorry to see you go," Megares murmured politely.

Jack stepped to the window and looked out. "I see guards below. I hear them in the hall."

Megares was no coward. Strapped to his side were two revolvers. Hadley was unarmed. The Mexican shrugged his shoulders.

"I had forgotten to dismiss them."

He strolled to the window and poured out a sentence or two of Spanish. He walked to the door, opened it, and gave the men outside a curt command.

"You have far from a trusting disposition, Mr. Hadley," he reproached.

"So I am free," Jack said. "I wonder."

"Free as the air. In fact, though I do not want to seem inhospitable, Miss Reynolds and I are ready to hear the word *adios* from you." With an apologetic

256

smile, Megares added a rider: "You will excuse the impatience of our ardor, Mr. Hadley. It is your Shakespeare, it is not, who tells how slow time moves till love have all its rites?"

"D'you think I'll be a party to your damnable bargain?"

"Not at all. You are an outsider." Megares turned to Lee. "We have our understanding, have we not?"

"No," Jack denied. "I'll not have it."

"Come, my friend. Since Shakespeare is on my mind today, let me recommend to you a line from 'Romeo and Juliet,' one I have found very useful myself at various times. By the way, have you ever seen Jane Cowl in it? If not, you've missed one of the most beautiful presentations ever given."

Jack watched him, closely. The man was enjoying himself immensely. The feline side of him, which found delight in playing with the victims, was to the fore. He was growing a little careless. Presently, if something did not drag him back from the mood on which he was floating, perhaps . . .

"No other play has so many quotable lines in it." The jet eyes of the outlaw chief sidled impudently to Lee. "Lines for lovers, dear my heart. In those good times ahead I shall take pleasure in calling them to your mind, when you and I are alone together and jocund day stands tiptoe on the misty mountain-top or night's cloak hides us from our enemies."

Not once did Jack's gaze shift from him. Megares knew it and was pleased. He did not quite read the thought in his prisoner's mind. He guessed it to be chaotic hate and jealousy and fear. This was as it should be. Let the gringo suffer.

"But I haven't given you yet the line I'm recommending to you, Mr. Hadley," he swam on unctuously. "It is worth remembering. 'I must be gone and live, or stay and die.'"

"If I go, I live?" Jack asked.

"Unless you should chance to meet a band of ruffians in the hills. The country *is* unsettled just now."

"I'm afraid I'd meet some, as I did once before."

"You might," Megares agreed. "But let us hope not. You have our very best wishes." He brought Lee into the talk again. "Is it not so, *muchacha?*"

"Yes." Lee aligned herself with him so reluctantly that both men knew fear alone had dragged the world out of her.

Here Megares made his mistake. The impulse to taunt the Yankee was too much for him. He bowed over Lee's hand to kiss it, slanting a smile of mock apology at the condemned man.

With tigerish swiftness Jack dived with the full weight of his hard-packed body. Megares dragged out a revolver just as the battering-ram struck his stomach. The Mexican went back as though shot from a cannon. His head crashed against the wall. He fell to the floor limp as a sack of flour.

Jack unfastened the belt of the unconscious man and strapped it around his own waist. He reclaimed the other revolver from under the table where it had been hurled by the impact of his charge.

"Get the key," he told Lee. "Lock the door inside."

258

She did so. With the rope that had been around his wrists Jack tied the arms of the Mexican behind him. He made a gag of his handkerchief and necktie. By the time he had fixed it in the mouth of Megares, the velvet-black eyes of the man were fastened on him savagely.

Hadley's blood began to sting with the excitement peril brought. "You were just a little careless, General. I expect you'll have a devil of a headache. Afraid I'm not in a sympathetic mood. Since you're so fond of Shakespeare, I'll recommend a line. From your favorite 'Romeo and Juliet,' by the way:

" 'Tut, man, one fire burns out another's burning,
One pain is lessened by another's anguish.'

"But to business. We're a long way from being out of the woods yet, Miss Reynolds and I. Some of your friends will be along presently knocking on the door. Yes, I see you've thought of that. Well, think of this, too. If they break in here, it will be to take me to that wall you specified this morning. I've nothing to lose by killing you and something to gain. For when I do, I save Miss Reynolds. You get the point. They can break in, to be sure, but they'll find General Megares quite dead."

The outlaw glared at him. But Megares was no fool. He understood quite clearly the kind of man with whom he had to deal. Hadley would not fire one moment too soon or a moment too late. He would be thorough.

"Don't make any mistake about that," the young man went on. "I'd as soon shoot you as I would a rat. You helped murder my father. Your life is forfeit a hundred times . . . Listen to me. I'm going to take the gag out of your mouth. If you call for help, you're lost. When some one comes along and knocks on the door, you're going to tell them to *vamos*, that you are with Miss Reynolds and do not want to be disturbed. Knowing you, the man will see what you mean without any further explanation. One point may not be clear to him. He'll wonder where I am. Perhaps he'll ask. Or an officer may come along later and ask. You'll tell any inquirer that it's all right about me. Just that, and no more. If you betray me by a word, by an inflection of the voice that arouses suspicion, I'll kill you before there's a chance of help. That entirely clear? Good."

Jack whipped out the gag.

Megares swallowed two or three times to relieve the strain on his throat.

"I'll pay you for this," he promised in a voice shaken by anger.

"You will if you can. I don't doubt that. But I advise you not to get anxious and try to hurry payment. Maybe you can think of a Shakespearean quotation to console yourself with pending the interim."

"Gringo pig!" Megares spat at him.

"Come, that's not from your favorite dramatist. You ought to do better than that," Jack told him.

A step sounded in the corridor. A knock on the door followed. Lee looked at Jack, alarm in her eyes.

260

"Speak your piece," Jack said in a murmur to Megares. At the same time he drew a revolver from its holster.

The eyes of Megares blazed furious hate. But he obeyed orders. He did not care to face the alternative. His hour would come, very soon, and his revenge on the man would be terrible.

"What do you want?" he asked in Spanish.

He could not entirely keep the anger out of his voice. This helped to serve the cause of his enemy, for it intimidated the soldier at the door.

"Colonel Pedro wants to know if the gringo is to be shot now, General."

"Not now. I will take care of the gringo at the proper time." The outlaw's rage choked him. For a moment it seemed that the man would burst through the barriers of caution.

The end of a revolver barrel pushed a little deeper into his stomach as a reminder. "Go," Megares went on. "Leave me. I don't want to be disturbed."

The shuffle of the messenger's feet died on the stairway.

"You did very well, General," Hadley complimented derisively. "All I can say, to quote the bard of Avon, is thanks and thanks and ever thanks."

"When I get you in my power again —"

"If, General, not when," the American corrected.

The teeth of the outlaw ground across one another. He was filled with a destructive fury.

"The upsets of life should be taken with philosophy," Jack reminded him. "It's all a matter of ego —

261

clamorous ego, I think you said. Subdue yours, General. What will it matter a few years from now?"

"What are you going to do now?" Lee asked Hadley.

"Nothing now," he told her. "Not till it's dark. We'll try and slip away then. If we have luck . . ." He smiled at her.

The hour before dusk deepened into darkness dragged endlessly for the two waiting to attempt an escape. Every moment Lee expected a knock on the door that would prelude disaster. The officers of Megares might leave him for a time, on the assumption that he wanted to be alone with the girl. But soon suspicion would begin to stir. An investigation would be made.

Two or three times Lee suggested to Jack that they had better go. He always told her not yet. It took nerve to sit and wait when the peril was so acute. But the one chance of making a getaway lay in the hope of not being recognized. Night was an ally they had to have.

Jack tied Megares as securely as he could and gagged him. This done, he unlocked the door and passed with Lee into the corridor. From the outside he once more turned the key.

Together the two passed down the stairs. They had decided to try the servants' quarters. It was almost certain that some of the officers would be in the living-room. Very likely a soldier or two would be hanging around Ysela, but that had to be risked.

They opened a door and walked into the kitchen. Ysela was washing dishes and a young fellow was wiping them. At sight of the two Americans, the young Mexican stared stupidly.

This was the gringo for whom a firing squad had been waiting for nearly an hour while the General made up his mind what he wanted to do. This was the *señorita* who was being talked about all over the place because she had been entertaining the General in her room. What were they doing here in the kitchen?

Ysela gave a little cry of welcome. "I am so glad, *señorita*. You are free again?"

"As you see, we are free, Ysela," her mistress replied.

"But the *señor* — it is far past time, and Rafael waits with his firing squad," the puzzled soldier said.

"Let him wait. I am in no hurry," Hadley said coolly. "Point of fact the execution is off."

"But the General —"

"Do you find fault with him because he has changed his mind?" asked Jack.

"Find fault with him? With the General? A thousand devils — no! Who am I to find fault with him?"

From above there came a sound of knocking.

Ysela looked up at the ceiling. "What is that?"

The eyes of the two escaping prisoners met.

"I think that must be Colonel Marcos's big dog beating its tail on the floor," Lee said evenly.

"But the Colonel has no dog," the soldier said.

"You mean he had not until today," Hadley corrected. "He seems to have one now."

The drumming continued. Megares was hammering on the floor with his heels to attract attention.

263

"I do not believe it is a dog," the Mexican trooper said uneasily.

"A big yellow mongrel," Hadley explained. "We left the brute upstairs not two minutes ago. Come, *señorita*, we must go."

The man let them pass. He had a feeling that all was not right. But it was not, after all, his business. The General did surprising things. Had he not sent the guards away an hour or so ago? No doubt the Yankees had come to an understanding with him. Still . . .

A tattoo of knocks drummed insistently on the floor above. Soon the dog would wear out its tail. The soldier decided suddenly to pass this responsibility to a higher authority. He went into the living-room to find an officer.

With her right hand in Jack's left, Lee moved along the shadows of the house.

"That fellow is suspicious," Jack said. "He'll get busy at once. We've no time to lose."

Voices drifted to them. Through the darkness they could make out men gathered around a horse.

"It belongs to the gringo Brennan," one of them explained. "He must have left it here to ride away upon before going in to kill the General."

"Take it to the stable, Juan," another ordered.

The group broke up and moved away, except for one man who stayed, lit a cigarette, and leaned against the wall. The two fugitives could see the glow of its tip. They waited, hoping the Mexican would stroll off. Yet Hadley knew they could not wait long. They must be on their way before discovery of their escape was broadcast.

The cigarette-smoker moved. He walked straight toward them. Jack drew a revolver from its scabbard and let it hang just back of his leg. If the man passed them, well and good. If he did not try to detain them the weapon need not be shown.

Abruptly the man stopped in his stride. Lee's throat grew tight. They were standing face to face with Colonel Pedro, one of the officers who had sat on the court-martial board earlier in the day.

"So!" he exclaimed sharply. "It is you. What are you doing here?"

"General Megares has released us. We have made arrangements with him. He said we might take a little walk after being confined to our rooms all day. It is a pleasant evening, Colonel. Not so?"

Hadley spoke quietly, in a voice unhurried and cool.

The Mexican was one of Megares's outlaw band. He had known his chief many years. It might be very true that he had released these Americans after making terms with them. But there would be no harm in making sure. There was something about the evening walk permission not quite like Manuel Megares.

"You will go into the house with me and if the General says —"

The words died on his lips. He was looking at a revolver pointed straight at his head. The Americans then had escaped and were running away.

Sounds of a commotion within the house could be heard. Men were running to and fro. Voices were lifted in excitement.

Hadley needed no explanation. Megares had been found.

"You will go with us, Colonel," he said quickly. "If you try to escape, I'll shoot you down. And if you betray us, you'll go first. Move fast, but don't run. But first I'll take your guns."

Pedro made no protest. He did exactly as he was told. The man behind the gun directed him toward the stable. Already people were running from the house shouting news of the escape. Jack's hopes chilled. It would be impossible to saddle and get away in time. They reached the stable.

To Pedro he gave an order in one curt word. "*Vamos!*"

Over his shoulder Jack could see pursuers scattering in all directions. He and Lee ran into the stable. At sight of his revolver the horse wrangler took to his heels.

Jack slammed shut the door and in the darkness climbed up a flight of wooden stairs to a loft room where the stable boy lived. He bolted the door.

"They've got us," Lee panted. "We've lost."

"Not yet. We'll try to stand them off."

He went to the small window and looked out. The pursuit was focusing toward the stable. Colonel Pedro and the wrangler had passed the news that they were here.

The stars were coming out and the night was lighter. Jack could hear a voice giving orders and could see soldiers moving forward. He dropped a bullet in front of them.

"I'll fire to kill next time," he shouted in Spanish.

The answer came from Megares in person. "For each one of my men you hit I'll shoot down a Lazy R vaquero. I'm going to get you, gringo dog, alive if possible."

Yet the attack was halted. Hadley wondered why.

Lee came close to him and put an arm around his waist.

"Don't get in front of the window," he told her.

The walls of the building were adobe and would stop any rifle ball, but any moment a fusillade might be fired at the window. "My dear, my dear!" she cried. "You have done what you could, but it is no use. What are we to do? If you give up to him, he'll kill you."

Jack kissed her. He had no comfort to offer, except to remind her that he was to have been shot at sunrise and yet was still alive.

From the grove of live-oaks a voice called. Once more Megares was speaking. Ten minutes before he had spoken in savage anger, but now his words came with suave cruelty.

"I've got some of your friends here, Mr. Hadley. We're having a little necktie party. I'll tell you about it as we go along. The first one is an old fool named Daggett. The rope is around his throat. Perhaps he would like to say a few words."

Dunc Daggett said a few words, in a falsetto voice quavering with excitement. What he had to say was punctuated with blistering epithets applied to Megares. The burden of his message to Hadley was conveyed in two sentences.

"Don't you let him bluff you, Jack, into giving up to him. Let him hang me, and be damned."

Jack's stomach turned sick. He could not let Dunc Daggett and the other Lazy R riders die on his account. He had to pay his own debts. That was so clear that he could not even debate it with himself. But he had to think of Lee. He could not surrender without giving her up, too.

"If I give up without a fight, will you turn loose Daggett and the other Lazy R *vaqueros?*" he asked.

"Yes," Megares shouted back. "I care nothing about them. It's you I want."

"Is Major Marcos there?"

"I'm here," some one answered.

"I'll surrender on one condition," Hadley called to him. "You and the other officers have got to swear that you'll protect Miss Reynolds from Megares just as though she were your own daughter."

To Jack's surprise, Marcos did not hesitate an instant. "I'll protect her with my life. This thing has gone far enough. I don't make war on women and I don't take orders from those that do."

Megares gave a roar of rage, but Hadley went on with the roll-call of the officers who had sat on the court-martial. The others were far less clean-cut in their answers than Marcos, but they came through with promises of a sort. The knowledge had come home to them that the insurrection was doomed and the influence of Megares was on the wane.

"I'll surrender within five minutes," Hadley told them. "The other men are to be freed and Miss Reynolds to be protected. That's understood?"

The officers assented.

"I won't have it, Jack. I won't have it!" Lee cried, clinging to him in terror. "Don't you see it doesn't matter what happens to me if I lose you? I'll not let you go. I'll not!"

He held her in his arms and spoke very gently. "It has to be, sweetheart. I can't let that ruffian hang Dunc and the other boys. It wouldn't do me any good if I did. I'm caught here like a rat in a trap. Maybe I could kill some of Megares's men before they dragged me out. But what good would that do? If I hold out and let them kill Dunc, I couldn't look you in the face. You must see that."

Even in his preoccupation Jack had been vaguely aware of a faint droning in the sky. Now it came unmistakably clear, the roar of an aeroplane above their heads. He and Lee stopped a moment, to listen.

"It's Harold coming back!" the girl cried.

The night woke to sudden noises. The sound of approaching automobiles, the roar of guns, the shouts and curses of men, blended into the inferno of battle. The horror of it seemed to leap out of the darkness as a flame shoots skyward when the dry leaves of branches catch fire, and as suddenly the storm swept away with

269

the end of resistance. Megares and his men were flying into the shadows.

A skirmish had been fought and won. Men had been killed, others captured. But with the egocentric urge of all human beings, the one important fact to the lovers in the loft room was that they had been saved.

They were free to love and be loved. The menace that had hung so heavily over them had been driven off as smoke is by a gust of wind.

They clung to each other in an ecstasy of emotion.

A trim young officer came forward to meet Lee and Jack. Beside him walked Dunc Daggett, talking volubly. The officer bowed.

"I am Captain Gonzales, a nephew of General Luna," he said by way of introduction. "I regret that the villain Megares has escaped after causing you so much distress. Your foreman here has been telling me that the outlaw meant to hang you in a few minutes, sir. Let me congratulate you on your close margin of safety."

"Let me thank you for your timely arrival, Captain, on behalf both of myself and Miss Reynolds, whom I take pleasure in presenting you to. My name is Hadley — Jack Hadley."

They shook hands.

"Though I am happy to have saved you, Mr. Hadley, I have failed in the most important part of my enterprise. I very much wanted to catch Megares and see him shot," the Captain said. "My men are still after him, but in the dark night I don't think there is much chance of finding him."

270

Daggett chipped in. "That fellow Megares is sure enough one scalawag I'd like to see bumped off. If you catch him, Captain, I wish you'd give me an invite to yore party. We've all done had an elegant sufficiency of Mr. Megares. Are you all right, Miss Lee?"

"I'm all right, Dunc," Lee told him. "I expect my hair has turned white, but I can have it dyed." She turned to Gonzales. "I want to thank you too, Captain, for saving us. Mr. Hadley and I are engaged to be married, so you can guess how terribly unhappy and frightened I was."

The old foreman gave a whoop of delight. "Now you're sure enough shouting, you two. Dog my cats, if it ain't worth having a rope around my neck for a spell to hear that."

"I heard an aeroplane just as we got here," Gonzales said. "It landed somewhere near. I'm wondering if it is a rebel plane." The captain smiled at Lee. "If I don't make enough of your happy news at the moment, señorita, please know that it is because I want to make sure your danger is past."

Hadley explained to the officer that they were rather expecting a plane from across the line to attempt a rescue and that probably this was the one. In a few sentences he sketched the story of their stay at the rancho and of the escape of Mrs. Silver and its consequences to those remaining.

The young Mexican summed up crisply. "The man's a murderous villain. For many years he has merited death. It would be a great pleasure for me to relieve the country of him."

271

They stopped talking, all of them, to listen to the sound of guns. It came from a distance of perhaps half a mile.

"My men must have made contact with some of the escaping rebels," Gonzales guessed. "I think I'll push on to them with reserves."

Hadley and Daggett released the riders of the Lazy R and armed them with weapons left by the rebels. There was a chance that Megares might have been reënforced by troops from his main army.

Half an hour later, Gonzales and his men returned. With them were Harold Silver and three other Americans. A prisoner also was brought in by the party.

The plane had made a landing on the mesa by the light of the stars. It had been a precarious business, but by good luck there had not been a crash. But there had been plenty of excitement. Half a dozen of the rebels had attacked the party, evidently in the hope of taking off in the plane. Silver and his men had driven them back and captured the most persistent of the assailants.

Gonzales had the prisoner brought forward to the light. At sight of the man, Lee gave a cry of surprise. He was Megares.

"You see I couldn't stay away from you, señorita," he said, with an ironical bow. "I had to come back, knowing how you must be longing for me."

He must have known what a short shrift was before him, but he was as gracefully graceless, as impudently raffish as ever he had been when he held all the high cards.

272

Hadley felt an odd, unreasonable wave of admiration for the man. He was a villain, beyond doubt. But he had the great redeeming virtue of courage.

"Who is this fellow?" Gonzales asked.

"Let me introduce myself. I am Manuel Megares, Commanding General of the armies of the patriots in this district. From your manner I take it that you are at least General Luna."

Megares smiled at the young man insolently. The Captain stiffened with indignation.

"So you are the murderer Megares. Very well. You will be tried at once," he said.

The outlaw lifted his eyebrows. "Why waste time, since I am to be shot in any case?"

"Or hanged," Gonzales added harshly.

The captured man did not bat an eye. "I shall be just as dead whether you hang or shoot me."

The trial took place in the same room in which Jack and Lee had been condemned. It was summary. Gonzales disregarded the criminal record of the man and tried him solely on the charge of having instigated rebellion against the government. Several of his men had been captured and there were no lack of witnesses. The verdict was reached on the first poll of votes.

In pronouncing the death sentence, Gonzales dwelt on the nefarious career of the prisoner. "You deserve to be hanged and not shot," he said. "But Miss Reynolds and Mr. Hadley, whom you condemned to face a firing squad, have pleaded with me for you to save you from this ignominy. As soon as possible you will be shot against the same wall where Mr. Hadley was to have stood."

"An interesting coincidence," Megares commented jauntily. He shrugged his shoulders. "Need I say I am at your service?"

"Take him away," Gonzales ordered.

Megares turned to Hadley. "No hard feelings. I played for high stakes and I have lost. No apologies. No regrets. I leave you the lady to console for my untimely end. Will you come to the little affair where I am to be guest of honor?"

"I think not," Jack said.

"As a favor to me?"

"Very well," the other agreed reluctantly.

The outlaw grinned hardily. "Your Shakespeare once more, if you'll excuse me:

"'Why, he that cuts off twenty years of life,
Cuts off so many years of fearing death.'"

He borrowed a cigarette from a soldier, lit it, and signified by a nod that he was ready.

He wore the khaki breeches, the leather puttees, and the pith helmet of a Mexican officer. The insignia had been cut from the helmet. His military blouse had been replaced by a dark civilian reefer jacket which was buttoned and belted. He walked out of the room as lightly as though he were going to a tennis court to play a set.

The moon was up now and a silvery light filled the court across which the condemned man moved. In a

274

few hours lizards would climb up and down the wall against which Megares took his stand, but he would not be there to see them.

He declined to have his eyes bandaged. "Why should I hide my eyes? Am I afraid?" he asked the officer in command of the execution.

"Can I take any message you wish sent to any one?" Jack asked.

"No messages. If you get a chance, will you tell the world how you saw a brave man die?"

"I will," Jack said fervently.

One of the soldiers standing in line with his rifle murmured to another, "*Que hombre!*"

The officer in command was a little nervous. Megares suggested that since it was not very light, the firing squad stand closer. The men moved forward.

"You are still too far away. A little closer. Let us not bungle this job."

Again the six riflemen stepped nearer, narrowing the distance to not more than fifteen feet.

The officer raised his sword and the soldiers took aim.

"*Adios!*" Megares called in a clear, steady voice.

The smile had gone, but there was no fear in the face. The bandit leaned forward, shoulders squared.

The sword swept down and the rifles cracked. Megares reeled and fell.

The tenseness relaxed. Jack walked forward, unsteadily, and spread a handkerchief on the face of the fallen man. All the wounds were in the breast close to the heart. Not a bullet had been aimed at the brown face which had looked so steadily at death.

Jack went back into the house to report to Lee.

"I heard the shots," she said, her face almost colorless. "It's over, isn't it?"

"Yes. He may have been a villain, but he was the bravest man I have ever seen." His voice was low and shaken.

She shuddered. "It came so near being you. I can't forget that. Thank God! Thank God!"

He took her in his arms and smiled. It was rather a wan smile, for the reflection of what he had just seen was still in his face.

"Yes," he assented. "He has gone, but I am here to love and be loved. We are both safe from his vengeance, and yet . . . I'll never see a man walk more gallantly to death."

"I know one who would have gone as bravely," she thought, but did not say.

Captain Gonzales came into the room. "My uncle heard just before I left camp that the rebels in the north have been disastrously defeated. The insurrection is crushed. All is well," he said.

Lee disengaged herself from the arms of her lover, but she looked into his eyes and repeated the concluding words of the officer:

"All is well, Jack."

He understood that the message was a personal one to him. All was well with them. There was an open road ahead for the golden gate of happiness.

Yes, all was well.